# The Journey Prize Anthology

# Winners of the $10,000 Journey Prize

1989
Holley Rubinsky (of Toronto, Ont., and Kaslo, B.C.)
for "Rapid Transits"

1990
Cynthia Flood (of Vancouver, B.C.)
for "My Father Took a Cake to France"

1991
Yann Martel (of Montreal, Que.)
for "The Facts Behind the Helsinki Roccamatios"

1992
Rozena Maart (of Ottawa, Ont.)
for "No Rosa, No District Six"

1993
Gayla Reid (of Vancouver, B.C.)
for "Sister Doyle's Men"

1994
Melissa Hardy (of London, Ont.)
for "Long Man the River"

1995
Kathryn Woodward (of Vancouver, B.C.)
for "Of Marranos and Gilded Angels"

1996
Elyse Gasco (of Montreal, Que.)
for "Can You Wave Bye Bye, Baby?"

1997 (shared)
Gabriella Goliger (of Ottawa, Ont.)
for "Maladies of the Inner Ear"

Anne Simpson (of Antigonish, N.S.)
for "Dreaming Snow"

# The Journey Prize Anthology

## Short Fiction from the Best of Canada's New Writers

Selected with Holley Rubinsky

**Canadian Cataloguing in Publication Data**

The National Library of Canada has catalogued this publication as follows:

Main entry under title:

The Journey Prize anthology:
the best short fiction from Canada's literary journals

Annual.
1–
Subtitle varies.
ISSN 1197-0693
ISBN 0-7710-4437-2 (v. 10)

1. Short stories, Canadian (English).*
2. Canadian fiction (English) – 20th century.*

PS8329.J68 C813'.0108054 C93-039053-9
PR9197.32.J68

We acknowledge the financial support of the Government of Canada through the Book Publishing Industry Development Program for our publishing activities. We further acknowledge the support of the Canada Council for the Arts and the Ontario Arts Council for our publishing program.



Typeset in Trump Mediaeval by M&S

Printed and bound in Canada

McClelland & Stewart Inc.
*The Canadian Publishers*
481 University Avenue
Toronto, Ontario
M5G 2E9

1 2 3 4 5 02 01 00 99 98

## About the Journey Prize Anthology

The $10,000 Journey Prize is awarded annually to a new and developing writer of distinction. This award, now in its tenth year, is made possible by James A. Michener's generous donation of his Canadian royalty earnings from his novel *Journey*, published by McClelland & Stewart Inc. in 1988. The winner of this year's Journey Prize, to be selected from among the fourteen stories in this book, will be announced in October 1998.

*The Journey Prize Anthology* comprises a selection from submissions made by literary journals across Canada, and, in recognition of the vital role journals play in discovering new writers, McClelland & Stewart makes its own award of $2,000 to the journal that has submitted the winning entry.

*The Journey Prize Anthology* has established itself as one of the most prestigious anthologies in the country. It has become a who's who of up-and-coming writers, and many of the authors whose early work has appeared in the anthology's pages have gone on to single themselves out with collections of short stories and literary awards. The Journey Prize itself is the most significant monetary award given in Canada to a writer at the beginning of his or her career for a short story or excerpt from a fiction work in progress.

McClelland & Stewart would like to acknowledge the continuing enthusiastic support of writers, literary journal editors, and the public in the common celebration of the emergence of new voices in Canadian fiction.

# Contents

# The Journey Prize Anthology

# STEPHEN GUPPY

## *Downwind*

The year I turned eleven, my mother and I ran away to Las Vegas. This was May of 1953, and we were going to miss the lambing. I was sad about that and about the fact that we couldn't take my pony, Bill, which I shared with my older half-sister. We were going to live in the city for a while, my mother had told me, and there would be no room to keep pets in the city. We were travelling light, my mother said. The way she said this made me believe that we were freeing ourselves of the weight of our lives, of the burden of our worrisome possessions. Everything we owned was in two cardboard boxes and a leatherette suitcase the colour of elderberry wine.

Mama took off her headscarf when we were still half an hour from St. George. She tugged the knot loose and let the scarf fall to her lap, then she gave her head a little shake and let her hair blow loose like mine. I smiled when I saw that, my mother with all her auburn hair streaming back around the collar of her car-coat. This is it, I thought. We're really going to the races now. In another half an hour, we'd be driving through St. George, but we wouldn't stop, we wouldn't even think of stopping. We'd drive right through, past J.C. Penney and the Big Hand Café, past the Desertet News and the Liberty Hotel and the Utoco Gasoline station. We'd keep right on driving for the rest of the day. When the dark came, we'd be in Las Vegas.

We were ten miles out of St. George when my mother saw the cloud.

"Look there," she said. She pointed south-west across the fields beside the road, towards the ridge of red mountains in the distance. There was something like smoke moving rapidly towards us, a wave of black dust maybe thirty feet high. The sky above the mountains was pink.

"Something's burning," I whispered. I started to roll up my window.

"That's no fire," Mama said. "I saw grass fires of all descriptions when I lived in Montana. There's no fire in the world makes the sky look like that."

Pretty soon, you couldn't see the road right in front of you. Everything was inky-black, and the headlights didn't help. Mama had to pull over and park beside the highway. The radio was drowned out by static, just this empty buzzing sound that echoed in your ears. Mama reached out and turned it off, and we sat there, the two of us, looking straight ahead into the smoke. There was no sound at all with the radio off, everything had gone completely silent. Whatever birds or other animals that might have been around at that time of the day must have gone to ground, I would imagine, when the smoke hit. Anyways, I couldn't help crying. I sat there in my eggshell-blue dress and sobbed, and my mother fished around in the pockets of her car-coat for a hankie. She had just pulled one out of her pocket when we heard this awful bang right close and the car lurched ahead a few feet.

"Lord! What was that?" Mama said. I could tell she was afraid from the way that she talked and from the nervous way she giggled when she'd finished what she was saying.

"Somebody's hit the car," I said. It amazes me now to think that I was calm enough to come to such a logical conclusion. I was right, of course; two vehicles that had been trying to make their way down the road through the smoke had smacked into each other, then one or the other of them must have nudged against a car that was pulled over by the side of the road behind us – we didn't even know it was there – and then that car rolled forward and bumped into us. When the smoke cleared enough that we could get out and see what had happened, there were three different vehicles beside ours all tangled up.

"I guess I better see what's going on," my mother said. She giggled again, and then she reached into the pocket of her coat and handed me a Kleenex. "You stay right here and keep the doors locked," she added. She got out and waited while I got back in and pushed down the button on the door.

I sat there in the Chevrolet and waited. Through the back window of the car, I could see my mother walking on the shoulder of the road. There was dust or ash of some kind falling just like rain or snow, and every few minutes Mama would brush it off the arms of her car-coat. She looked as if she was having trouble walking in the new shoes she'd bought for the trip. She had rarely worn heels on the farm, and now she walked as unsteadily as a teenager trying on her first pair.

The car that had bumped us was parked about thirty feet back. Whoever was driving it had managed to back up. One of the other vehicles involved in the collision, a pickup with a bulbous hood and two bales of hay on the flatdeck, was still out in the middle of the road. Mama walked over to the truck and started talking to the driver, a man about my daddy's age who looked as if he needed a shave. They talked for a while and then the man with the stubble got out of his truck and so did a boy about my age. While they were conversing with Mama, the driver of the car that had hit us came and joined them. He was older than the other man and wore a neat grey suit and glasses. They all had a look at our bumper, and I turned away and pretended to fiddle with the radio knobs so's not to seem to be taking an interest. By the time my mother got back into our car, the other people had already started theirs up.

Mama settled in behind the wheel. She waited until the other car had pulled away before she pressed the starter. I could tell she was thinking hard about something by the way she knit her brows and looked straight ahead at the windshield as if she still couldn't make out the road.

"That was one of those atomic bombs," she said quietly. "They let it off an hour before daylight, and this dust has drifted out here from Nevada."

It was after nine o'clock in the morning. The sun had been up a couple of hours before we'd left the farm and started driving. It seemed to have taken a considerable time for the wind to blow all that dust across the state line and up through the canyon. I thought about the light from stars, how many generations pass before it travels through the space between worlds.

My mother had grown up in Bitter Springs, Montana, which is just southeast of Billings. The farm where she'd lived was between two reservations, one Crow and one Cheyenne. She'd talk about Sitting Bull and General Custer and Little Big Horn, which I guess was what they'd taught her in school. When she married my father, she had turned into a Latter Day Saint, but somehow her conversion never changed her. She was one of those people who likes a good time. When Daddy was off working, all we did was joke and laugh, Mama and me and Big Sister.

It was a cool enough morning, but sunny. My mother turned on the radio as soon as we got to the highway. She liked to listen to cowboy songs, mostly, and I fiddled around with the dial until I found her a station that played her favourite tunes. We rolled down the windows and cruised towards St. George, Mama in her headscarf and me with my hair blowing loose. Our car was a 1942 Chevrolet sedan, one of the last American cars made before the factories switched over to war production. It was silver-grey, like an airplane, and had tall white-wall tires. My father had bought it for my mother to drive us to Gleaners and Bee Hive Girls and to pick up things we needed from the city. Later on, when Daddy took on the Utah distributorship for Francis Luscomb Seeds, Mama would hop into the Chevy when Daddy was away and drive to St. George. This time, we were going all the way to Las Vegas, where Mama was going to look for a job. She had worked as a waitress, she said, before she and Daddy were married, and she figured she could find work with one of the hotels.

"This reminds me of home," Mama said. "Saturdays, we'd climb into your grandfather's truck and drive into Kayopa or maybe Bitter Springs, Papa and me and my brothers. We'd roll down the windows and let the wind blow in. That always made me feel so free and happy."

I smiled, not knowing what to say. The people she was talking about, her father and her brothers, I had never known nor even seen. I had never even seen a photograph of my mother as a girl, nor been to the place she'd grown up in, and it was hard for me to visualize her childhood. I knew what she meant, though, or at least I thought I did. I always liked driving with the windows down, too.

My mother rarely spoke about her childhood in Montana, but she did tell me once that her father, who was a stockman of some sort, a man who worked with cattle, had occasionally lifted her up by her hair. I was terrified at first when I heard this. I imagined this brutal man, my grandfather whom I had never seen, grasping my mother's long, reddish-brown hair in his rough cowboy's hands and lifting her clear off her feet. I visualized her screaming, clutching at his arms as he heaved her up clear of the carpet. My mama laughed when I told her this. Apparently, I had formed the wrong impression. Lifting my mother by her hair was a magic trick, a party piece my grandfather had performed with my mother, like making a lady float through a hoop or cutting her in half with a saw.

"Pull my hair," my mother told me. She started taking bobby pins out of her hair and putting them between her lips. When she had loosed her hair completely, it fell down in waves to her shoulders, luminous auburn-red, soft as meadow-grass after a rain.

"Go on," she said, talking out of the side of her mouth, "pull it!"

I grasped a thick, plushy rope of her hair between my fingers, and gave it a tentative pull. I could smell my mother's Palmolive hair shampoo, which she purchased at the druggist's every second or third time she drove to St. George.

"Oh, come on!" she said. "You can pull a lot harder than that! When you were little, three or four years old, you used to grab a whole little fistful of my hair and yank on it hard as you could, like you were trying to pull a heifer out of a mudhole by its tail.

I remember that distinctly. I didn't mind one bit, though, did I, baby? It didn't hurt at all."

We stopped at the first café we came to, a bright little place with a KikCola sign on the door. There were cars parked all along the street, and the café itself was so full that we had to sit on stools up at the counter.

"You go ahead and ask for a glass of milk, baby," Mama said. "I'll just go and freshen up a little." She walked towards the restroom. I took off my cardigan sweater and put it on Mama's stool to save her place, then I pretended to read the menu while I waited for the girl. Every time I glanced up, I saw my own face looking back at me, reflected in the mirror that ran the whole length of the wall behind the counter.

I didn't much like to admire myself in those days. My skin seemed rough and sallow and my eyes too narrow-set. My face as a whole was thin and undistinguished. It's the bones that make the beauty, Mama had told me many times, but my cheeks looked merely angular and horsey. There was nothing in my image that foretold a special charm; I'd have laughed if I had somehow glimpsed the future.

There were two policemen sitting next to me at the counter, a deputy with a round, smooth face and a balding man with glasses. They were both drinking coffee and conversing between sips. They both looked straight ahead as they spoke, and they both talked in calm, quiet voices. From the little I could overhear of what they said, they were talking about the bomb.

"It's up around a hundred rads," the deputy commented. "Hotter than a two-dollar pistol."

"That Snow Canyon?" the other man asked him.

"Around there. The road down from Alamo, mostly."

"A fellow from one of those silver mines called Jurgens on the phone about eight. Said there were flakes of hot iron coming down. Some sheep and his horses were burned pretty bad."

The deputy shook his head.

"It's worse on the Vegas road. Been raining. Fellow said his meter went right off both scales."

"They washing cars down there?"

"Couldn't tell you."

The waitress and my mother arrived all at once. I ordered a small glass of milk from the girl, and Mama said she wanted some water. More people started to come into the café, and pretty soon there were men and women standing in the aisles between the tables, and the waitresses were having trouble moving.

"Well, isn't this just like a party!" Mama said. She smiled at the deputy and he smiled – a tight, contained smile like he was smiling at her out of simple politeness. He was drinking black coffee out of a white stoneware mug. All the men were drinking coffee, some taking it black like the deputy and some adding cream from the little chrome jugs on the counter. I wondered what that coffee would have tasted like if I'd ordered some instead of my milk. There I was, eleven years old that winter, practically a teenager, almost a woman, and I had never tasted coffee, could not even visualize what coffee might taste like, having grown up under the rules of my church. That simple fact seems remarkable to me now. I can scarcely believe I was once that poor child.

We finished our drinks and got up to leave. It took us a while to weave our way through all the people to the door. On the way out, I heard a tall man saying something to a woman with a crushed-looking green velvet hat.

"This fall-out, it'll get into everything," he said. "Water. Milk. The air you breathe. It'll shine right through your body, make you sick in your blood and bones."

"The AEC people said it couldn't hurt a fly," the woman with the green hat objected. "Less than you get from a Timex wrist-watch. Less than you get from the noonday sun."

The man repeated what he'd said about the fall-out. How it would get inside your body, make your bones sick, sour your blood. I wanted to hear more, but Mama was right behind me, prodding me to hurry through the crowd and out the door.

A philosopher determined that there were one hundred billion demons that came down from heaven when Lucifer fell. That was one hundred evil spirits for every person who had ever walked the Earth. They were all around each of us, every waking hour and all night long, tempting each and every one of us to renounce and forsake the Lord. Big Sister told me this; she got it from my Daddy, who heard it from an elder of the LDS church.

"If you're genuinely faithful to the Lord," she said, "you can see every one of those demons. They're wisps of air with little eyes, or flames or just reflections on the surface of some water, the farm pond or a fishing hole or a shady spot out on a river. If your soul hasn't been protected by God, they can get in through the holes in your body. Your nostrils and anus and ears and other places. That whole yard out there is full of them, and so is the air that we breathe."

It was bed time when she told me all this, and I lay there awake half the night full of worries. Was the house safe from devils? Could the evil spirits filter through the lapped wood on the walls? Close to dawn, I got up and looked out from between the curtains on my window. I could hear Big Sister breathing in her bed across the room, and somewhere far below me I could hear my daddy's snores. There was just enough light in the yard for me to see the yellow, threadbare meadow grass that grew between the porch and the hog barn. I could see our old dog Rusty sleeping curled up in the shadow that the moonlight cast around Daddy's moon-blue Fargo truck.

I imagined spirits, wisps of air, curling in and out of Rusty's nose, writhing through his gold-red hair, raising twisters in the Utah dust around him. Could the spirits pass through glass and wood? Could they enter your bones and your bloodstream?

I should not, I guess, have asked myself these questions. My daddy was a priest of God; he would surely preserve and protect me. There were times, though, when I'd pause in the shade and imagine that I felt them – writhing spirits, cold as wind – coiling in my nostrils and the flesh around my eyes.

We sat for quite a while in a line-up of vehicles, just south of St. George on the highway. Nobody seemed entirely sure what it was we were waiting there for. Mama told me it was an accident, a car crash up ahead someplace, or maybe they were working on the road. After what seemed like a very long time, a deputy came walking slowly down the line of cars. People rolled down their windows, and the deputy bent down and had a word with each of the drivers in turn as he walked along. Every once in a while, he waved a car out of the line-up, and it drove along on the shoulder and left the rest of us behind. When he came to us, he asked my mother how far we'd driven that morning, and Mama told him we had just come from St. George.

The deputy nodded and continued along down the line. He was taller and thinner than the officer at the café, and he seemed for some reason to be terribly angry, as if there were something in what he had to do that made him mad. When we finally got going, we saw the cars and trucks they'd waved aside lined up at a Utoco station. Some boys and men were washing them down, hosing them off and scrubbing. There were quite a few people, old men and cowboys, people of all descriptions, standing around on the tarmac conversing, waiting for their cars to be washed.

It was dark before we got to Las Vegas. I was almost asleep, and I let myself slouch down and rested my head on Mama's shoulder. The city was a ball of light, and we drove towards it through the darkness, winging straight for the luminous core. They were playing Nat King Cole songs on the radio that night – each tune seemed to last for hours, until I thought that I could feel the singer's velvet, crooning voice against my skin. When we reached the Strip, I opened my eyes and sat upright in my seat to watch the sights.

We rented a room at a place right on the Strip. I had never stayed a night in a hotel before, at least not that I could remember, but I was so tired out I hardly even glanced at the people in the lobby or paid any attention to the elevator ride or the room in which we stayed. We undressed and put on our night clothes and climbed into the bed. I suppose I fell asleep straightaway. I was awakened a few hours later by the sound of someone moving. Mama wasn't in the bed with me, and I could see that the bathroom light was on through the gap around the partially open door.

I got out of bed and went into the bathroom. Mama was standing there over the vanity, holding up a hotel towel and sobbing. Her head was half-bald, like a middle-aged man's head. There were clumps of her hair, black and shiny, lying every-which-way in the sink. The towel she was holding up was also full of hair, clinging to the nap of the terry-cloth. I sat down on the carpet just outside the bathroom doorway, too stunned to say anything or even to cry.

In the morning, Mama's head was bald, and we were both of us feeling ill. She made herself a turban out of a scarf she'd got herself for her birthday with some money my daddy gave her as a present. She put on make-up, lipstick red as cherry pulp, eye-shadow, mascara, every single thing she had in her handbag, I think. I wondered if she had bought this stuff recently, the last time she drove down to St. George, for instance, or if she'd always had her makeup, kept it secret all those years. She looked like a lady, anyway, sitting there with her head all wrapped up in that scarf, looking down at me through those heavy black lashes.

"This just doesn't mean a thing," she said. She had sensed, I believe, that I was anxious, and she wished to reassure me that our lives would go on as planned. That evening, though, my mother was ill, even sicker than she had been before. The skin of her face and arms was red, though she was tanned from working outside at the farm and she never had the type of skin to sunburn. She brought up what little food there was in her stomach and then lay in the hide-a-bed the rest of the night, not sleeping a whole lot but too weak to move. I brought her a cake pan from the little kitchenette, in case she felt the urgent need to vomit, and then curled up on the loveseat to sleep. The furniture in the hotel room was some kind of plastic leatherette, and I woke up after midnight drenched in sweat. I opened the only window and let the noise of the Strip come in, then I drank a glass of water looking out at the neon signs. I wondered what my daddy and Big Sister were doing at that moment of their lives, back up on that farm in Utah. Were they worried and bereaved about us leaving like we had, or were they sleeping in their bedrooms just like always? I visualized them in different ways, Daddy standing at the porch door, looking out into the night, Big Sister in her flowered housecoat weeping. Or both the man and girl asleep, the big house still and dark, impervious to cares and drifting spirits.

By dawn, my mother was well enough to sit up and drink some tea. I went out and found a corner store and bought a small bag of necessary things, then I came back to our room to be with Mama. She was sitting up in the bed in her new flowered housecoat, with the scarf around her head. She patted the bed beside her and I kicked off my shoes and sat down.

"I've been thinking," she said.

She stopped there and took a deep breath, as if something was weighing on her, putting pressure on her chest.

"When I married your daddy," she finally continued, "I went over to the LDS church. I wore my garments every single day. Your father was an Adamic priest, with the power to speak to God and enter heaven. I most honestly and truly believed that. He would speak to me in no more than a whisper, those hard, hurtful eyes of his probing and prodding, and I'd feel like he was screaming from a mountain. He used to go to the Temple every week to perform vicarious baptism, did you know that? He would find the bones of Utes and Shoshoni in the fields, just turn them up with the plough or harrow, and the very next time he was at the Temple he would baptize that Ute who was no more than bones, just a handful of sticks like a scarecrow. He traced his own ancestors back a dozen generations, and over several years he baptized every one."

This speech seemed to take all the fight out of my mother. She lay back against the pillows and started fussing with the sheet.

"I wish you could have met your natural father," she said. This surprised me, because she seldom mentioned the man who'd fathered me; she rarely, in fact, said much about anything that had happened before she'd come down from Montana and married Daddy. I listened attentively, hoping she'd tell me some special thing about the father I'd never known.

"He was someone who liked to see a pretty thing when he had the chance to," she said. "He'd drive all day to watch the sun come down and turn some worthless little sump-hole yellow, and he always liked to watch me take my hair down."

The mention of her hair distracted her, and she had nothing more to say about my father.

"I wish I was little, as young as you are now," she said. "I wish someone would lift me up and spin me by my hair. I've felt so thick and heavy ever since I had you. Women feel that way after a child."

She reached out and touched the crown of my head, as if to confer some small blessing, then let her fingers run down the curve of my face. I flinched, which I hadn't wanted to, because my hair was lank and greasy and my skin was greasy too. We sat there for a long time, tired and speechless.

When I was old enough to work, an acquaintance of my mother's got me a part-time job in a diner in Henderson, which is just south of town towards the Hoover Dam. My mother and I moved down there from our place in North Las Vegas and I drove to work each morning in our car. The clientele were drifters, mostly, though at the time I didn't see that. I'd been raised to take people pretty much as they came, and the broken-down cowboys and servicemen let go from the Air Base seemed no different to me than anyone else you might meet in this world. In the evenings, when my shift was done, I would count up my tips at the counter and write the amount in my little book, then say goodnight to the fry cook and the fellow who did the books and drive back home to have my dinner with Mama.

Nothing had been right with my mother for years. She was tired all the time and couldn't work. She complained that the strength had drained out of her arms and her legs; even walking up a flight of stairs would make her feel sick and exhausted. A woman she'd waitressed with, Jeannie Craig, came to live with us in our apartment. She chain-smoked and butted her Camels on her plate, right in with the ketchup and left-over food. Mama told me to call her "Aunt Jeannie" and to treat her like she was my true-to-life aunt. After dinner, Jeannie Craig and Mama would make highballs and drink. They would listen to the radio or play records on the hi-fi, stack five or six platters on the automatic changer and listen to Peggy Lee or Frank Sinatra half the night. Years ago, when her hair had come back in, my mother had let it grow until it was halfways down her back, and she'd kept it that way even though it was partially grey now and the ends looked split and kinky. She would sit there talking away to Aunt Jeannie and play with her hair, rubbing those frazzled hanks between her fingers, feeling the texture in an absent-minded way.

Those last days in Mama's apartment were a difficult period for me. I got so I hated the company of women. Their nylons draped over the towel rack. Their cigarettes, smudged with pink lipstick. Their misshapen girdles. Their yellowing lingerie hung up to dry. I hated their weakness, their endless complaining. I would sit at the kitchen table looking out at the moon and wish I were anywhere, even back home in Utah. Aunt Jeannie's things got mixed in with mine and my mother's, and once she accused me of stealing a brooch of hers that had amethysts and sentimental value. The stink of her perfume seemed to fill the apartment. If I opened a window, my mother or Aunt Jeannie closed it. It was a place I couldn't be.

At the end of my junior year in high school, I left my mother's home and went away. I travelled to Los Angeles, to see the ocean and learn about acting, two things that I had always dreamed of doing. I dyed my hair blonde before leaving Las Vegas, and a girl I knew gave me a Toni home perm. My hair was so blonde it was silver, not gold, and I swept it away from my face in two wings. I wore a blue dress the colour of Navaho dream stones, with a low neck that showed off my cleavage, and my mother's pair of shiny black heels.

I went with an ex-GI named Larry Dean Palmer. I had met him at the place where I waitressed. He had learned to play the vibraphone when he was in the army, and he intended to form a jazz band when we got out to the coast. We drove up through Caliente, Alamo, and Ely, then headed west towards the Sierras with the top of his Mercury down. Larry had a brother in Carson City who he thought would lend him money. We were going to California, where we were going to make it big.

One afternoon, we stopped at a road house. It wasn't anything you could honestly call a casino, just a little flat-roof structure like an Esso garage with a sign that said SLOTS LIQUOR FOOD. Inside, it was all one big room, slots at the one end and a bar at the other, with some tables in the middle for those who wished to play cards. The air was full of heat and smoke. There were three men playing blackjack at a table near the fruit machines.

One was middle-aged and fat and wore a charcoal-grey fedora. The other two were boys who looked like soldiers out on leave.

We sat down on leatherette stools at the bar and Larry ordered me a soft drink and himself a shot and a beer. While we waited for our drinks to come, he lit a cigarette.

"Dig the bones," he said, waving his smoke at the wall behind the bar. At the top, near the ceiling, they had hung up the bleached-looking skull of some animal, a small cow or a sheep perhaps, it was difficult to say. The creature had been so deformed you couldn't tell what it should have looked like. There was a socket for a single eye, and one horn was branched and twisted, like the limb of a leafless tree. It could have been a demon or a figure from make-believe.

"Cool," Larry whispered. When the drinks came, he threw back his head and took his shot in one hard, sudden mouthful. Then he tapped the ash from his cigarette and lifted his glass of beer as if to contemplate its colour in the murky, inadequate light.

There wasn't much to look at in the road house. The three men at the table seemed to have as little interest in card games as I did. They lounged in their chairs and blew smoke rings, threw coins and folded bills across the table when the occasion required that they do so, and spent a lot of time shuffling cards. More than once I caught the younger fellows looking at my legs. Around dark, a couple more men arrived to play blackjack, and not long after that a dilapidated woman in a stained khaki car-coat shuffled over to the slot machines with a paper cup full of change. My boyfriend nursed his second glass of beer.

"We ought to get going," I finally told him. "We ought to get along to Carson City. It's getting on night now, we ought to be gone."

Larry waved to the bartender for another beer-and-a-shot.

"Anywhere I am, I'm gone," he said. His voice was hardly more than a whisper. He smiled and flicked ash across the counter. His eyes had already taken on that smug look that a person's eyes get when they know that they're going to be drunk. I told him once or twice more that I wanted to get going, that I'd have voted not to stop there in the first place if I'd been asked. Pretty soon, I went into the foyer, where I'd seen a good-sized armchair, curled up in it under Larry's black windbreaker, and drifted off to sleep.

I was awakened near dawn by the noise of someone shouting. I heard the sound of splintering wood and some woman's hysterical laughter. I walked right through the road house from the front to the rear and went out into the yard behind the building. There were eight or ten people out back in the lot. The glass panes in one of the outside doors were smashed, and the door itself was hanging off its hinges. Larry Dean and another man were fighting. By the looks of things, they'd been wrestling around in the dust for a while. They both looked beat and heartsick, as if their bodies were two tired animals that had no wish to fight.

It was a scene that should have made me blue, but though my back was sore from lying on that lumpy chair all night, I felt strangely fresh and clear-headed. I could visualize the whole of my life, every hour of it flowing into the next hour, all the days of my existence laid out there right before me like a Rand McNally map. I would drive to California, if not with Larry Dean Palmer then with someone else entirely, some other man who owned a car – with one of those fellows in the road house, perhaps, or with someone I would meet in Carson City. I would act in many feature films, playing beautiful girls who had no luck, who were married to unworthy men or who were menaced by evil-doers or troubled by terrible fears. I would swagger through elegant parties, let my blonde hair fall across my eyes. I would laugh out loud, drink cocktails, and walk for miles beside the sea. I would never think of Mama, or that road house, or my life.

Over thirty years later, I wait for Pilar. It is late in the day, and it's my custom in the evenings to take a drink of plain club soda on the deck above the pool. Pilar brings my drink on a tray, just as if she were a waitress in a night club. I expect this amused me years ago, when I moved up to this house. Lyman Whyte, my second husband, was the one who hired the help, though at that time it was someone other than Pilar, someone smaller, cleaner, and less good-natured, though also a Spanish-speaking person.

The summer has pretty well played itself out. The pool is streaked with curled brown leaves from the Japanese maple, a pathway of babies' hands, reaching for light. I sit on the balcony, looking down at the yard. I am wearing wide palazzo pants and an equally loose-fitting jacket. My head has been wrapped in a turban. This is also Pilar's job, to lay out my clothes on my bed in the morning, to wind the scarf into a turban, to get me undressed before bed. Neither of us looks at the other while she performs these operations. At night, before she comes upstairs, I take off the turban myself. I sit down at the vanity and look at my white, oval face. Without hair, I seem unearthly, like a crone who has come back from the dead. My hairless visage fascinates me, but I regard it without much emotion. What has happened has happened; there is nothing to be done. Time is just a treacherous thing, my mother would have said. Whatever you build, it blows away; whatever you put a shine on, it'll tarnish.

Not long after Mama and I moved down from the farm to Las Vegas, I pulled off one of my fingernails when I was lying in the bath. We were still in that room on the Strip in those days, and my mother was in the bedroom, listening to the radio with a cold towel over her face. I was listening to the music too, and thinking about the farm. My mind was full of farmyard scenes, like a pack of picture postcards. Big Sister dressed for Beehive Girls. Mama and me climbing into our Chevy. My daddy's footprints pooled with shade in the dust beside the steps. I rubbed at an itch on my finger, and the nail curled away in my palm. It was tougher than pigskin and seemed as foreign as a claw. I put it on the side of the white enamel bath and resolved to say nothing to Mama. It would soon grow back, I told myself, and in this I was correct. A brand new nail, baby-pink and pearlescent, formed gradually in place of the old one. I awaited other portents, but nothing else occurred. The spirit was inside me, marking time.

The fistfight seemed to have been going on for quite some time. Both Larry and the other boy were stumbling on their knees. The spectators had begun to lose interest. Some had wandered back inside the bar and others were laughing and talking. I walked around the knot of men and went out to watch the dawn.

The man with the grey fedora was standing a ways beyond the rest, looking out at the southern desert. There wasn't much out there but creosote bushes and the odd twisted tree. The sun had come up just enough to paint the mountains red. Some kind of bird made mournful sounds. It was an ordinary south Nevada sunrise.

"Seen one, you seen them all," I said. I was making conversation, that was all.

"Hey, it's the Blonde Bombshell! Where you been?" he said. He grinned at me in a friendly way and tipped back his fedora. His face was fat but not gross or unpleasant. He seemed, now that I looked at him closely, a more refined sort of man than his companions.

I shrugged and gathered Larry Dean Palmer's windbreaker around my shoulders, to show him that my whereabouts were no concern of his. He shook his head as if amused and went back to staring at the sunrise.

"There's a test shot at oh-five-thirty. That's any minute now," he said. He pushed back the cuff of his shirt and took a glance at his watch. "Keep your eyes on the edge of that ridge, it's worth watching."

When the bomb flash hit, I flinched and screamed. The world became transparent. After that, there were winds and the terrible cloud. We all stood and watched without speaking. Larry Dean Palmer left about half an hour later, the Mercury spraying dust across the lot as he peeled out. Later on, I took a ride with the older man and made my way west, crossing through the hills into my future.

Pilar comes out onto the deck with my club soda. She puts it down without a word and then goes back inside. I sip my drink and watch the leaves floating motionless in the pool. Like all inhuman things, they wait, their bodies changing form, abandoned in the arid light of heaven.

## CHERYL TIBBETTS

# *The Flowers of Africville*

Viewed from a certain angle, Africville in its last days looks much as it did in its first. A sprinkling of clapboard houses in various salt-faded shades, and here and there an outhouse or a well. A tidy white church, a piece of dirt road, a red row of gladioli. It perches on a rim of land where the North Atlantic spills into the Bedford Basin, and the ocean shines beneath the burning sun like the bath of God.

And it is His bath. For a moment, time collapses to a string of Easter Sundays, and a procession of Baptists threads its way from the small church to the rocky shore. Their voices rise up in an anthem of praise – the very soul of soul – that ricochets off the floorboards of heaven and reverberates in ripples across the face of the water below. A few bodies plunge into the liquid element, where the winter ice broke only weeks ago, its particles spattering like shards of glass across their purified skin. But their fervour insulates them from the cold, and the song grows stronger. They squint into the holy skies though the brilliance of the sun blinds them.

Then the image is lost. The years expand like an accordion and in its pleats there are other days of the week. Other eras.

A man stands alone on the pebbled beach, small stones cutting their way into the soles of his toughened feet. He examines a piece of paper he cannot read, and doesn't understand he holds a ticket instead of a land deed. Doesn't understand that generations will pass upon this soil and yet the hour will come when the piece of paper will matter. And it wouldn't make a difference if he did understand. Unlike the paler loyalists, he owns nothing.

The man becomes obscured by the slow roll of a fog bank. When the mist clears, he is gone.

A hundred yards offshore, a group of small children push and shove one another atop a wooden raft. They squeal in fear and joy until, one by one, they fly into the August air then slip under the swells and squirm like tadpoles. "Ma!" they yell at the height of their glorious flights. A woman sits shucking peas on a doorstep, hears their distant cries and stops her work to wave.

The woman is obliterated by a cloud of dust and time shifts once more. It is a bulldozer making its way alongside the railroad tracks to the schoolhouse. The bulldozer reaches the schoolhouse, pauses, reverses, then advances with its ram. A clutter of noise. Windows smash, wood splits, and walls collapse into rubble. Somewhere a piano plays. The dust thickens.

When the speckles of plaster dissipate and gradually float back to earth, it is possible to see her. Abigail Downs. She who has seen all this and more. Abigail has her father's memory and, beyond that, her own recollections are long. This bolsters her as she becomes aware of her slipping hold on the chronological ordering of things. Learning just now, as she is, mercifully late in life, what happens to humans afflicted with age. How the distant past grows larger while the recent years recede.

This is how Abigail is found: still planted firmly in her chair the day the bulldozers arrive in Africville. One hundred and four and nothing but black hair can be seen in the fastidiously tight braids she fashions so closely to her head. Smiling because her descendants believed they had outsmarted her with the distraction of a party to celebrate the new residences that had been constructed to house them elsewhere. Public apartments. It would be better there, they assured her, as they unwrapped her fist to insert the five hundred dollars she had been given in exchange for her home. Not bad, they said, since it developed it was never really Abigail's anyway.

She stares at the remaining furnishings in her tiny house, which, until three days ago, had been cluttered with the accumulation of the generations who had lived there. Now only her own things are left, awaiting the momentous decision of who she would choose among her family to die amidst. Of course, she has already decided to remain with the family of her favourite grandson, Ruevin, whom she's lived with ever since they temporarily moved into her own house almost thirty years ago. But she wants to stall to gain a little time by herself.

She's never had such a thing before. Whether it was a new brother or sister being squeezed into her childhood bed, or a forsaken aunt setting up a cot in the kitchen. That's what happens when land gets passed down. All the offspring have an equal right to be there.

Abigail surveys her life's belongings. Not much of an assortment, but then there have been many purgings over the years under the ever present strain of always having to make room, which became so much easier once the mayor decided to turn their back yard into the town dump. Abigail knows the value of finding the bright side. If you looked at it the right way, and didn't mind the vermin and the smell, it made life easier, really. At least they didn't have to go begging for the loan of a truck to get rid of that old chesterfield. And spring cleaning had always been a snap. Yes, she nods to herself, there was a certain convenience to having the dump so handy.

Now those five rocking chairs really should have gone too. Five. It would be an imposition to arrive at Ruevin's with that pack of sticks in tow, but she can't help smiling to herself and thinking how they deserve it. It seems a woman gets to a certain age and everybody likes to believe she would be happier with the universe tilting at all angles under her feet. Let them enjoy it if they think it's so dandy, Abigail reasons, smiling to herself a little vindictively. She had let the number get to five before she had insisted these prized gifts be placed around the supper table, and was satisfied to see that she never did receive another rocking chair gift since. She lets out a high laugh thinking of Ruevin's family careening about through their evening meals, lunging for the butter in the centre of the table and involuntarily rollicking back again before it got within their reach. While she, Abigail, sat at the head of the table in her favourite wooden armchair, its four legs and her two feet attached solidly and unwaveringly to the earth beneath her.

It is the same armchair she sits in now, though it has been pulled out from the table to the middle of the living room, facing the big picture window.

Through the corner of the window, Abigail can just see two bulldozers plodding down the road. Her eyes are bad enough that she doesn't see the man with the big camera who is walking ahead of them until they come to a full stop in front of her. The man frets back and forth with his camera, a few paces this way, scowls over his shoulder at the sun. Reaching for that consummate photograph of one of the last remaining structures in Africville: the home of Abigail Downs.

She watches. Waits until she hears a polite tapping at the front door.

It is him.

Abigail doesn't stir. "Come in!" she calls from her chair, almost as if she has been expecting him. And in a way, she has. The man pushes the door open and peers tentatively into the living room with one hand still on the doorknob as if in preparation to bolt should internal circumstances demand. Seeing only Abigail, he apparently decides it is safe to step inside.

"I'm a reporter from the *Transcript*," he says.

Abigail is not surprised. He looks as a reporter should. Eager. with a camera slung around his neck and a pencil and notepad in hand. A little young maybe, but it has gotten difficult for Abigail to discern age in those beyond her great-grandchildren's generation.

The reporter strides over to Abigail's chair and extends his hand. Abigail doesn't take it. She is in no mood to indulge this man who sees fit to impose such foreign customs upon an old black woman.

"Sit down," she says, motioning her head towards the fleet of rocking chairs near the wall.

He remains standing. An impatient shift of the feet. The bulldozers are waiting outside. "I won't take much of your time. I just need a quote. Something on your thoughts on leaving Africville."

Abigail considers this. "My thoughts are that it stinks."

"Um. The dump, you mean? You're glad to be getting away from the dump?" His pencil hovers over his pad.

"No."

"Well, it *is* kinda close to the houses. I've never been down here before."

"No call to, I don't imagine." Abigail feels irritated.

"Would you object if I took your photo for the paper?" He starts to adjust the viewfinder, expecting a positive response.

"I thought you wanted a quote!"

"Well, I do."

Abigail expands her nostrils and inhales deeply. She holds her breath for a moment while the reporter waits.

"It's been a fine place to be a nigger," she exhales.

She is tormenting him, she knows, but she has to take her opportunities for fun where they lie.

"Aw, come on!" he says, tapping his pencil impatiently against his notepad. "You know I can't use that. No one can get away with using the word 'nigger' any more."

The reporter is young, but it turns out that he has more spunk than Abigail had thought, and this somehow pleases her.

"I can," Abigail shoots back. "Folks can call themselves whatever they please, and I say it suits the bill just fine."

"You know it's not going to look good. I can't pass it by even in a quote. I'm supposed to be writing an article about you people moving up from here."

"Moving up? Whoever heard of moving away from the sea being moving up?"

The reporter is becoming cautious. He says nothing.

"Free fish," Abigail challenges. And her mind turns like the tide.

There were provisions, her father had often proclaimed, that could be had as simply as walking a few hundred yards to drop a line into the Bedford Basin. And Abigail's mother knew lots of good ways to cook fish. She would even save their skeletons and boil them down to the secret seasoning she added to her delicious black-eyed peas. Never waste food. All parts of the fish are good if you just let your mind get around eating them. The

Micmacs had taught them that. Abigail's mother said she didn't know if they would have survived the first year if the Micmacs hadn't come to the Basin that fall. Her in a fever and without family or a man. Nothing but the dress on her body and a high talent for needlepoint inherited from an aunt who had made cushions for fancy southern ladies. The Indians will outnumber the white folk in the end, her mother had told her.

Abigail, with a certain blasphemous guilt, has begun to suspect that her mother might have been wrong on that score. Then she scolds herself. Knowledge is a confidence of the young.

"The Basin is polluted now," the reporter states.

Abigail greets this interruption with a start. Maybe she's been rambling again.

The reporter repeats himself, increases his volume. "I said, the Basin is polluted now."

Abigail snorts. She knows his type. He buys his fish in boxes in the frozen food section of a supermarket. Always had. Probably that High Liner brand she's seen advertised on the television.

"I heard you," she says.

He says something else, but this time Abigail doesn't hear him. His words are lost to a passing train and the responding rattle of glass.

The reporter walks to the living room window and stands looking out with his back to Abigail. She hears the pitched squeal of steel against steel, shuts her eyes and clenches her fingers around the arms of her chair.

"Stay put," Abigail whispers to herself, but the past rises heedlessly around her. Her mind slips a notch, and catches on the year of the hard winter.

Almost midnight. She scrabbled along the track. Her frozen knees pounded on the wooden ties, sodden skirts heavy across her calves. Lumps of coal glittered blackly in the fresh snow. Too far apart. Already she was half a mile from home. Her wide eyes watered in the rising wind, as she stared into the drifts on the left side of the rails for the precious scatterings of freight. She reached out, her fingers dipped into the frost, retrieved another piece to stow into her apron pocket. So cold. Her daughter, who was covering the right side of the rails, called out from behind, "All right. I've got all I can carry!" Abigail laughed in relief, carefully arranged the coal in her apron pockets as she rose to her feet. "That's good, girl."

They'd staved it off another day. Her eldest son would not have to cut the last standing tree for their hearth. Not yet.

Where was her husband? Four months at sea and he was supposed to be gone for only three. Just then, Abigail was sure, he was tightening his grasp on the mast of the drowning ship. Or trying to board an overcrowded lifeboat, perhaps. In her mind, an oar extended and pushed him away.

The shriek of the locomotive dwindles into the distance.

The reporter is facing Abigail again. "Phew! There is a reminder to look both ways."

"We've made the best of it. It was better when it was steam."

The reporter regards Abigail anew. Scrutinizes the veined hands clutching the chair arms, allows his eyes to float down to her feet. Abigail wishes she had remembered to wear her slippers.

"Would it be impolite to ask your age?"

"My name," she tells him, "is Abigail."

"Oh."

She is about to disclose her age – it is cause for boasting after all – but she is distracted by the commotion of Ruevin pulling up in his station wagon.

Abigail shakes her head. A heap of scrap metal as sorely in need of a new muffler as Ruevin is in need of customers who can afford to pay.

Through the window, his eyes lock with Abigail's as soon as he pops out of the car. For the first time, Abigail realizes that Ruevin has grown old. Why, all his hair is grey!

"Grandma!" he bellows as he slams his car door. He motions for the bulldozers to drive away. "Do the white bungalow and that blue place first," he hollers. "Give us a chance to pack the car."

Abigail hears him through the pane. Feels him stomping up the front steps.

"Now what's this all about? Kevin just came back and said you wouldn't drive over with him. You should be ashamed of yourself. Him all upset. Now how's a young boy like that gonna handle a crotchety old lady like you? And I thought you said that this was all fine in the end."

Abigail adores Ruevin. He has the gift of gab.

Ruevin throws open the front door and quickly adjusts himself upon seeing the man with the camera standing next to Abigail.

"Ruevin Downs," he says, walking forward to offer his hand. Abigail is still contemplating the matter of the muffler and Ruevin's job. Her father had been much better at attracting the right sort of customers, Abigail decides.

Her father had managed to get by with his trade in the beginning. Helping rich white men build their houses in return for meals. Hammering up the wainscotting, carving the chair rails, sleeping in their cellars through the frigid winter. No one was better at fretwork than old Ben. This was one thing Abigail's particular so-called shanty still had. Its presence was so familiar she had completely forgotten about it until this moment. A sculpted chair rail ran like a fine leather belt around the belly of the living room. Abigail made a mental note to ask Ruevin to take it down and reaffix it in her bedroom in the new place.

Now, where was she? She could barely keep track of herself any more. Oh yes. Her father spending the winters in white men's cellars. Just dirt and stone back then. But the winter nights were warm enough in Africville once he started keeping house with Abigail's mother. A nice, solid woman with heat enough to keep ten men warm for a year of Januarys, Abigail's father had been heard to brag.

And times were good enough. "There's always some kind of job to be found by a man who is inclined to work," her father said. And what a luxury, being free to stop labouring when his leg started acting up, instead of waiting for it to sneak off on him like it belonged to someone else. When he was a young man, his master broke it in three places because he caught him sleeping under a tree one hot afternoon during the tobacco harvest. It was so hot that day, never in his life would he find fault with even the harshest of northern blizzards. He long remembered how the skin on his face blistered and bubbled like a pot of coffee on an open fire. And he recalled how lucky he was to have had such a kind master. Others would be dead.

His master grimaced when he heard the leg breaking under his club. "You've forced me to do this to avoid inciting the others!" he angrily hissed.

The professor who came down to Africville from the university had tried to dredge all kinds of stories like this out of Abigail's father, and was perpetually dissatisfied by his laughing renditions. The white history man, her father had called him.

"But weren't you enraged?" the professor demanded, flushed and obviously feeling quite furious himself.

And her father laughed again, and shooed at the professor with his hand. "Hell, no. Ask any man who has been to war. If they let you go with nothing but a bullet in your foot, it's a gift. You can't help wondering if such a God-given soldier is even doing his job."

Then the professor shook his head in annoyance. "But wouldn't you?" he persisted. "Wouldn't you let another man live?"

And her father shrugged his shoulders and squeaked out another maddening chuckle. "I don't know, my friend. Maybe these are easy thoughts for an old slave and a northern white man."

"No. They are not," the professor stated tightly. "The moral choice should be perfectly clear."

"Well, I can't speak for everyone. But I believe that master of mine was a good man."

A disgruntled rumble from the professor.

"Then get some fresh opinions," Abigail's father encouraged. "There's lots of people still being used as slaves in this world. Ask them."

Afterward, he explained to Abigail what the white history man would never understand. That his master was better than he had to be, and this is why he was a good man. If the professor understood that, her father said, he might learn to be of some help yet. He had enough money. Sitting around and yakking about right and wrong was no more good than a rotted cod.

Decades later, Abigail would boil this down and deliver it to Ruevin in a much-rehearsed lecture series. "Rise above the demands of circumstances," she would expound. "There is the test that defines a good man."

But to Abigail's dismay, Ruevin in this respect had something in common with the white professor. Ruevin didn't see how it could be a happy fortune to merely have your leg broken in three places for falling asleep on an enslaved job. Laughed. Said Abigail's father had perfected the quest for that elusive silver lining.

Eventually, that bad leg would refuse to bend, forcing Abigail's father out of the wainscotting business when he could no longer work on his knees. A turn of events well worth the variety it offered, he argued. There are plenty of options available to an industrious man.

Now, being a self-employed knife sharpener: there was not a grander career. Abigail got plenty of mileage out of that one while Ruevin was still in law school. She had determined that, with all the airy ideas he was getting at the university, he might need a bit of old-fashioned tempering at home.

Abigail spent many a delightful afternoon in her armchair devising new speeches around this theme to deliver to young Ruevin when he got back from his classes. Special scholarship. They paid him to go to school clean through high school, and the social workers were just falling over themselves with glee when he said he'd like to continue on to university. He would have been half crazy to do otherwise with all the money they were paying him by then. A social services triumph: a black law student! A lineman on the football team and third in his class. Whoever would have thought it possible?

Ruevin had hit a lot of firsts, and the government people took note. It was good for publicity, and Ruevin was affable enough to make himself available for the odd photo with this official or that. Abigail noticed the cameramen were predisposed to focus on the joining of the black and white hands, but if you followed the black hand up the arm and over the curve of the broad, suited shoulder, there was her Ruevin smiling away. And Abigail, though she tried to fight it, was a damned sight proud.

"But it ain't any better than what my daddy was able to achieve for himself in his day," she would spit whenever pride threatened to overcome her. And she was off again. The business of sharpening knives.

Her father had rhymed off all she needed to know. "First, you've got to work up a solid route and get a good bell so they can hear you coming. The thing is to make everyone else's life a little easier. Be friendly, wish all your customers a pleasant day. It's all part of the job." Abigail's father even arranged to pay a man who ran a dry goods store to accept messages for him when he was urgently needed to get the knives ready for a big dinner celebration. In all the hustle and bustle of a party, the state of the cutlery was one of those details that often went overlooked until the hour was nigh. And the last thing a decent white woman wanted was to be seen scrambling down to Africville after the knife sharpener.

The storekeeper's name was Jake. Abigail could easily summon his stony face on the day she first accompanied her father into the store. Jake was already an old man, even then. Initially, he was reluctant to listen to her father's anxious proposal. But Abigail's father offered him a one-dollar bank note to allow him to tell folks they could leave messages for him at the store, and five cents for each message relayed thereafter. It was a lot of money, but it was worthwhile if they could come out even a few cents ahead.

Abigail, who was the only one of the three who could read, would be sent to check for messages every day at high noon. She was seven years old, and the year was 1871.

It seemed Jake had his doubts regarding Abigail's reported literacy. He looked sceptically at Abigail then said to her father, "What did you say your name was?"

"Ben."

"And what's that a shortcut for? Benjamin? Benedict?"

"It's just Ben."

"Surname?"

"It's just Ben."

Her father had never known a family and a white man had named him.

And, miraculously, Jake agreed to her father's scheme. He took the bank note from Ben and handed it to Abigail to read.

The note was crisp and new.

"One dollar. The Dominion of Canada." Abigail slowly read.

The two men nodded solemnly and the agreement was sealed. By the time Jake died, they were almost friends.

And so Abigail began her daily visits to the storekeeper who never asked her name.

"Oh, Ben's girl," he would say as she arrived each noon. Then, if any knife customers had called, he would reach into the envelope kept behind the counter and his fingers would hunt for the slips of paper inside.

"Anything to know?" he would sometimes inquire hopefully as Abigail silently read the messages in the store.

My name, Abigail would think, not fully realizing her own reverence for the only white man she knew. A gentleman. Why don't you want to know about me? And depending on Abigail's mood, she would choose whether to answer him. Candy, six for a penny, was magically free if he was curious enough. Abigail had become the gatekeeper of social news on the Halifax elite.

It would have been different if Jake could read.

After Jake's funeral, she went uncertainly to the store and found his brother there. Abigail was a young woman by then.

"This is from Jake," the brother said.

He pressed a worn envelope into her hand, marked with her own seven-year-old handwriting: MESSAGES FOR BEN.

Abigail accepted the envelope mutely.

"Jake said, 'Give this to Abigail,'" the brother explained.

And Abigail cried on the spot, stricken with sudden grief to learn Jake had known her name.

"If I knew that," Abigail sobbed to Jake's bewildered brother, "I would have told him where the parties were for free."

Inside the envelope, Abigail found the bank note, no longer crisp and new.

More than four score years it has rested now between pages 256 and 257 of her Bible. Ruevin has told her it is a first edition Canadian dollar bill. Eighteen-seventy-one was the first year they rolled them off the presses. He thinks it may be worth something, and he is right. Before it's over, Abigail thinks, she must educate Ruevin on the real value of that dollar.

Abigail realizes her eyebrows are tightly knit together and feels angry somehow. She wonders how long Ruevin and that young reporter have sat in front of her. Right now the young man is talking to Ruevin and happily scribbling away on his pad. Ruevin knows how to tell people what they want to hear, and he has the desire.

Abigail feels she's missed something. Tuned out too long again. This has been happening to her more and more lately.

Now the two men have stopped talking and are smiling at her like a pair of birthday clowns.

"Grandma?" Ruevin says. "Are you not paying attention again?"

He turns to the reporter. "Look. She's tormenting you like an old cat with a tennis ball the one minute, and the next she doesn't even know you're there."

"Is it okay to take a picture?" the reporter asks. He is pointing his camera lens at Abigail but is directing the question at Ruevin.

"Sure, sure," Ruevin booms confidently. "Show those teeth, Grandma." He shows his own to Abigail. "They're all her own, you know," her says to the reporter.

"No kidding?" The reporter sounds genuinely impressed. "And a hundred and four," he breathes in amazement. "I can't get over it. No grey hair!"

"Teeth, Grandma," Ruevin reminds Abigail.

She grimaces, then lets it relax into a nice, white smile.

"Great teeth, too," the reporter exclaims encouragingly while he frames the shot.

Abigail feels like a lamp. Flash. She sees spots.

When her sight returns, she sees Ruevin slapping the reporter's back as they head for the door. The reporter is leaning confidentially towards Ruevin. Her eyesight may be poor, but her hearing is as sharp as ever.

"She'd be an excellent candidate for a human interest story. When's her next birthday?" the reporter asks.

Abigail stares at the retreating reporter in annoyance. That reporter hadn't even heard her out, she thinks. Just ended up chatting with Ruevin and then tried to sail on out. Ruevin. What did that young whip know about Africville?

"I know what you've got down in that chicken scrawl," she snarls after the reporter. "Ruevin complaining about the town dump next door. Ruevin moaning that we got dirty wells and no running water. How hard it is just to get a taxi to come down here. The bad reputation. How they shoved the prison and the slaughterhouse right on top of us. Nothing to show for our taxes . . ."

Abigail is suddenly exhausted and ceases enough to notice Ruevin grinning uneasily at the reporter. She begins to feel a bit guilty about all this back-talk of hers. Ruevin had worked hard on the Africville committee. His well-meaning rhetoric pounds in her brain, and she falls silent. Young and naive, she thinks, though he is almost fifty-five.

Ruevin appears relieved. "Sometimes she's got this sort of delayed reaction thing," he explains to the reporter as the two men resume their walk towards the door.

Abigail, imagining herself admonished, ponders this. Why is it that some folks speak in the presence of the very young and very old as though they're not actually there? She tries, unsuccessfully, to pinpoint the exact age when she graduated to being directly addressed by adults.

Her mother arriving home from needle-pointing the napkins for a wedding: "What did Abigail do today?"

Her father: "She came with me. Ran up and rang doorbells for me so folks wouldn't have to come out into the rain, while I stood and did my sharpening in the street. Asked folks right nice, I could hear her little voice all clear and polite, 'Excuse me, ma'am, do you need any knives sharpened today?'"

"That's nice," her mother replies. "Abigail can be a good girl when she wants."

"When she wants," her father agrees.

Abigail sighs. The old woman and the young girl merge, and Abigail understands she will have to make the best of it and be good. There is a need to make room again. Except this time, it isn't just a matter of another pair of cold feet in her bed or children being told to play outside. No. Everything and everybody will have to turn to dust to make room for the white people's highway. More traffic lanes than her youngest little descendant could count, and they'd never even been able to get the city to pave so much as a single footpath down here in a hundred and fifty years.

It will be as though they were never here.

Abigail gets as close as she ever has to allowing herself to recognize irony. But it is too bitter, and she has resolved to be good. She draws in her eyebrows and concentrates. Ruevin had said there would be water running from a tap right inside the new house. No more beating the bushes for volunteers to take a bucket to the well in the dead of winter. And hot water too. No more boiling. Clean hot water right inside the house. Now that would feel nice on an old body. Just imagine the convenience of that.

Abigail smiles then, having opted for the pleasant thoughts instead. She watches, as if from a great distance, the slow slide of a bead along a rusted rod of the abacus on which she counts out the lessons of her life. "Ma!" a child calls from a raft. Abigail hears, and raises her hand, waves and imagines an ocean breeze touching her face. A little girl throws herself into the swells, bobs up and turns to shore to see the village has vanished like Atlantis. The little girl floats onto her back. She studies the clouds and she is singing.

## JOHN BROOKE

# *The Finer Points of Apples*

"Mmm! You smell like apples." Bruce was nuzzling her hair, pushing his knee against her thigh.

"Le vinaigre de cidre," said Geneviève, "the apple man sells it."

"Cider vinegar?"

"C'est bon pour le . . . how do you say it? . . . itching."

"Smells good." Then Bruce asked, "are we going to make love tonight?"

"Pense pas."

"Ah . . ."

"You would like that?"

"I could."

"Pas moi . . . trop fatiguée." Geneviève rolled over.

"Maybe the apple guy has something for that too."

"Peut-être . . . bonne nuit."

In fact, the apple guy did.

Gaston Le Gac had long fingers that knew how to reach deep into her different openings to places Bruce had never been, or scratch her breast at *le moment juste*, or slap her bottom with a calculated measure of playful malice which could make her insides flow. Or baking the apple: He would disengage completely – maybe softly kiss – while pressing an apple against her. She would ply herself upon its smoothness. It was birth in reverse, the head of the child she had never made. No, she had no regrets on that score. It's far too late for that. Rather, it was this sense of being removed, of falling into a space between herself and the life around her. Pure imagination. The erotic far-side of procreation . . . The apple, after all, is forever. Gaston brought Geneviève fresh sex and immortality.

And it was conversation – of the kind Bruce, eight years into their liaison, had never quite caught onto. Oh, his French was mostly fine at this point; but what could an English Canadian ever really know of a French traveller's soul? Of her blood-borne feelings?

They had determined that Gaston had arrived from Quimper via Paris the very week she had walked off her flight from Toulouse. That was twenty-three years ago. Now here at long last was the inevitable meeting with a fellow countryman, the kind she vaguely imagined as she'd set out, footloose, excited . . . then nibbled at from behind loneliness for the first two years at wine and cheese things at l'Alliance or brunches at friends of friends', then forgotten for a time when she'd met her first stranger at a fern bar in Vancouver, and then encountered again from a different kind of distance as the trail had wound in ever more diffuse circles, back here to Montréal.

Where there are lots of us.

Yes, but all re-attached, she thought. To them.

Twenty-three years, and it was this scruffy Breton, coming up from Freleighsburg to sell his apples at le Marché Jean Talon.

His wife's apples, to be more exact. Well, her father's, really. But almost hers and so Gaston's. Geneviève had heard that part too. It meant this could only be *une aventure*. A fling? An affair? Something on the side? Positioning it in English was something she would leave for the time being. Just *une aventure*, thought Geneviève, without a sense of any wrong. Because we have the passion and the practicality, and these are meant to be separate. The ability to keep each in its place is in our blood. It's what they know us by, our calling card . . . Gaston's wife was a sturdy Québécoise. Micheline. She worked the stall the occasional day but there was no threat. And there were three children, and perhaps the eldest girl sensed something as she observed her papa chatting with this regular customer. This Française. But that girl was half French. His wife? Not a problem. She wouldn't know. Too far from her. Just like with Bruce. Never in a million years.

It was a question of breathing the same way. Or the finer points of apples. They could talk for hours if they had to, right there in the middle of the market. The locals' eyes would glaze over and they'd get on with other things. It was a kind of natural protection, especially here in Montréal.

They were settling on Empire. The acidy element made the sweet more precious, the pulp required real teeth, had character. But Gaston was still loath to dismiss the McIntosh.

"This is your basic apple," he said. "Sure, some will call it bland, flaccid. Myself, I say it's soft, welcoming. This apple is fundamentally sweet. Sweetness is a quality where degrees begin in the ineffable and descend from there. A child will eat six of these McIntoshes before she realizes she is ill. None of them can match that. We are talking fruit, remember, something the Lord created and the Devil put to use."

"It is like our vin de pays," countered Geneviève; "solid, and there for anyone. But low. No, there are no two ways about it – the McIntosh is low. If you want to know quality, you have to move up."

"True. Absolutely true."

"Now the Cortland," she ventured, "is almost a McIntosh. That soft taste, as you characterize it . . . and almost Empire as well. Cortland's pulp is a force to be reckoned with. And it lacks the sour bite. Yes, I would almost say Cortland is the best of both worlds."

"But are we here to deal in almosts?" queried Gaston.

"No . . . no," sighed Geneviève, smoothing her palm along his hairy back, "we've come too far for that."

"If you want to challenge Empire you must side with Spartan. You must go past the threshold of stringency. Spartan compels the mouth to draw in upon itself. Not pleasant to my taste – but vital!"

"But if we must explore those areas," and Geneviève was at a point in her life where she did not like to speak of dryness, "we must surely say Lobo is king."

"King of dryness, yes, no argument there . . . But it is flat. Lobo is soft but in all its negative connotations. Sweetness, character . . . there is nothing there! . . . much like those waxy things they send us from the west. *Delicious.* There's a marketing triumph for you . . . Lobo is entirely too easy. If McIntosh is for a baby, Lobo's for a sauce and not much else." He rolled over, sipped on her nipple. "It's my biggest seller though. I have to love Lobo regardless of what I know is true."

"I know the feeling," said Geneviève, fingers in his stringy hair – jet black and so familiar.

"Do you?"

"Oui," she mused, suddenly weighed down by subtlety, ". . . some things are made to test us."

That morning she had tried to give Bruce a reason why *fini* could not be used to express his feeling of exhaustion after a fourth piece of toasted baguette, smothered, as usual, with peach jam from her mother's village in the Midi, a half-hour north of Sète:

"Yes, to say you are finished – as in *through eating,* which anyone would be . . ." Bruce never flinched at her jabs. "And yes, if eating four pieces of toast like that will serve to break your reputation into crumbs. Your social standing, or your business credibility: these both could be fini . . . Mais, tu ne peux pas dire pour le moral. Jamais."

"I don't mean to use it for my morale," said Bruce. "I feel fine. Wonderful! I'm just wiped out from eating four pieces of toast and two bowls of your beautiful coffee. Je suis fini. As in *fatigué.*"

"You can't."

"You can in English . . . whew! I'm finished!"

"Faux amis."

"Why?"

"C'est le moral."

"No . . . c'est le physique."

"No, Bruce . . . non."

"Think you're wrong this time, Gen."

So she'd got the dictionary and it took an hour.

She should have been used to it by that point, but no, it was still surprising how much time they spent working with words. The mechanics. They were a shield against the gap and why deny it. Not a bridge; one cannot bridge a gap that will always, like sweetness, be ineffable. Just a shield. One more way to work around the gap so a bond could form. And it was not only with Bruce . . . with the English. It happened with all the Québécois she knew as well. Gaston had said "and how!" (*tu parles!*) to that, referring to the three children he had engendered, but who lived *here,* in this slightly less-than state of culture.

Geneviève did not need to explain or argue language with Gaston. Of like generation and both with a *Bacc A* . . . philo or literature; not much real use like the *B* which was the economic sciences, and from a system that was now obsolete; but it meant they could speak the way one was meant to. So they did, and were free to delve straight into each other. Which is not to say that Geneviève and Gaston went gouging through the body to devour the soul. Not at all. A passion of sorts, yes, some days (self-respect demanded some); savagery, no. They were both too old for such behaviour. They both had things worth guarding.

She had Christmas in English now. Bruce's blue-rinsed mother refused to consider chestnuts in the stuffing. His too-polite father really did believe in the English queen. But Geneviève had found the beginnings of a new family over in the western reaches of crumbling Montréal. Sure she fought it – the bond that could never be perfect. She was fighting it in this thing with Gaston. Or was wavering the better word? *Balancer.* Her instincts . . . fears? Something had latched on to these people even while her mind continued to dissect their ways. Because Bruce had helped her shift up, at long last, into a more civilized way of living. He sent his daughter to college, and he kept his son supplied with music and those ridiculous clothes; yet he still contributed enough to allow Geneviève's one-woman translation operation to be enjoyable now. No more panic if the calls did not come. Since leaving his disaster in Westmount and moving in, Bruce's presence had allowed her to work with a view of the poplars in the lane and the Italian neighbours in their gardens, then, if she felt like it, leave it in the afternoon. Bruce and their home together: the practical side . . . She would take her bicycle and pedal to the market, ten minutes away, for bread that was improving, sausage she had learned to like, real cheeses from France, good fish from the Greek, decent tomatoes in September. And apples.

Les Pommes Le Gac. You had to pass it. It was dead-centre, where the two closed-in aisles met in winter, the nexus of the expanded open-air arrangement that came with summer. There were eight varieties of apple, six of which came from Le Gac's own orchards. They also offered apple butter, jelly, juice and cider, pies, a syrup . . . a taffy in the winter, and the cider vinegar – with herbs, or straight. Geneviève had a healthy *mère* growing in a large jar of wine vinegar and replenished it with the dregs from each and every bottle opened in her home. So she had never tried this product. But she was a regular. She had been stopping at the stall for several years with no real thought for the proprietor with the Breton name. Bruce took an apple in his briefcase every day.

It was September when it started. It had been hot, Montréal humidity lingering, but pleasant by then, and even cherished, with only three, maybe five more weeks till the seasons changed. She and Bruce had gone for their three weeks in Maman's house, then come home to pass August in the back yard. A cousin – Yves, on her father's side from Nantes – and his family had stopped over for a couple of days on their drive through Québec. Visitors always liked the market so she'd brought them along. Yves and Gaston traded pleasantries in their Breton dialect, everyone was delighted . . . they came away with a complimentary bottle of the cider vinegar. Four weeks later Geneviève approached with a postcard from her cousin, to be forwarded to Monsieur Le Gac, and a bottle of the chewy southern wine she always brought back from Maman's village.

"You must drink it with me," said Gaston.

Yes, she thought, chatting on about Chirac and his atomic bombs in Polynesia, perhaps I must.

It was not difficult. He kept a three-and-a-half opposite the police station on St. Dominique, hardly a minute away. Ramshackle. In need of a good fumigating. She watched officers tucking in their shirts as they got out of their patrol cars and slammed the doors.

". . . handy," offered Geneviève.

"Practical," corrected Gaston, "otherwise I'd never sleep."

So it was September. But they did not rush into it.

They kissed on Referendum Day. A cold day, the bitterness of Québec winter just arriving. It had been a joke actually, to show their own small solidarity. Yet it was also, they both knew, a recognition of its inevitability – the thing that was going to happen. But they did not consummate it until January, with Christmas and family well out of the picture, the day after Mitterrand died.

Not difficult at all. There was the grotesque cold since New Year's, historically unusual amounts of snow, a strike by the blue collars which meant it stayed there, and, of course, the politics. Apple buyers were sparse and sombre. Gaston wore two sweaters and a Montréal Canadiens toque, making him look more of a *nul* than Bruce's son. Not difficult . . . But neither was it passion that first carried them through.

Her Bruce was disappearing into the cold several nights a week and on Sunday afternoons, leaving shows he loved unwatched to drive through the cramped and broken streets, out to the West Island, Westmount, and NDG, or down to McGill for these meetings.

"*Seinfeld*, *The Health Show*, the hockey game, even his stupid Super Bowl! . . . And twice to the Townships, just near your place."

"They call it l'Estrie now," muttered Gaston, whose Micheline had put everything aside while she prepared a speech she would give at the town hall down in Burlington, Vermont, less than an hour from the border which was five minutes from their farm, "to tell them the real history of Québec . . . and not to be afraid of it. That's her message. They have a network. They're determined to spread the good word from the Adirondacks over to Maine."

"Bruce's group is going over to the Outaouais next week . . . a weekend workshop, is what he's calling it."

"They don't have a chance."

"They don't care. They're expecting contingents from the Gaspé, the Megantic, Pontiac County, even from up in Val D'Or."

"It's provocative."

"It's what they're thinking," shrugged Geneviève. "He says they've got the Indians on their side."

"Not really. That's a whole other thing."

"Try telling him. He says his country had a near-death experience and he's vowed never to let it happen again. It affected him."

"Micheline says she has never felt more alive." He rolled his bony jaw around in its sockets, shook his head and stared down at the messy melange of police cars amid the drumlins of dirty snow. ". . . alive in front of the computer for sixteen hours a day. My children have it too. Not just from Maman. It's their teachers."

"So where do you stand, monsieur?"

"I don't care," said Gaston, glum. "I don't feel it."

"Mm," agreed Geneviève. "It all seems so unnecessary."

"Yes," reaching for her, "and so does all the snow."

"I've never been homesick," whispered Geneviève, "but I feel quite left out by all this . . . I feel cast aside."

He nodded. He knew.

And so, like that, they made love.

Then, sitting there in the apple farmer's pied-à-terre, they watched a tribute to the wily Mitterrand. *Wily?* Some American's word. But yes: a survivor – in the face of controversy and even, for a while, mortal illness. They both identified with that.

They continued making love through the winter into the spring. It was nice. It was necessary: a step back from the tense bleakness colouring the cold. Endless Montréal winters made life seem directionless in the best of times and these were anything but. She was glad she'd done it . . . In the rusty shower, Gaston showed Geneviève the right mix of water and cider vinegar. A simple rinse, to close the follicles after the shampoo. With regular use, it worked; her itching all but disappeared. So did Bruce's, once she'd started him on it. (It was, she felt, the least that she could do.)

Yet, when it's up in the air like that – in three lime-coloured rooms with water marks on the ceiling – you have to begin to wonder where it could ever lead. Gaston seemed sustained by the sex, a sharing of the odd perception, a laugh together at *Paris-Match*. But Geneviève felt a need to push it; she found herself saying things she had tried to stop thinking. "Every time I go back I marvel at the cleanliness, the stream in the gutters every morning. It's such a beautiful place because they keep it that way."

"They?"

"We . . ."

"That's more like it."

"But if I went back, I'd be taxed through the nose the second I put out my little shingle."

"To keep the water running in the gutter."

"They don't give you time to get going like they do here."

"But your money's stronger there. The *franc fort* – European money . . ."

"But would I make any? Who needs a French translation in France? and especially in the south. I won't live in Paris . . . never again."

"They still take care of you if you fail."

"They're trying to get out of it . . . they seem determined this time." Juppé had sat tight and taken the strike right through Christmas. "Can't afford it, just like anywhere. We're supposed to care more about Europe than France now – for our own supposed good."

"You know that's impossible," scoffed Gaston. "Besides, there will always be a place for you. Monsieur Le Pen will see to it."

True. Fifteen percent last time out and expected to rise.

"But do I want that," she asked.

"Do you want a job – or a clear conscience? The man speaks from the heart . . . our heart."

"Not mine . . . not the one I left there."

"Nor mine," he sighed, eyes on the ceiling. Gaston could make the dream of returning difficult.

But Gaston was all she had to share it with, and she persisted. Some days it would be the fast train and the brilliant autoroutes, signs at every *rond-point* that never left you guessing. And look at Mitterrand's new monuments; only a true giant would have dared! Pride was an ongoing sub-text; even, ironically, pride in Algerian bombs along the railway track – as if to say, what do Canadians know of trouble? Or the climbing rate of male suicide, the highest rates of AIDS and psychiatrists, the neurotic line-ups at pharmacies for sleeping pills and tranquillizers. (She and Gaston both admitted to having brought this inclination with them to Canada.) The declining state of French film was discussed at Oscar time. And how the rampant cheating, from Juppé's rents to Tapie's matches, was making the best and brightest look so bad. And the growing malignant shadow behind the Church that was *l'Opus Dei* . . .

Everything, good and bad, was set against the obsession surrounding her. Her adopted home was trying to kill itself. The wish was building, morbidly – *les moutons de Panurge*; or as the English would say, *lemmings to the sea*. Either way, Geneviève did not need that. She was a citizen, but she did not know how she was meant to participate. She could not see herself as one of them. She should leave it.

Yet the more she prodded her lover and explored her Frenchness . . . and the France that existed now, the more she thought maybe she was too old and too far from the France she'd left to really think of going home. *Cosmo* magazine had even determined that 87% of married French women were faithful. Well, she was not married, but –

"Home?" asked Gaston, to challenge her . . . to keep it going, the talk that sculpted clarity. That very French thing.

"Home," she murmured, "like Bruce says: where does it start? Where does it end?"

"And like Micheline," echoed Gaston, soothing her. "We'll see what happens . . . Look," slicing an apple into perfect halves, "each side shows a five-pointed star, the sign of immortality, the sign of the Goddess in her five stations from birth to death and back to birth again. It's a Celtic thing. You have that. Lots of it, according to your cousin Yves. Who you are lasts forever."

"I suppose it could."

And *une aventure* could become a holding pattern.

The Jean Talon Market is a cultural crossroads in the north end of the city proper. The stalls in the centre are owned mainly by Québécois farmers selling fruit, flowers, vegetables, and eggs. But there is an Italian with his own kind of tomatoes, an Anglo egg man called Syd. Merchants in the surrounding shops are Greek, Italian, mid-eastern and north African . . . with one Québécois butcher, baker, one more selling fruit. Everything is fresher and cheaper, and every sort of Montréaler goes there. Some Chinese can even be spotted, lured away from their own market downtown, and also some regulars from the cluster of Thai and Vietnamese grocery stores two blocks away at the corner of St. Denis. Any politician fighting for the hearts of the people will naturally find his way to the market, to glad-hand and smile, and be seen with all the various kinds of faces. *Look!* says the image, *our bustling community, happy together amid the bounty of our land.*

It was May and finally warm. Six months of soul-draining winter lay between the comfort of that morning and the cold night of the former Premier's ugly words in the face of a narrow defeat. The idea of partitioning Québec still simmered, but without the fervour of those initial cries of war. It was a good time to start reaching out again. The new Premier showed up in corduroy and cashmere with his wife, two sons and the usual entourage of handlers and media representation.

Geneviève and Gaston had adjusted to Bruce on a Saturday. They dealt with it without a blink. And they surpassed themselves when Micheline would decide to work the weekend, with the silent daughter behind her, keeping the $1 and $3 baskets full.

Bruce was deliberating between Cortland and McIntosh when everything suddenly stopped. A crowd formed and pressed close. Lights went on over the eyes of the cameras. Gaston pushed the hair off his forehead and Micheline, looking good in tight denim (Geneviève always gave credit where it was due) beamed as the two boys sampled her apple juice. The Premier chose a basket of Lobos, and, being from Lac St. Jean, made a glib comment about blueberry season, still a good three months away.

"We close up for three weeks," joked Gaston, "they make our apples lose their point."

That was untrue. Les Pommes Le Gac was never closed. But it sounded good and everyone laughed.

Then Micheline presented his wife with a bottle of the cider vinegar. It came with Gaston's small brochure explaining both the gastronomic and medicinal uses. The woman, an American, seemed impressed.

Yet no one paid for the apples. Geneviève wondered if anyone else had noticed. Perhaps money was not a part of this sort of thing, and someone else took care of it later. Then the Premier, just another shopper with a sack of fruit, moved to shake some hands.

What are you supposed to do? It's Saturday, the market . . . Geneviève took his hand, looked into the baleful eyes and said, "Bonjour."

But Bruce, who was beside her, said, "Are you kidding? No way!"

"Dommage monsieur." In that rumbly voice.

"Hell of a lot more than a pity, monsieur."

"I mean your manners. You are very rude."

"And you're dishonest."

"I am a democrat."

"Try dema*gogue* . . ."

Geneviève watched it from that distance she had been allowing herself to feel, the voice inside saying *oh these people* . . . and still from that removed vantage as Bruce was suddenly yanked away from in front of the Premier's face – and smacked. By Micheline.

"Va-t-en! We don't want the likes of you around our stall!"

"No . . . I'm sure you don't," said Bruce when the blush had faded. "Well to hell with you and your apples, madame. Your children won't thank you when they wake up in the third world!"

A dour man in sunglasses made a move, but Bruce indicated there was no need. The cameras panned away from the Premier, following as Bruce pushed through the throng and walked away.

Geneviève hurried after him. Of course she did.

Her *aventure* was over before the next weekend. Gaston's daughter had said something in the aftermath of the ugly incident. Something about *la Française*, the Anglo's wife. Yes, he knew she was not Bruce's wife. That was not the point. *He* was someone's husband and that someone had caught on. Gaston said that's it – *fini*.

Geneviève would have said the same thing, regardless of his wife *la militante*. It was as good a time as any. She and Bruce would be gone by mid-June, back to the village in the south – for a month this time. She would be re-charged. Maybe they would be renewed. Even Bruce wouldn't be able to think about his politics with all those topless teenagers wandering around on the beach.

But that was cynical and, happily, something that was burned away by the Mediterranean sun.

Because she had watched the thing on television, in both English and in French, and then again at eleven, with the sound turned off. In fact she had taped it, and watched it again, alone, brown and relaxed, the night they got back. Geneviève watched herself: her reaction, the way she went straight-away after her man – no hesitation. She realized she had a purpose, if not a cause, right there in Montréal. A passion for something new had brought her life to Canada and now she was involved in it. The place and its people. She had been re-attached through love. Yes, she thought – it had to be. It was there on Canadian television . . . just look at my face: Jeanne Moreau. Arletty. Deneuve or Fanny Ardant. Very noble. Very knowing. Very right. Surely Gaston would have watched and seen as well.

Bruce never knew. For his sake, Geneviève bore the prick of feeling like an enemy whenever she passed Micheline Le Gac, there most days now, defiant in her stall. The apples were just as good at the other end of the market. Apples are apples. Unfortunately none of the other merchants was as ambitious or creative as Gaston when it came to developing spin-offs. No more cider vinegar. Although her scalp itched in the dryness of the next winter (Bruce's too), Geneviève forced herself to live with it. Besides, it was $10 a bottle – an outrageous amount to pay for vinegar.

There would be something in France to solve the itching. They would find something the next time they went, and bring it back.

# MICHAEL CRUMMEY

## *Serendipity*

When my father was finally assigned a home by the company and moved out of the bunkhouse, we carried our belongings by cart and boat from Twillingate across New World Island and down to Lewisporte, where we caught the train for Black Rock. Fourteen hours in the single passenger car at the end of a line of empty ore boxes and most of that time in darkness. Clatter of the rails carrying us deeper into the island's interior, into the unfamiliar shape of another life. I woke up just after first light as the train leaned into the half-mile turn of Tin Can Curve. Out the window I could see a rusty orange petticoat of scrap metal poking through the white shawl of snow at the foot of the rail bed: hundreds of old barrels and pieces of abandoned machinery junked there by the company. Twenty minutes later we crossed a trestle and chuffed into town. My father met us at the red warehouse that served as a train station, his lean face dwarfed by a fur hat, his grin lopsided like a boat taking on water.

I had never been away from Durrells before. Everything in this new place looked the same to my eyes, uniform, indistinguishable. Streets as neat as garden furrows, rows of identical quads painted white or green or brown planted on either side. For the first three weeks after we arrived, my mother tied a kerchief to the door handle so my sister and I would be able to find our house in the line of uniform, indistinguishable houses.

Even my father got confused on one occasion, coming home from a card game at the bunkhouse: he'd been drinking and turned onto the street below ours, mistaking the third door in the second building for his own. Only a small light over the stove on in the kitchen, the details of furniture and decoration draped in darkness. He took off his shoes in the porch, hung his coat neatly on the wall, and was about to have a seat at the kitchen table when Mrs. Neary walked in from the living room. "Can I get you a cup of tea?" she asked him.

He was too embarrassed to admit he'd made a mistake. "That would be grand, missus," he said. "I wouldn't say no to a raisin bun if you had one to spare."

"Carl," Mrs. Neary shouted up at the ceiling. "Come on down here and have a cup of tea. We've got company."

For years afterwards, my father dropped in on Mr. and Mrs. Neary for tea on Saturday evenings. They became regular visitors at our house too. My father and Mr. Neary hunted together, played long raucous poker games at the kitchen table with my Uncle Gerry.

My mother said that was just like him, to find his best friend that way; that everything that ever happened to my father was a happy accident. She said it with just a hint of bitterness in her voice, enough that I could taste it, like a squeeze of lemon in a glass of milk.

When I turned thirteen, my father began taking me with him to check his rabbit snares on the other side of company property. We'd set out before dawn, following the Mucky Ditch that carried mine tailings across the bog until we reached the trees and struck off for the trails. We hardly spoke a word to one another as we walked and at first I didn't understand why he invited me along or wanted me with him; it wasn't that he needed my help, not with his luck. Every winter he took twice as many brace of rabbit in the slips as Mr. Neary, for no reason but chance as far as anyone could see. Of ten hands of poker, my father won eight, sometimes nine. Mr. Neary swore never to play another game on more occasions than I could count. "That man," he announced often and loudly, "has a horseshoe up his arse."

My father smiled his lopsided grin as he shuffled the cards. "One more before you go?" he asked.

It's hard not to feel ambivalent about someone that lucky, and that casual about his good fortune. "How can you love a man," I once overheard my mother confide to Mrs. Neary, "that you never feel sorry for?"

I wouldn't have gone into the woods with my father at all if my mother hadn't encouraged me, and it was mostly for her sake that I paid attention when he showed me how to tie the slips, and how to use boughs to narrow the run where the slip was set. He explained how a night of frost set them running to keep warm. He tied the feet of the dead rabbits together with twine and let me carry them, the bodies stiff as cordwood against my back. I suppose he was trying to soften me up a little, to make me like him.

Around noon we stopped to boil water for tea and eat the sandwiches my mother made for us before we left. "You've got a good head for the woods," my father told me one Saturday. "Why don't you see if you can find us a bit of dry stuff for the fire."

I tramped off into the bush, annoyed with his irrepressible good humour, with his transparent praise. He had no right, I thought, and as I moved further into the spruce I decided to keep walking, to not go back. Getting lost would serve my father right. I wanted him to panic, to feel his world coming apart, to hear him crashing through the woods yelling my name. I wanted him to feel the sadness my mother felt, the same sick regret. I kept my head down, not bothering to check my trail, working deeper into the green maze of forest. When I stopped to catch my breath I closed my eyes, turning three times in a circle before looking up. A light snow had started falling, stray flakes filtering through the branches of the spruce like aimless stars. I had no idea where I had come from, or where I was going. I was completely, perfectly lost.

My father always said that he and my mother were meant to be together. That it was their fate.

Before he moved to Black Rock, he worked as a fisherman in Crow Head on Twillingate Island. The year he turned eighteen he courted a girl who lived with her parents down the Arm in Durrells. Every night of the week he'd walk the six miles in from

Crow Head to have tea and shortbread cookies with Eliza; then he'd walk home again, arriving after one in the morning, crawling into bed for a few brief hours before heading out on the water by six.

During the winter, he walked both ways in total darkness, often in miserable weather. On a particularly blustery evening in February, Eliza's family tried to convince him to spend the night, but my father politely declined. His mother was expecting him at home, and the bit of blowing snow wasn't bad enough to keep him in. The old man tapped the weather glass beside the front door. "She's dropping fast, you'd best be going if you're going."

There were no roads through Twillingate in those days. The paths quickly covered in snow. The wind pummelled the treeless shoreline, visibility dropped to zero. My father walked for half an hour before he decided to turn around and spend the night. An hour later he had no idea where he was. His hands and feet were numb, his eyelashes were freezing together. He hunkered below a hummock to catch his breath out of the wind. He leaned against the face of the small hill and fell backwards through the door of a root cellar. There was a bin of dark-skinned potatoes, shelves of onions, parsnip, cabbage. He was near a house. He stared through the snow looking for a sign of life in the white-out, and then marched towards what he thought might be a light in a window. My mother answered his knock at the door. "Can I get you a cup of tea?" she asked him as he unwrapped himself from his winter clothes.

My grandmother went into the pantry, digging out a plateful of buns, cheese, and crackers. "Sarah," she called to my mother, "get a few blankets upstairs, we'll set him up on the daybed for tonight."

The storm went on unabated for four days. On the fifth day, my father left my mother's house to walk back to Crow Head. On the way he met his father, who had set out to look for him as soon as the weather eased up.

"Well," my grandfather said, "you're all right then."

My father grabbed both his arms through the bulk of his winter coat. "I'm getting married," he said.

My grandfather turned and they began walking back home through the thigh-deep snow. "It's about time," he said finally. "We were starting to wonder about you two."

Eliza's uncle was the merchant in Twillingate, and after my parents married he refused to give my father credit to outfit himself for the season. It was unfair and petty, but there was no recourse. My mother's oldest brother, Gerry, was working underground in Black Rock at the time and he had a word with his foreman who spoke with the company manager. When my father left in July to start work in the mine, I was already lodged in my mother's belly, undiscovered, like a pocket of ore buried in granite.

For the first eleven years of my life I saw my father only at Christmas, when he had enough time off to make the three-day trip to Twillingate by train and boat. He stayed with us from Christmas Eve until Boxing Day, then began the return trip in order to be back at work on New Year's Day. I looked forward to his appearance with the same mix of anticipation and anxiety my sister reserved for Santa Claus. As if I suspected he was not quite real, that this year my mother would sit me down and explain he was simply a story made up for children. He arrived with my Uncle Gerry, carrying boxes of presents; he sat us on his knee, holding our faces to the wool and oil smell of his face, buying kisses with nickels. Then he disappeared for another year.

As I grew older my simple disappointment with this arrangement soured. I began to suspect that the man chose to live away from us, chose to visit only four days a year. It made no difference how often he explained that the company had yet again refused his application for a house, or how lucky he was even to have a job. The promise of moving us to Black Rock was like a gift my father was constantly saving for, but could never quite afford. I had been waiting for so long that I stopped expecting it would ever happen. Had stopped wanting it altogether. I sat on his lap, I took the coin he held between his thumb and forefinger after I kissed his cheek. But I no longer believed my father loved us as much as he claimed he did, and I did not believe him when he said we would someday live together.

Like her children, my mother became more and more accustomed to the idea of life without him. During the summers she tended the garden with my grandmother, helped her brothers cut the meadow grass for hay in the fall. She sewed and mended and knit through the winter, she taught me my sums by the light of a kerosene lamp in the evenings. For eleven years she lived alone, married to a man she knew only through occasional letters, a brief annual visit. It should have been no surprise to anyone, least of all my mother, that she was no longer in love when he finally sent for us to join him in Black Rock.

It was a Christmas tradition at the house in Durrells, before we left for Black Rock, that the story of how my parents met and became engaged would be recounted by the people present during the storm. It was an informal telling, a story thrown out piecemeal, with everyone describing their own particular role or viewpoint on this detail or that, as if they were discussing a movie they had seen together years before. My father got lost and fell backwards into the root cellar, my mother opened the door to a hill of clothes covered in snow. My mother's youngest brother caught them furtively holding hands as they sat together on the second day. Uncle Gerry slams an open palm on the table, making the glasses of whisky and syrup jump. Nothing at all would have happened between them if he had been at home at the time, he announces, and what was my grandmother thinking to allow such a thing in the first place?

My grandmother lifts a hand from her lap-full of crochet cotton to dismiss her son's feigned outrage. "When Sarah came to my bed that night and said he had proposed I thought, What odds about it? You lot are all alike under the clothes anyway. Go ahead and marry him if you want to, I told her. One man is as good as another."

Everyone laughs at this, my mother included. I am too young to think there could be anything prophetic in my grandmother's words.

My father says, "It was fate is what it was. It was in the stars." He digs in his pocket for a ten-cent piece. "Come over, my darling," he says to my mother, "and kiss me."

"You men," my grandmother says, "you're all alike."

Whatever her feelings about leaving Durrells might have been, my mother was determined to make the best of our new life in Black Rock. She thought that pretending to be a family long enough would make it real for all of us, hoped that would be the case. She insisted we see my father off to work before each shift, turning our faces up to receive a ritual peck on the cheek. We took the company bus out to the lake on weekends, summer and winter, sitting on a blanket on the sand or skating across to Beothuck Island. We went to matinee shows at the theatre, standing with the rest of the audience to whistle and slap the seat of our folding chairs when, inevitably, the film broke and Smitty had to splice it together before continuing.

My sister joined the Brownie troop, the school glee club, played hopscotch and cut-the-butter with a half a dozen other children on our street. She sat in my father's arms as he played poker with Mr. Neary and my uncle, sleeping through the laughter and cigarette smoke and the cursing. She couldn't have been happier, and I was angry with her as a result, as if it was a personal betrayal somehow. I sulked in my room for hours on end, refusing to be placated by my mother's trays of shortbread cookies, by the second-hand pair of skates my father left on a nail in the porch for me. "I don't know what we're going to do with that one," my mother said.

"Don't worry," my father reassured her. "He's just missing Twillingate. He'll come around. It'll all work out in the end." More than anything else, it was his assumption that blind luck would carry him through that infuriated me.

Eventually, I forgave my mother as her own unhappiness became apparent. My parents never fought, but there was a distance between them that living together did not reduce, as if the miles of bogland and forest between Black Rock and Durrells had come with us on the train, was laid out across the kitchen table, the living room chesterfield. I don't believe she disliked or distrusted him in the same way I did. It was feeling nothing that made her unhappy.

When my father worked the night shift, my mother often sat in the living room with the lights out and cried. I stood at the top of the stairs, listening as she wept into her fists, forgiving her in my wordless unconscious way and blaming my father for everything. More and more determined to show him how wrong he was about the world. How his luck had finally run out.

The further I walked through the bush, the more dense it became. Branches scraped my face and hands, but I hardly noticed. I was elated. I felt like shouting, but didn't want to give myself away. Instead I kept walking, putting as much distance between myself and my father as possible, falling deeper into the forest like a man walking into a river, his pockets full of stones. I pictured my father scrambling through the woods behind me, calling helplessly, blaming himself for letting his son wander off alone. Knowing his wife would never forgive him if anything happened to me.

Minutes later I broke through a web of alders into a clearing and stopped dead in my tracks. I felt something falling inside me, a toppling of some sort, and I had to work to hold myself upright. Twenty yards from where I stood there was a fire burning. My father crouched beside it, chewing nonchalantly on a sandwich. Lost in the bush, I realized, I had walked in a perfect circle.

"I was starting to wonder about you," my father said. "Did you find any wood for the fire?"

It was hopeless, I decided. I walked towards him, empty-handed, defeated. Finally convinced there was no way to fight destiny, that I would never be free of my father's luck.

The following summer my mother slipped into the same posture of defeat that I had adopted. She abandoned her attempts to force us into the shape she thought a happy family should take, began complaining of headaches, bowing out of regular excursions and events to stay at home alone. My father took my sister and me to the movie matinée without her, bought us popcorn or candies, joking with my sister as if nothing had changed. I sat sullenly through war movies and westerns starring "The Durango Kid," or a white-hatted hero played by Rocky Lane. Even during barroom brawls that hat never left the man's head, as if it had grown from his scalp like hair. Someone in the audience inevitably shouted "Knock his hat off!" and everyone cheered in response. It was enough that he always came out on top. The hat was simply flaunting it.

When we arrived home I brought my mother tea or juice where she lay in the dusk of the heavy curtains in her bedroom, her hair splayed against the pillow like meadow grass cut and drying in a field. The air in the room thick with the smell of cloistered bodies. "You're a prince," she murmured, distracted, as if I had woken her from a dream. It was all I could do to keep from crying. Winter was coming. My mother was retreating into a world I wasn't privy to or part of. The stars, I couldn't help feeling, were aligned against me.

Fate is simply chance in a joker's hat.

The Black Rock ore deposits were discovered when the stones around a prospector's cooking fire began flaring, the seams of ore in the slag bursting into flame and melting. A snow storm threw my parents together for four days and they married. My father happened on his best friend by accident. In retrospect, it can all seem inevitable, unavoidable. I think about that now, how I might have gone on hating my father forever if not for the intervention of serendipity.

Two weeks before Christmas, the company held its annual party for the children of employees, at the Star Hall. My mother stayed at home, complaining of a headache. I dressed reluctantly while my father and sister stood in the porch, ready to go and sweating under coats and scarves, shouting at me to hurry. I lagged behind them on the street, scuffing snow with the toe of my boot. My sister was in my father's arms, and they were laughing. I hated them both for being so oblivious, for carrying on as if there was nothing in the world that was wrong. Other families on their way to the hall congregated around them. I walked more slowly, watching as the dark cluster of people and conversation moved farther and farther ahead of me, like a train leaving a town behind. Finally, I stopped altogether, angry and curiously satisfied that they seemed not to notice I was no longer beside them. I could just hear their voices at the bottom of the street and then they turned the corner towards the hall.

Back at the house I pulled off my boots in the porch, feeling vaguely triumphant, as if I had accomplished something of minor significance, won a symbolic victory. My mother and I could spend the evening playing crazy eights, drinking tea. I knocked my boots together to clear the bottoms of snow, then set them neatly by the wall. Beside Mr. Neary's boots. I walked into the kitchen in my stocking feet. Only the light over the stove was on, there was no sound. I was about to call when I heard my mother's voice upstairs. "Who's there?" she shouted.

"It's me," I said.

"Where's your father?"

"Is Mr. Neary here?" I asked, unsure what was happening.

"Russell, you go straight to the Star Hall. Right this minute. You hear me?"

I didn't know what to say. It was like walking into a house you think is your own, taking off your shoes and jacket in the porch, sitting at the kitchen table. And suddenly realizing you are in the middle of something completely unfamiliar and unexpected, something foreign. I was too embarrassed to stay.

"I forgot my scarf," I lied, and I left without saying anything more.

Halfway to the Star Hall I met my father, on his way back to look for me. "Well," he said. "You're all right then."

I looked at his face, at the complete innocence of it. The wind had brought tears to his eyes and he was grinning his lopsided grin at me. My mother, I was thinking. My mother and my father's best friend. He had no idea what was happening behind his back and for the first time in my life I felt sorry for him. I wanted to step into his arms and hold him.

"I forgot my scarf," I lied again.

He turned towards the Hall and we walked together in the darkness. "If the wind dies down there'll be a decent frost tonight," my father said. "Tomorrow should be a good day to check the slips."

He really had no idea. I pitied the man. I reached out and held his arm through the bulk of his winter jacket.

"I'd like that," I said. "I'd like that a lot."

## LIZ MOORE

# *Eight-Day Clock*

The first time I met Zoltan he took my face in his hands like a bowl of soup he was about to sip from and told me I had paprika in my soul. He had barged into the dressing room and made himself comfortable, propping his feet up on the counter, and said, "How's the Wig Girl?"

"Premenstrual," I said. "Who the hell are you?"

He laughed – a bark – and stared at me in the huge mirror as I clamped the comb in my teeth and fastened perm rods into the Mary, Queen of Scots wig, a do, I knew, that would be detested by the lead. Actresses hate ringlets.

Zoltan was difficult to ignore. He practically hummed with confidence. But I was determined to work alone, which is the best thing about doing wigs, and did not find his casual invasion amusing.

He smiled, a patronizing smile, underneath his bushy, grey moustache. "I am Zoltan Toman," he said. "I am director for the children's shows. How do you do?" He smelled slightly of spiced cologne and body odour. He had unruly hair and too much of it for his face, the moustache and greying strands sprouting like an over-fertilized plant.

"Is there something I can do for you?" Directors hardly ever bother me – I usually know more about what they want than they do. As far as hair goes, I mean. I wiggled the long-handled comb in my fingers to show him my impatience.

"Just hanging around, you know, haunting the backstage." He took out a cigarette and lit it. He had a slight accent –

Hungarian, I found out later – that became thicker with desire or when he had an audience. "You still haven't told me your name." He ran the tip of his tongue along his bottom lip. He dragged on his cigarette and crossed his legs, knees together, like a woman. I felt his eyes, like a warm wind, on my back and legs and elbows.

"Cheryl," I said, and went back to combing.

"Ahh, Cheryl. You are very beautiful."

My mother says I'm immature for twenty-nine, and I know I am not worldly. I also know I am *not* beautiful. I have my father's pointed chin and heavy wedge of a nose. I can look okay. But not beautiful. People who say stuff like that want something, as sure as if they just came right out and asked for it.

I slammed down the comb, ready to give it to this guy, but he leapt out of the makeup chair and before I could speak he was close to me, very close, his nose almost touching mine. He whispered, "Yes you are, Cheryl, that *paprika* in your eyes, in your heart . . . delicious." And he smiled into my face, the cigarette still burning by my ear. Then, he dropped his hands and stepped back. "Come home with me, *Baba*. Let me rub your feet. You will come," he said like a dare, in a voice that made me already feel his moustache bristles on my skin.

I went with him to his house on Albert Street with its dusty plants and abstract art, and there he undressed me in a demanding, pawing way, pulling me out of my clothes like he was pulling groceries from a paper bag. I felt his rough skin on mine, his heavy arms, his legs encircling me like walls. I was pulled up high above myself, out of my own ordinary-ness. This was something different.

He smoked American cigarettes and rubbed my feet with vanilla-scented oil, not using a tender or romantic motion, but vigorous, intense, as if he still had need. My feet, by then, were smooth and tingling. And beautiful. Stupendously beautiful.

"Forty-two, forty-eight? What?" my mother asked me.

"I don't know. I'm guessing," I said. "Maybe he's older, maybe he's fifty-something and just doesn't show his age. It doesn't matter." It did not occur to me that there was anything my mother did not need to know.

"Still seems too old for you. He won't want to start a family. For God's sake, don't get pregnant. That's all we need." She was at the sink, washing lettuce, her glasses perched on her nose so she could look over them at me from time to time.

"I may never see him again. He's just an exotic man."

"Well, *exotic* doesn't put food on the table. Huh." She pushed her glasses onto the bridge of her nose and went back to tearing lettuce.

It was unusual for mother to comment on any man I saw. But then again, there had been very few in my life in recent years, ever since the parade of grunting, ball-capped boys I brought home as a teenager – guys Mother mostly ignored – had ended. My coming-of-age was spent entangled in the raw, sticky rumblings of young male passions on our living-room couch while my mother slept upstairs. I was vaguely comforted when they held me, danced with me. But I lost interest as I grew older and took my place in my mother's house, sequestered in celibacy.

Mother has never urged me to date, rarely even spoken of men in relation to me. Except once, when I did Christopher Plummer's hair for his one-man show. She liked that and brought it up whenever anyone visited. But she would never ask me about boyfriends or even girlfriends, for that matter. I thought she would at least be curious. Motherly guidance and all that. I guessed that she was probably afraid. Afraid that I'd leave.

"Tomorrow's list is on the fridge there, see it?" She nodded at the envelope with her list of needed items and banking documents, my chores. "'Kay? And I made your favourite supper tonight. See? Spaghetti. And salad. Your favourite."

"Mother, we always have spaghetti on Thursdays."

"Yes," she took off her glasses to look at me, "but it *is* your favourite."

"Did you bring the tickets?" she asked me. Her face was round and soft with an air of panic folded into the creases, as if the thought of going outside, out *there*, was always with her, a shadow. Her hair was curled all over her head; it was coarse and full and held the curl well. I envied Mother her hair.

It did not happen suddenly after my father died, though that might have been expected. There was no single moment of which I could say my mother stopped leaving our house. My sister and I cracked up a little, each in our own way, after watching Dad disappear in that hospital bed. I dyed my hair black and hung out with a new set of friends, and Dianne, she eventually got pregnant and married young. But Mom kept on, kept driving us to piano lessons and freezing shepherd's pie for suppers and going to work. She just started staying home more and more nights – a homebody, she'd call herself – until finally she retired and the school presented her with an eight-day clock in gratitude for her twenty-six years of faithful secretarial service. She brought it home and never left again.

I handed her the lottery tickets and she taped them to the peeled patch on the wall where past weeks of losing tickets had waited. She taped everything to the kitchen wall, abandoning anything like a filing system or bulletin board. Newspaper articles, recipes, TV listings, letters. She had transferred her life, Scotch-taped it, to our kitchen wall.

Occasionally, something my mother was reading or thinking about would stir her and an expression transformed her face, an expression I knew from the past, giving me a glimpse of my old mother, my father's wife. I remember her laughing around the supper table – you know, shooting the shit. The way she used to be when Dianne and I would hear her and Dad partying from our beds upstairs. Then the expression would evaporate, cut off by a pang of such regret that I felt guilty about all the resentment I'd built up against her, the grudge I held against her for wasting her life.

That was my chance, when she brought home the clock. I didn't realize it at the time, but that was my chance to leave like my sister. Now, every day, when I go to work, the wisp of terror in my mother's eyes is what makes me glad to go, anxious to step outside and breathe in the cold air and bus fumes. But then I see a look on her face, a look that comes and goes, and I know

Mother really *is* my mother, and I guess that's what keeps me coming back.

Zoltan made me soup, thick with meat and vegetables, and spiced heavily with paprika and hot peppers. We ate it on the floor, on the rug, facing each other. Zoltan devoured his in huge spoonfuls, while I sipped and took gulps of water to cool my throat. He rubbed my feet and lectured me about the revolutions and uprisings in historical Hungary.

I wanted to wash his hair, to knead it in thick lather and wring it out in warm water. I wanted to wipe shampoo from his hairline and massage his temples and forehead. But he wouldn't let me and shrugged me away if I tried to touch or brush it. He let his hair grow long, not caring how greasy it got.

At work Zoltan threw himself into rehearsals for a new show. He never paid attention to me, never came looking for me. He fawned over the actresses, the lead in particular, speaking to them quietly, putting his hands on their shoulders. Once he called me out on the stage and yelled at me in front of the whole cast because Anne of Green Gables' wig wasn't green enough.

But, later, at his house, when his door closed and we lay down together, he would need me. He would press me to talk. He urged me to tell about my father's illness and death. Again and again, he coaxed me to go over each detail, the way my father wasted away, his body shutting down like a power outage in a storm. He wanted to know my mother's grief, how we mourned, my sister and I.

"It is the drama, *paprika*," he whispered thickly, close to my ear.

His whisperings, desperate and demanding, annoyed me. If I refused to go along with this fetish, he would have a tantrum, stomping ridiculously around the room, the white flesh on his bare legs wobbling. I hated this kind of weakness, hated it in men. I preferred his bullying at work. But, when I gave in and told the story in the dark, my voice a plume of smoke, he curled his naked body into a fetal position, resting his head on my breast, a baby. He was placated into someone gentle, almost loving.

Soon I became intrigued by the ritual. I began to anticipate my role, rushing through my tasks to be with Zoltan. To perform. I started exaggerating and adding little details to the account, making the story more sweet, more tragic. I'd have Dianne holding a bible, or a lock of Dad's hair as she sat by the bed. The more melodramatic I made it, the more it stirred him, softened him. The play could have been called *The Taming of Zoltan*.

"I know what you are doing," my mother said to me. It was very late and she sat by her wall in her nightgown, her hair in curlers. I took off my coat. I had forgotten to call, to tell her I would be late.

"For that matter, you know what you are doing," she went on. "This man, this Zoltar –"

"Zoltan."

"Zoltan, he is a replacement for your father. You are looking for an older man to fill his shoes. It's simple. Textbook."

"I don't think so, Mother."

"And this *talking* you do, this infatuation with Dad's illness, it's not healthy. It's not right. It's not healthy to talk to *him*. Go see a professional, someone who knows, Cheryl, if you want to talk so much."

"You want *me* to see a shrink? You're the one who hasn't set foot outside the door in five years, but you want *me* to see a shrink?? Jesus, Mother! Just because you can't control what I'm doing, just because I'm developing a *life* . . ."

Mother sat still and stared hard at me. I couldn't tell if I had hurt her or jolted her with logic. After a few moments, she took a deep breath and let her gaze settle on the clock on the bookcase.

"I love that clock," she said, and I believed she was talking to herself. "I only have to wind it every eight days."

"He's just quirky, Mom."

"You know?" she said, turning to me. I let her ramble. "I worked hard, every day for twenty-six years. Now I wind it every eight days. The rest of the time, I just look at it."

I pulled out one of her loose curlers and recoiled the lock of hair securely. "He makes good soup." I tried to laugh, to lighten things up. "I'm sorry I forgot to call. To tell you I would be late. I . . . lost track of the time."

"Have your fun, Cheryl," she said, getting up from her chair. "But don't give everything to him. Don't give him all of us."

Zoltan was growing bored with my story, I could sense it. He was restless, could not lie still. He glanced around in the dark, I was not sure he was listening. I wondered what the young actress told him, what stories she wrenched up from her past, from her subconscious to seduce him with. Were they better than mine?

I became more daring; Dad's death became more violent, more torturous. "His nails turned blue, his eyes yellow," I told Zoltan. Soon, I described graphic, bloody scenes, veering further away from the truth. I told him about my mother, how she held herself prisoner in her own home, an agonized wretch whose torment practically breathed in the room with us. I wove detailed plots about Mother's dependence on me, and how I toyed with it, staying out later, abandoning her. It brought him back. He whispered excitedly into my ear again, lying close to me, suckling.

"Yes, yes," he would urge me, "do it, stay tonight, leave her to wait at the window, to wonder, *piros* . . ." I indulged him and my cruelty towards Mother was strangely invigorating. My fingertips tingled as I pushed the limits.

So this was how I was going to do it. This was how I was going to leave my mother, leave home: by satisfying the odd fetishes of an older man. I would gradually extract myself from my mother's house, slowly trade in the paling, fading version of my mother for the one I had invented – a night, two nights, a week, until I was living with Zoltan. On the other hand, I would maintain my power over Zoltan by going back to my mother each day, by leaving him wanting more. I could keep him needing me, something the actress could not do.

It went on, this vicious circle of heady game playing. Zoltan. Mother. Zoltan. Mother. I felt as if I had actually grown in size. Larger than Mother, bigger than Zoltan. Bigger than my sister or her kids or even my father. I was huge. I was beautiful. I could keep this up indefinitely.

I stopped telling Mother the details of my relationship with Zoltan, mainly because she no longer asked. Soon, she was not speaking to me at all. And I didn't care. It just made it easier to go on.

One morning I woke up in Zoltan's musty bedroom on his creaking wooden bed and could not remember my father's face. A blank form was there, in my mind, left over from sleep. I lay on the bed not moving, straining to fill in the eyes and nose. I couldn't remember. I saw the scene I made for Zoltan and I saw my sister, virtuous in white, blood on her dress. My mother bent in pain, my wretched self.

I sat up and shook my head, put my cold fingers to my forehead. No.

Zoltan was in the kitchen. I could smell his cigarette smoke as it drifted into his room. I got out of bed and hurriedly dressed.

A photograph, I needed a photograph.

I could not hear my father's voice, could not even remember what he said to me, anything he'd ever said to me.

Zoltan ran water in the kitchen and did not see me come down the stairs, did not know I'd opened the door and left without shutting it behind me.

I tore scraps of paper from my mother's wall. I was still wearing my coat, and when Mother came down from her room I must have looked like a mad woman. I ripped down calendar pages and tickets and drawings made by Dianne's kids, taking more circles of paint from the kitchen wall. Ann Landers clippings, lists.

"I need a picture of Dad," I muttered under my breath. "You must have a picture of Dad here somewhere."

She stood in the middle of the room with her arms folded, her bare feet white on the floor. She watched me stand on a chair, pulling, pulling off a map of the city, a graduation photograph of myself, birthday cards. I turned to her, out of breath, and said, "I need a picture of Dad. Come *on*." But she just watched, fascinated, until I had pulled everything down, everything off the wall, all the tape, some with chunks of drywall attached.

I got down from the chair, still panting, still wearing my coat.

"I just need to see his face." My voice cracked and I wished it hadn't.

My mother's face hardened just a little for a moment and I wondered if she was going to refuse me, kick me out, say, "I told you so." Then she shrugged and went upstairs. She returned, holding a framed photograph of my father, a picture I'd forgotten had been on her bedroom wall all along.

"Oh," I breathed as I sat down and felt the smooth wood of the frame in my hands. It was a posed picture of him in a shirt and tie. And there was his face, his pointed, harmless face. My face. The relief I felt was physical, like eating when you're hungry or sleeping when you're tired. "Oh, yes."

Mother sat down at the table with me. She said, "Cheryl. *Cheryl.*"

I looked up at her.

"You can leave if you want, you know," she said. "You can get a place of your own."

I was hugging the photograph of my father. My mother's words were flying around, hitting the empty wall – I couldn't quite hang on to them. She looked prim, sitting there in her long robe, her wrinkled hands folded on the table. Not mad or tormented at all. I felt bulky in my heavy coat.

She spoke again. "We all make choices," she said. "Me. Dianne. Now you. Make a choice." Her hand made a move towards mine, rested on the table surface. "I just want you to understand, Cheryl. Every eight days, I'm going to wind my clock. That's what I want. You're free to go and do whatever you want."

She looked quite lovely at that moment, soft. Like I hadn't seen her in a long time. Like I remember.

## JEAN McNEIL

# *Bethlehem*

She is running back and forth to the bathroom, getting towels to put underneath the man. The boy is sitting on the edge of the bed.

"I'm not gay, *Senhora*."

"That's reassuring," she says, in English.

The boy scowls. "*Qué?*"

She switches to Portuguese. "He's my husband."

"Sure." The boy shrugs. He can see she wears no ring.

Behind the boy his hands are tied to the bedstead in a loose noose. They rotate gently within the confines of the rope, which has been covered in strips of pillow-case.

She disappears into the tiny bathroom. When she emerges she is carrying a towel. She wrings her hands in it first, noticing a dark brown ring underneath her nails, next to the skin-dried blood. Suddenly her hands look alien, like mandibles, or claws: the appendages of another species.

She flicks the wall switch, turns on the fan. "I have to dress his wound first."

"What's wrong with him?"

The boy's copper skin has turned to onyx in the soupy light. It is the rainy season and dark has fallen at four o'clock. Peru-shaped clouds bloom: the rain clouds that float across the Amazon basin every afternoon. She doesn't answer the boy. She concentrates on dressing the wound, slapping on the yellow lotion and winding the gauze around his midriff. He whispers something in her ear, but she misses the sense of it. She kisses his forehead. She does all this with the same detachment she would feel if she were watching herself on film. Everything she does seems to happen too slowly. Even the walls of the room look very far away.

"I've been shot too, *Senhora.*" He pulls up his shirt to show her a tiny puckered scar just to the right of his abdomen.

"Good for you. Here, catch." He claps his hands over the small packet. The boy opens his hands and grins. She leans against the wall. "Put it on."

As the boy unbuttons his jeans she goes to sit in the chair by the window. The sheer curtain floats in the breeze and brushes her hair like an insect. She watches them closely, noting all the manoeuvres and sequences, as if she were cataloguing them. The only thing that still surprises her is how men can become aroused without really feeling any particular desire. Otherwise she is not shocked. It is really heterosexual sex she finds most disturbing: the appendages fitting each other with the puerile facility of Lego.

After a while the boy begins to moan.

"*Basta,*" she says. Enough.

She pulls him off the bed. She hates it when they moan: it sounds like the death cries of animals. She stuffs some *cruzeiros* into his hand. He scowls. He had been expecting dollars. He trips into his trousers, his graceless movements revealing his youth. He is all gangling adolescent limbs.

When he is in the hall she shuts the door behind him and turns to the man on the bed. He is sweating. She goes into the bathroom to get more towels to wipe him down. When she pulls on the light cord she cannot help seeing her face in the mirror. She grabs another of the too-thin towels and quickly pulls off the light.

I love to watch the rains come. It doesn't get dark so much as the sky seems to become coated with metal. Then it comes, bulleting and horizontal. Potholes open in the streets, as if they've always been there, like wounds underneath the skin of the asphalt, waiting to open.

About once a week, after the rains, I go to buy earrings in the market by the cathedral. I make a lot of friends in the market because only tourists usually shop there, and they speak little or no Portuguese. I have picked up the deep-throated, meowing accent of Pará. I even use the *tu* and conjugate it correctly. This is an interesting regionalism; nobody but people from Pará do this in the whole of Brazil.

The Basílica de Nossa Senhora de Nazaré is my favourite church in this city of heat-stunned churches. It is modelled upon St. Paul's in Rome. Not far from our apartment building is the quarter where the rubber barons used to live. The best of these Portuguese mansions have been built, natives of Belém tell me, by Antônio Lemos and Lauro Sodré. Brazilians say their names with the gravity usually reserved for military heroes. It's one of the things I like most about this country: they hold their architects in reverence. The buildings are the colour of faded lime, oyster-hued, and peeling, as if they have been attacked by some kind of eczema. In the middle of a rainstorm the whole city looks like a torched Versailles, or the earthquake-smashed apartments of ancient Pompeii.

I go out so often that a lot of people know me on sight by now. There is not a large foreign community, so people are not exhausted and surly in the face of my inevitable foreignness. I could love this city if I were here under different circumstances. I even take an interest in the riot scenes in the supermarkets, when shoppers discover rice has been made more expensive yet again. Inflation is running at forty-six percent per month. To a degree I am protected by my cache of American dollars.

I don't know why he is indifferent to the city. He behaves like someone who has come here to die. He has become very interior, fixated upon himself and his reactions. As far as he is concerned, he could be in Calcutta, or Toronto. Maybe this is just his way of saying he wants to go home.

I love to watch the rains come but sometimes I wonder why I stay here. We're young: he's twenty-four, I'm twenty-one. We're almost out of money. We should go home; I should leave him. But I'm still edgy, still hungry for experience.

The nearest slum neighbourhood, *favela*, is where she goes to make her contacts for him. Without Lourdes, she could not have dreamed of entering the *favela*. Lourdes has lissome legs, trim and pretty. She can see the girl takes great care with her appearance; her hair is always neatly clipped in pink plastic butterfly-shaped hair pins, her shirts always spotlessly white. Most days she wears the same pair of blue shorts, but every day they are pressed and clean. She manages to keep up this level of hygiene and meticulousness in a one-room tin shack where she, her father, and half-brother live.

As she enters with Lourdes through the darkened house, shapes shift in the corners – people rising from the floor, or falling down; she can't tell which. They pass through the house and emerge through the back door into narrow alleyways of corrugated tin-roof dark squares. As they descend the stairs to the alleyway, Lourdes walks in front of her, putting each foot delicately on the mulch-soft wooden steps.

Then she sees him, or at least she thinks it's a he, judging from his bulk. He lies on his side, his head propped up by an arm. Folds of fat droop where his bicep should be. Lying on his platform, which has the slab-like aspect of a masseur's table or a surgeon's bed, he looks like a whale or a beached seal. His mouth is lipsticked; his hair drawn back into a bun. He wears a purple piece of material – the exact colour of *açaí* berries that come from the jungle – draped over his flounderous body in the style of a toga. His dark skin glistens as if it has been greased. His eyes, she notices, are extremely cunning.

"Is he a man or a woman?" she asks Lourdes when they are past him.

"Who? Gorda?" the girl grins, hiding her mouth behind her hand. "Who knows? A man. We think."

"Then why is he called Gorda, in the feminine, as you would call a woman?"

"I don't know."

"Is he homosexual?"

Lourdes considers this for a few seconds.

"What do you mean?"

She gave her mock-severe look. "You know very well what that means. Don't tell me you can live twelve years in a place like this and not know. It means a man who likes men, or a woman who likes women."

Lourdes screws up her face. "Will you buy me an ice cream?"

"Sure," she says, taking her by the hand. "Let's go."

"It's not really a zoo," Lourdes corrects her, pointing to the sign, *Bosque Rodrigo Alves*. She has taken Lourdes there to buy her an ice cream. "It's a Bosque. How do you say that in English?"

"Wood."

Lourdes shifts her mouth in emulation of her consonants. "Voooodd."

"That's right. You've got it."

"There are more animals at the Goeldi. Do you want me to take you there?"

"Sure, let's go." She does not tell the girl she has been to the Emílio Goeldi museum at least five times already.

They enter the gardens, following a path of gravel the colour of wood chips. On either side of them are clumps of tropical vegetation. It is early morning and a weekday, so they almost have the place to themselves. She reminds herself that she must avoid the snakes, but they go up there anyway, she and Lourdes leaning over the railings, looking at the boa and the anaconda which are kept in cages placed next to each other. The boa drapes itself over a bare, constructed tree branch like an exhausted inner tube. The anaconda lolls in the water. They can only see its eyes and its massive head.

"Which do you think is bigger?" Lourdes' vanilla ice cream drips down her fingers. She extends her tongue, small and feline, to lap it up.

"I think the anaconda is the biggest snake in the world, so it must be bigger."

Lourdes licks her ice cream thoughtfully. "I like them."

"I hate them."

They move on to the alligators. "These are imported alligators," Lourdes informs her officially. "They were brought here from Florida."

"They should have only Amazonian animals here. It's not as though there aren't enough of them, or that they don't need protection."

Lourdes looks at her sharply. She has to remind herself that most Brazilians are unused to hearing opinions about the United States that are not entirely positive.

They move on to the aviary where the macaws are making a racket. Lourdes has finished her ice cream and is looking longingly at her soggy napkin, which has mopped up most of the melted vanilla.

"There's one more thing you have to see before you go," Lourdes says, pulling at her arm. "The Amazon is famous for it. Do you know what it is?"

She smiles, and shakes her head.

"Oh, come on." Lourdes doubles her body up into a burlesque of impatience. "It's this big." She throws her arms out on either side of her body, her face turning pink with strain.

"*Não,*" she shakes her head, trying not to laugh. "*Não posso imaginar.*"

"The Victoria Régia lily. Do you know, this flower is like Gorda. It is both male and female. It changes overnight. That's why it's so big."

Lourdes begins to frown in concentration. "It begins the day as a male, but then at dusk it traps this insect, a beetle. And it uses this beetle to pollinate" – Lourdes grins, proud of her use of the word – "to reproduce itself. And then, by morning, it has become a female. The plant, not the beetle."

"And does it let the beetle go in the morning?"

Lourdes frowns. "I don't know."

They go to the indoor exhibit, billed as The Natural History of the Amazon. "*Belém,*" Lourdes points to the sign on one of the bird displays that recounts the importance of the trade in tropical birds to the city. "I can read that word. Do you know what it means? Bethlehem." The girl stumbles over the consonants, unable to aspirate the 'h' and concretize the 't,' so that it comes out sounding like *Betchleheem*.

"Bethlehem."

Lourdes cracks up laughing. For the rest of the morning she coaches the girl to say it properly, in English. Lourdes insists. Still, she wonders if she had been cruel, teaching the girl to say a word she will never use again.

At noon, they part.

"You have to get back to your *namorado*," Lourdes states, a little flatly.

"Yes." *Namorado* means both 'boyfriend' and 'betrothed.'

"I know a good new boy for you, Ana," Lourdes says, using her name. She doesn't normally do this; she's doing it for the same reason a salesman would: to pretend or invite familiarity.

Suddenly, she feels sullied. She wants to let the girl know that their friendship can be pure.

"He's not for me."

Lourdes says nothing, just walks away from her, turning to look over her shoulder from time to time, but she keeps on walking without turning around, heading for home.

Lone taxis scoot up and down the wide streets that lead to the docks like frightened rodents. Massive gutters are built alongside each *rua* and *avenida* to trap the daily deluge. They are so big that in any other city I'm sure they would be called canals.

Every day, all year, it rains twice a day. Once at one o'clock, once at five. The second instalment of rain is less predictable. But the sky is almost always clear in time to see the sun disappear into the river.

Our apartment is on the eleventh floor. We live in the highest high-rise in Belém, on Praça Tiradentes: "Toothpuller's Plaza." It is American in style, furnished in chrome and mirrors, but Brazilian in intent. The kitchens all have a maid's elevator leading onto them, and a small maid's room right next to the laundry room. For a Brazilian, an apartment like this costs a fortune, but we have American dollars.

Every evening at five-thirty I go out onto our balcony and watch the sunset. To the right are the docks: the oblong forms of warehouses look like greased lozenges in the setting sun. Cranes tower above them, lopsided, delicate. In the distance is the Ilha do Marajó: a wedge of green dotted with what looks like lakes. This time of year the island is a virtual flood plain.

To the left is the river, heading towards its intersection with the Xingú. And to the north, nothing, at least for us city dwellers. Only an untransversible forest stretching from here to the Guyanas. For most of the foreigners and the wealthy Brazilians, the only thing north of Belém of any significance is Miami. Both Varig and VASP have daily flights there. I see them taking off from the airport, which is also visible from my balcony. Planes are so different when they fly in; they seem to come in at half-speed, hovering like exhausted metal angels. When they take off they are as clear and intentful as an arrow. In their burning thrust into the stratosphere they almost seem to write MIAMI OR BUST.

One or two nights a week we go out to eat. We always end up in one of the many very good seafood restaurants.

"We should stop eating so much shrimp." He makes a face, as soon as we have ordered shrimp again. "I never thought I'd be sick of shrimp."

I like *vatapá*, a shrimp dish in a rich sauce made from Amazonian fruit. But my favourite is *maniçoba*, shrimps cooked in leaves from the bitter casava, which are also toxic, at least under most circumstances. To be used in cooking, its leaves first have to be simmered for a full eight days to drain them of their natural poison.

She opens the door to their apartment. As soon as she opens it she feels a wave of tiredness wash over her. The plants look plastic, she notes for the hundredth time, even though they are real. Then, that's the tropics. He sits watching a *telenovela* to improve his Portuguese. Its name translates into *As the World Turns*.

"Hi," he grins, and turns his eyes upon her.

She has seen them hundreds of times before, but she will never exhaust their magnificence. They are dark green, not large, but perfectly framed by thick ginger eyelashes. Chapped skin flakes off around his straight nose and thin, svelte eyebrows. His lips are full, criss-crossed like the stitching in a quilt. His hair is red-gold; a prominent, but not jutting, jaw line, and wide-sprung cheekbones show traces of Slavic ancestry. His face, as always, causes her to think of unlikely foreign phenomena: the loping walk of the Bushmen of the Kalahari, the disdainful turned-down mouths of the ancient Incas. Every time she looks at him she feels a kind of exquisite shifting taking place inside her, as if she were made up, not of veins and organs, but of sand bars.

He is not a large man, but his limbs are perfectly in proportion. He is still almost as muscled as he was when he went to the gym every day. She has never seen anyone, not even Lourdes, who has such beautiful limbs: his forearms, for instance, which are tendon-hard and transversed by a riverine network of veins. Sometimes she runs her forefinger along them, pointing to the places where they branch.

"That's the Tapajós," she says, where one thick vein departs from another. "That's the Solimoes."

His skin has the delicacy of parchment. She can swing next to him in a hammock and not say anything for hours. They don't need to talk. But she doesn't like the burnt-metal taste of this supposed languor or ease, this relatively cheap idyll.

She's aware that this is not real life, even though she enjoys her friends and her life, her students. She loves the city. Even in the midst of her experience of living here, she already knows she will never forget it. But she also knows it is a place to be left behind in favour of more rigorous realities. He does not seem to realize this. Sometimes she thinks he has no aspirations in particular.

Later, they sit together in the darkness in front of the window, illuminated by the sodium light of the docks. Flecks of white dot the river: the headlamps of boats. On the ink-viscous river they seem to form a mirrored pattern of the stars.

"You are everything to me."

Does she say this, or does she just think it?

From the moment she met him – when she had to lean against the wall for support, such was the impact of seeing someone for whom she'd been waiting – she had never expected not to know, at any point, where he was; whether he lived or died.

Sometimes she has this vision of him out in the world, without her. He is in Srinagar, maybe, the hue of his beautiful ochre skin the exact colour of deserts waiting for the rains to come. He has the grace that all people whose fingers are longer than their palms have. In his every movement is the same fluidity as that of a lazy swimmer, heavy with supper, about to go under.

Between her fingers is his hair. It feels as soft as the tendrils of sea anemones. Noises from the docks, twenty blocks away, crackle into the apartment. Eleven stories up, she thinks, you hear everything.

Night falls. On the equator, she has the impression that the world does not turn.

When they left behind the northern winter and came to Brazil she thought she would hear sounds of dense forests at night. She wanted to be surrounded by a breathing, whispering conspiracy of trees. But it was the sounds of the city that came to her every night: Rio de Janeiro, Salvador, Sao Paulo, Manaus, and finally Belém. She could only make money teaching English in the cities.

When they first came to the Amazon they flew in from Brasilia. In the plane, she saw Manaus rise up beneath them like a giant satellite dish. Fifty feet from the edge of the airport runway was the rainforest.

A few days later they flew to Belém. The plane took off just before dusk. From her window seat she watched the night come over the river. They flew into its mouth in increasing darkness; to her left, towards Venezuela, the sky was streaked purple. Then she lost the shape of the river beneath her in the night.

That night in their hotel in Belém, he took a wisp of her hair in his hand, twirled it between his fingers.

"It's not you I need."

"Who is it," she said. "*Who?*"

She thought she was shouting; her voice came out a whisper. In that way it was like a dream.

"What," he said. His lips were dry and they smacked as he said it, the sound of desert-bleached bones brushed by wind. "What I need."

That night she went out on her own into the still-baking thoroughfares, clogged with vehicles whose axles and undercarriages were caked with red dirt from driving the Trans-Amazonica highway. Curtains of rain brushed her cheek. Steam rose from her linen and cotton clothes – once crisp, now soaked as sex-soiled sheets.

From our balcony eleven floors above the city, I can see the ferry to Macapá wandering into the river. I've never been there, and from what I've heard I don't want to go. It is a heat-ragged city on the northern rim of the Amazon with a soccer field, a landing dock, and not much else. I've seen the ferry leaving the dock, barely moving as it slogs through the licorice viscosity of the river. It's an old rusting tub by any standard, so it won't have any navigational equipment. By some sonar instinct – like bats – it dodges the hulks of big cargo boats, the Amazon steamers. The boat leaves Belém at midnight and takes twenty-six hours to cross the Amazon. That means it arrives at two in the morning. The transport schedules in the Amazon are unreal: buses leave at three or four in the morning and arrive at the same time. No wonder no one gets any sleep.

Caracas is a four-hour flight away. The cities which are near, at least in relative terms – Cayenne, Manaus – are still jungle backwaters. Even Lima or Bogota is five hours' flying time away, including the inevitable stops in Letícia. Rio and Sao Paulo are about five hours by air, in the frigid south. Only the very rich of Belém go there with any frequency. Everyone else takes the bus to Brasilia, if they really have to. That takes two and a half days. New York is an impossibility, Paris so remote as to not exist at all. Although I still hear people talk about it occasionally in the tone usually reserved for speaking of jewels, or jaguar pelts, or other endangered or near-destroyed objects: *París*.

Instead of the Seine and its bulb-garlanded tourist boats, I have the *açaí* boats landing at 11:30 each night. The berries are brought to Belém from all over the mouth of the Amazon. Some evenings I watch them come in to their docks below the Círculo Militar, the army fortress compound. They look like migrating eels: long thin boats, their cyclops' eyes piercing the night like fireflies. When the boats land, small, dark men scuttle to unload the heaps of fruit.

*Açaí.* I love the name, its medicinal, swishy sound. I like the taste even more, even though on their own the purple berries are far too sour. They can be mashed with sugar and mixed with manioc to make a purple couscous. More often, though, they are sugared and used to make ice cream the colour of virulent bruises.

At these moments I don't feel I occupy a periphery, somewhere dreamed of only by centuries of scientists and merchants and other alarmists, but forgotten by everyone else. I feel I am at the fulcrum of the universe. Nowhere on earth is as flat and broad and significant as this part of Amazonia. All along the two-thousand-kilometre length of the river, the elevation barely rises 200 metres. I really believe those *National Geographic* sentences, the ones that tell me I am living in the lungs of the world.

They are having breakfast. As always, he seems nervous when he eats, trembling, plucking at his napkin as if it were a chicken that needed to be defeathered.

"The newspapers in the Amazon are such crap." He points to the corner of the table, where one of the body-count papers that dedicates itself to corpses and accidents lies in a frustrated heap.

"You knew that before we came here. Why don't you go out and buy the *Folha de São Paulo*?"

"Because my Portuguese isn't as good as yours. I can only look at blood and guts pictures."

"I'll translate for you."

"No thanks. I'm dependent on you for enough already."

"You'd rather complain."

"I would." He smiled. "Oh *God*," he groans. "Another story about the damage anthropologists are wreaking. This is a great joke," he grins. "What's a typical Kayapó family? A mother, a father, five kids, and an anthropologist."

She moans and rolls her eyes.

"Why don't we go to Salinópolis this weekend?" he says. "I want to go to the beach."

"I don't think we can."

"You mean we can't even afford that? A weekend in Salinópolis, the Daytona Beach of the northeast?"

"This apartment costs a lot. You know that."

"So," he shrugs. "Let's move."

"We can't."

"Why not?"

She pauses, and looks down at her hands. "I need the view."

We can't afford to go to Salinópolis on the Atlantic so we go to Icoaraçi, a good river beach only half an hour by bus out of town. For a river beach, it's okay. There are not many piranha, and almost no chance of bilharzia – the water is too swift-moving. There are crocodiles, though.

The beach is crowded on the weekends with Amazonian families and their children, who glisten like lizards. The fresh water seems heavy and sticks to my skin like mercury. We drink chilled coconut milk, he meets sylph boys at beach bars. In the distance I can see the low flat shape of Marajó island. I wonder where the crocodiles are.

"I have to go out."

He eyes her. "Okay."

"Do you want me to bring anyone back?"

"No," he shakes his head far more emphatically than he has done in a long time, except during sex. "Just go out and enjoy yourself."

He hardly goes out now. On the nights when he used to accompany her ventures into the city, they would sit in the Bar do Forte, built on the battlements of the old *fortaleza*, the one that overlooks the Ver-O-Peso market. The Fortaleza once defended the entire Amazon against the English and the Dutch.

From there they used to watch ships sliding like giant glass structures over the Amazon. At night the river and sky are a seamless horizon of black, occasionally sequined by the lights of the massive dock cranes, which warp and wink like the eyes of dinosaurs. Some nights they would go on to the Clube Lapinha, which she knew Belém natives avoided. Tourists are always fascinated by it because there are toilets for three sexes: Men, Women, and Gay.

Now she has become so used to being alone in the city that she finds his presence obtrusive. Other men never look at her in the street when he is with her. She is treated deferentially in bars and restaurants. She knows why: with him she is a *Senhora*, an attached woman. Historically, women's survival in the Amazon depended upon having the protection of a man, she knew. Either that or they could become prostitutes. Most of the time he stayed in their apartment, reading Classics on their eleventh-floor balcony. She would come home to find him in the chair, sometimes asleep, with Ovid and Aeschylus and Plato and Cavafy sitting at his feet like puppies.

She misses seeing him in action, out in the world, because his being was calibrated on the cusp of action-obsessiveness and languor, and she knew this was unusual. When he did things, even if it were just buying fish at the Ver-O-Peso, he did so decisively, and with a need that was ragged, intense and controlled at once. He kissed her like that too, but there was also a languor in his limbs and lips. He let them linger on hers until something inside her became insupportable. If she could X-ray him and see his innards she was sure she would see something that was in the process of melting. That's how he felt when he touched her: frozen maple syrup or chilled chocolate warming up, returning to its natural viscosity.

When she enters the air-conditioned office that afternoon, the one that pays her her meagre salary, or into a travel agency to investigate flights they cannot afford, her body breathes a sigh of relief. Her business done, she goes back onto the cracked pavements – insane carapaces driven by rain and rot – and into the shoe stores tumbling onto the sidewalk.

The Organization of American States is in town. Heat-stunned gringos wander the broken pavements, avoiding crevasses, stepping delicately, like storks. All the minor statesmen and their acolyte bureaucrats have convened on the city for six days. She tries to avoid the North Americans; their pale and fleshy faces remind her too much of what she herself is. Still, just for a moment, she wants to go home.

The nights have gotten worse, not better, since they came to Belém. Most nights now he has to uncurl her from her screwdriver sleep postures. In the middle of the night all her muscles contract, as if she were a stroke victim, and she doubles up upon herself. He prises the pillow out of her hands. He sits at her thighs. The click-click sound of the docks filters in through the window. Light from the halogen floodlights used to illuminate the nighttime loading makes its way in too, bathing them in a sick hospital yellow.

He sinks down onto one elbow and swings his legs up on the bed. All this time he says nothing, but begins to stroke her hair, moving it off her forehead. Then he lays himself out against her and straightens her out, limb by limb, like a store mannequin.

From time to time she would picture herself, or at least try to, with someone else – someone who returned her love at its exact pitch and frequency. Then she would replay their conversations. Every time she talked to him, she felt she was going somewhere she had never been before. No one else had ever given her that sense of possibility, and she clung to it even while she understood that its promise was false in the way that a journey undertaken in a dream does not really get her anywhere, at least not when judged by the moment of waking.

Although he is in a way every inch the Western man, his smooth limbs and chiselled face suggesting infinite progression, she can tell he is becoming increasingly dark, interior. Just talking to him is like entering an abandoned labyrinth. He often takes off his glasses to look at her, and even in the moment she would wonder if this was a calculated move of his, as if he knew the effect of the jade-threaded clarity of his eyes.

Still, she can't imagine he has any need to manipulate her. They can sit together happily for hours on the couch, facing the window of their apartment, their fingers twining and untwining. She runs her fingers through his hair, rubs the point on his neck where his hair stops and his skin begins. Her body flushes hot, just from this activity. If he falls asleep beside her, their thighs running alongside each other, she fingers his eyelashes very lightly. They are extraordinarily long, like a camel's. She runs her finger through the whorls in his ear. She can do this for hours and not be aware of time passing. Then she might look up, suddenly, and see that outside the sky has turned to aluminum: rain's coming.

The OAS conference had brought opportunistic traders from all over the mouth of the Amazon. After she encountered a glut of

Canadians, she walked down to the Ver-O-Peso. Under a massive Amazonian sky, pelicans fell like bombs into the brown waters. Or they waited opportunistically with the hunch-shouldered posture of diplomats next to the fish stalls. Some of the pelicans were as tall as the women minding the tattered stalls. The late afternoon light was silk-washed. The sun would go down in less than an hour.

"*Senhora, Senhora.*"

She turned around to see a man, his face creased with the lines of too many false smiles. His forehead wide, his hair cut by some maniac. She could see immediately that he was a *caboclo* – of mixed indigenous and Portuguese blood. He wore a brown-stained white sleeveless shirt and blue nylon shorts. On his feet were flip-flops.

"I have something show you," he said, in burring English, and winked at her.

"*Qué?*" She pretended not to understand.

He switched to Portuguese.

"*Vem conmigo.*"

She did not know why, but she went with him. It was not a safe face, but she went with him anyway.

He turned his back to her, bent down, and reached into a box carefully, all the while whispering, "*Mínha amor, mínha amor.*"

From the box he pulled what looked to be an animal.

She stood back. The first thing she noticed was the smell: like rotting leaves. The animal's fur was grey and wiry and was covered with what looked to be a dark green slime.

The animal faced the man, gripping his shoulders with two short arms. Then it rotated its head, very slowly, and turned to look at her. Its eyes were the colour of black licorice streaked with amber. Its stare was inquisitive, and sad.

"Don't cry, *Senhora*. Here, she's yours."

She approached the animal. Its nose was squashed, button-like. Over its eyes was a band of dark hair, like a raccoon's mask. She realized its benevolent expression came from its upturned mouth: two thin black lips, smiling.

"Only thirty dollars, *Dona*," he said, addressing her as Mistress.

She took it in her arms. The animal gripped her shoulders with its claws. She was made nearly delirious by the heat and damp coming from its body.

She turned to the man, smiling. "She's beautiful."

The sloth gripped her just like a child, each leg splayed on her hip bones, its claws, snug but not biting, on her shoulders. It seemed to move very slowly, like a computer-generated animal.

She could hear the thump-thump of its heart. It was very slow. The sloth had extremely long claws. She felt her skin being serrated, but the sloth did not puncture it.

She looked into its face but wasn't sure what it was she could see there. Its nose touched her forehead: it was hot and wet. The sloth put its nose in her ear and she flinched, then smiled.

"She's trying to tell you something," the man grinned. Then he pried the sloth off her body.

"Thirty dollars, *Senhora*." He put the animal back in the box.

"Wait here." She thrust fifteen dollars into his hands. "That's a deposit. I'll be back this afternoon."

She wanders in and out of the afternoon rainstorms, going nowhere. She stands beneath their waterfall wetness, emerging from time to time into curtains of sunshine.

Near dusk she finds herself in Lourdes' neighbourhood. She can't remember going there. She has no appointment to meet her. He doesn't need a boy tonight.

She passes through the undergrowth of the house and into the courtyard of neatly arranged tin shacks. As she descends the stairs she expects to see him there on his slum divan, but Gorda is not there today.

She arrives at Lourdes' shack and, as there is no door, steps into the gloom of the shed. She steps back, blinks a couple of times, re-enters. By this time the girl has lowered the gun and holds it limp, at her thigh. She blinks again. It is unmistakably Lourdes. She looks just as she has always looked: a twelve-year-old girl, long-legged and intelligent.

"What are you doing with that?"

The girl shrugs. The gun falls out of her hand, thumps to the dirt floor.

"That's loaded. You never, *ever*," she steps forward to take Lourdes' face in her hands. "You *never*," she nearly squeals, her voice still constricted, "let a loaded gun drop on the ground, do you hear me?"

Lourdes doesn't look at her.

"If you load a gun then you use it. You point it at someone and you *use it*." She is shouting now. She is shaking the girl by her shoulders. "Who were you going to shoot?"

The girl goes limp as a mollusk, comes to her, slides against her body.

"Oh, Ana."

She has to remember that this is not her real name, only what she told Lourdes she was called. She feels guilty, suddenly, that this girl who trusts her thinks her name is something that it is not.

The girl puts her arms around her chest. Her flat body pinches itself against her breasts. She takes Lourdes' oblong face between her hands.

"Who were you going to shoot?" Lourdes lowers her eyes. "Who?" She shakes her.

"I don't know."

She felt sad, immediately, as soon as the girl had said it. She didn't need to know who Lourdes had intended to shoot. She didn't need to ask that question.

Later that night, as they lie entwined together, listening to the fizz of rain on the tin roof, Lourdes stirs, turns to her, only a shard of her face visible in the moon's knife coming through the window.

"Will you do something for me?"

She fans the girl's eyelashes between her index and third finger. Lourdes closes her eyes.

"I'd do anything for you."

She unbuttons her shirt and reaches both arms to her back, unclasps her bra. She releases her arms and lets her breasts spill out. Lourdes moves her mouth towards the nipple, closes over it.

On her breast the mouth is delicate, unscarred. It does not feel like a child suckling her breast. But it feels very different from when he does it. He does not close his mouth over her nipple softly, but devours it, seems to want to swallow it. Lourdes stays like that for what seems like hours, until she falls asleep with the nipple in her mouth.

For the first time since she met him, she sleeps with her body relaxed. No one has to come in the night and pry her apart. About an hour later, after the rain has stopped, she gently extricates her breast from the girl's open mouth, picks up the gun from where it had fallen, and leaves.

Much later that night she sits in the Tip-Top ice cream parlour licking her favourite flavour, the bitter-lemony *cupuacú*. Families take desultory promenades around the square to the rattling sound of axle-battered cars: combatants of too many Belém potholes. The sky is clear, but it is a sideways, neon night.

In the park, women are arguing with their boyfriends. The women always take the initiative in an argument, she observes. The men are pliant, as if drugged with heat-stunned lassitude. They go along with everything until they start drinking.

She has only a thousand *cruzeiros* left. Not much. She has spent the fifteen dollars she was going to use to buy the sloth on ammunition.

In the window she sees the reflection of her face. Then she sees his reflection in their apartment window, superimposed on the river-cranes. The cranes are sawing the sky, groaning forward and back. On the bed, he is thrashing back and forth, too.

I didn't mean to hurt you.

He is barely conscious, and gasping.

"We're the same," she whispers.

Then she mops up the blood, makes him a torque bandage, takes him to the hospital. Everywhere she looks in the ward, malarial men lie like exhausted bread loaves. Whenever anyone is shot in the conflicts of the garimpo, the nearby gold mines, they are taken to the hospital in Belém.

"To your knowledge, has your husband ever had dengue,

malaria, or HIV?" they ask when she fills out the forms. In Portuguese, HIV sounds like *Ash ee va* – soft, she thinks. Almost benevolent.

"We'd like to keep him overnight for observation and run blood tests," the doctor tells her. "It's just a grazing. He was lucky. Or it was meant to be just that."

When she has told him the story about the robbers, the doctor shrugs.

"It happens a lot. And you live in a rich neighbourhood. You should move downmarket. You can take him home in the morning."

The doctor looks at her, sudden and sharp. "You're not going to report this to the police, are you?"

She shakes her head.

"Good." He clips a piece of paper onto his board, turns away from her. "That would get you nowhere."

She makes sure he is asleep, then she walks out of the hospital, catches a taxi and asks the driver to take her to the ice-cream parlour.

As I work my way through the riot-coloured ice-creams – *Açaí, Cajú, Cupuacú, Castanha* – I run through the possibilities of what I have begun to call "My Future."

I will go and live with Lourdes and her brother. We will save our money, the three of us, and I will take them to Miami. There they will learn English, and instead of a prostitute, Lourdes will become a dark-skinned secretary in an air-conditioned office.

I will leave this city. I will swim out to the one or two ships that still make the journey up to Manaus and back again and then are spit out the mouth of the giant river and go to Port-of-Spain, to Monrovia, to Panama. There I will meet a Belgian businessman in a bar and we will become lovers and he will pay my passage home. Or I will go with him to Antwerp and work there for the tourist board, guiding English people around the city.

I will use all my savings to buy the sloth. I will return her to the forest. I will journey for many days in small boats, dependent upon the kindness of the people in the river settlements.

They will understand what I am doing. They will help me. Even if by that point I smell of piss and green slime because the sloth will not let go, even at night, of my shoulders.

He had been out of the hospital for a week. The boy had just tripped into his trousers, closed the door. That night, like many nights before, she sat in the corner of the room, the one beside the tall faux-French window. She sat so that her hair was brushed lightly by the once-white gauzy curtains as they swung in the breeze. In front of her was the bed which took up an obscenely large area of the room. Her legs – tanned, mosquito-bitten – were curled up underneath her, and she sank down as far as she could into the chair.

She loved to watch his face when he came close to orgasm. It twisted into an almost phantasmagoric mixture of pain and waiting. Waiting, waiting . . . and then relief. Like the slow opening of a flower, or the open mouths of bears, rabbits, small animals as they died, caught in the steel trap in the winter forests of her childhood.

She could do this too. It wasn't just the boys she brought to him. They were made for each other. His penis was thin and long, delicate. She was small. They fit each other perfectly. Sweat even ran down their chests in synchronized rivulets.

In the morning she would change the dressing on his wound. This would bind them more to each other. There was nothing about him that was foreign. Not his ruptured skin, the scar he would always carry. Every part of his anatomy seemed made to inhabit her body. And it had been even better between them ever since he had told her she was not what he needed.

He would watch her change the dressing on his wound, following the complex instructions from the doctor, which he could not understand because his Portuguese was bad. At these moments, he looked at her face with an expression approaching benediction.

Later that night she lay beside him on the big bed, so hot she thought she might be breaking into a fever. She rolled over, away from him, careful not to touch his body.

In the morning, she got him a glass of water, took his gold-rimmed glasses delicately in her hands and cleaned them with her silk scarf. She replaced them quietly on the bedside table.

Quietly, without looking him in the eye, she went around the room gathering her things. She stuffed them in her bag. The claustrophobia was getting worse with each second, but she tried not to appear rushed. He looked like a wounded animal, faultless and uncomprehending, lying tense and waiting for the moment to be over, the one when she would close the door behind her.

## EDWARD O'CONNOR

# *The Beatrice of Victoria College*

Arthur McGrievey hadn't been married two years when his wife Sheila packed up and disappeared, running off with one of any number of men she'd got to know on the street corner where she plied her trade. She wasn't a prostitute but a jewellery vendor who sold mostly necklaces and earrings she made herself at a fantastically messy worktable in the living room of their tiny apartment on Gloucester Street. Arthur, a failed academic, had been putting in time for several years as a copyeditor for a publishing company, but when his wife took off he had something of a nervous breakdown and either decided or was asked to go freelance.

He also began to drink considerably, at least on the weekends. He was in his mid-thirties by then and felt he'd missed the boat in more ways than one. In spite of his weekend binges and generally lugubrious attitude, Arthur thrived as a freelancer. He developed the valuable habit of finishing his projects on time, and he was able to maintain unusually cordial relations with authors while still getting them to do everything his employers wanted. For these very simple reasons, publishers were mad about him, and Arthur succeeded in doing something that had always eluded him till then, that is, he began putting a little money in the bank. This allowed him to be choosier about the projects he accepted, and the choosier he got, the more eagerly the publishers sought him out and the better they paid him.

In the meantime, in what might be called the editorial community in Toronto, Arthur acquired a nickname. They called him Fireface, this from the condition he habitually assumed at parties, where he would drink until his face and the high crown of his nearly bald head turned a flaming crimson. He was uneasy with women and never danced himself, but once he'd had several drinks, he loved listening to music and watching other people cavorting to it. When he was standing off to one side like that, face aflame and watching the dancers, his yearning to be part of something he disdained was so palpable it was funny, if not to himself then certainly to anyone who looked at him.

By far the majority of freelance editors in Toronto were women, a number of whom worked sporadically but were married to men who pulled down massive salaries. At the parties sponsored by the editors' association, there were always a few of these husbands present. They could be identified by their taste in clothes. Though conservative, their suits were so finely tailored and the fabric so expensive the men ended up peacocks in spite of themselves. Arthur, on the other hand, took pride in dressing like a sloven. He let his greying beard grow long and the horseshoe fringe of hair around his head he left unattended so that it hung lank and scraggly to his shoulders.

At a party in the fall of the year after Sheila left, Arthur found himself standing off to the side of the area where a few couples were romping to the music and next to a man about his own age who was dressed in a jacket and tie. When the music stopped for a moment, the man spoke to Arthur.

"What do *you* do, anyway?"

Arthur thought of asking the fellow why he didn't just piss off. He knew he'd had enough to drink by then that if he didn't keep his answers as brief as possible the words would come out slurred and in a sing-song cadence.

"Freelance."

"Freelance what?"

The man placed the accent on the second word, as if to say, "Well I knew that much, for God's sake." To Arthur his face seemed unutterably coarse, brutalized by a lifetime of greed and self-assertion.

"Oh, anything. Jack of all trades."

"And master of none, it follows."

He spoke the words in a pointed, biting fashion and fastened his eyes on Arthur's. They stared at each other for a long moment, two men who despised each other instinctively, and then the stranger laughed hatefully and strolled away, manifestly pleased with himself.

Anyone who reads very much has favourite passages, scenes from stories or novels that occupy a place of honour in his memory and cannot be dislodged by time or alcohol or any subsequent reading, no matter how disruptive these forces may prove in other ways. Arthur had always loved the beginning of *Wind, Sand, and Stars*, where Saint-Exupéry describes the bus ride he takes in the blackness of a rainy morning. He is on his way to the airfield where for the first time he'll fly the mail plane to Africa. He's a young man about to embark on a great adventure, flying over the mountains to Spain and then over the sea to Casablanca, and he knows he could very easily lose his life. In the bus he directs the reader's attention repeatedly to his fellow passengers, all of whom are bureaucrats on their way to work. "Worn old clerks," he calls them, preoccupied with "shabby domestic cares." They lead lives of such contemptible dullness, Saint-Exupéry wonders that it does not kill them or drive them mad.

Arthur always soothed himself after encounters like the one at the party by thinking of this passage. In fact, he didn't have to make an effort to resurrect it, it simply came to him of its own accord. He told himself that under the circumstances, because of the occasional nature of his employment and the complete lack of financial props like pensions, insurance, and paid vacations, that he was the nightflier, the explorer; while the person mouthing the words "And master of none" was the drone, the termite, the fear-mesmerized bureaucrat with a face like a baboon's ass.

He was mulling over just such thoughts as these the night after the party when the telephone rang. Arthur had just achieved that stage in hangover when the pressure in his skull had eased enough that he felt like weeping with relief into the chapel of his two cupped hands. The ringing of the phone harrowed him with fear. He glanced at the clock on the wall and saw that it was just after ten. When he lifted the receiver a woman asked for Mr. McGrievey and then identified herself as Jenny somebody-or-other, her voice so faint he could barely hear her.

"You'll have to speak up."

"I got your name from the book," she said, making no effort at all to raise her voice. He was annoyed enough to speak sharply.

"What book? What in hell are you talking about?"

"The editors' association. Am I calling too late?"

"Oh, the directory. Are you with a publishing company?"

"No, I'm not. I'm in school actually, at university."

She stopped. There was dead silence.

"Yes?" he said finally.

But he knew it was hopeless, that there would be nothing in it for him. The only time he'd had profitable relations with a student had been years before when he was still in school himself and had written a term paper for the daughter of a Mafioso from upstate New York. She'd paid handsomely on delivery but couldn't resist issuing the warning that if she didn't receive at least a B-plus for the paper, she'd get her money back. She hadn't said "want" or "appreciate"; she'd said "get."

"Well, in your listing it says you're a writer as well as an editor."

The trace of an English accent held in the voice. The accent became more pronounced as the voice grew more emotional.

"You're not really going to ask me to do one of your papers, are you?"

"No. No, of course not."

Then she said, "Not a *paper*."

He waited.

"It's my dissertation, actually."

"Ah Jesus, you must be joking. A doctoral thesis?"

"Well, yes, but it's really not writing it needs so much as just giving it a good, thorough edit. All the parts are there, they're in place already. They only want to be fitted together a bit more snugly."

Arthur didn't reply immediately. Instead he opened a new pack of cigarettes. He took his time removing the cellophane and then the foil, drawing the first cigarette out of the tight pack and lighting it up. He hadn't allowed himself a cigarette all day, and the smoke had a fine toasty flavour. The woman on the other end said nothing, waiting.

"But look, don't you have a supervisor to advise you about exactly that sort of thing?"

"Of course I do. But at this point we're not speaking to each other."

A thought came to Arthur so suddenly and vividly that he never considered questioning its truth. They'd had an affair, and it had ended unhappily. That also explained why she couldn't finish her thesis. A picture of the woman began to form in his mind. A bit overweight, a little frumpy but with sex appeal. Soft around the edges, blond frizzy hair, and a welcoming smile if you could coax one out of her.

"I've been working on this thing for twelve years now and he's simply fed up. Won't see me or speak to me until I'm finished, he says."

She sighed softly. The sound, coming to him over miles of tightly stretched wire and through the inanimate piece of plastic in his hand, poured into his ear like molten lead. He knew at once that there'd been no affair, that the woman he was speaking with was simply a lost, feckless soul, one of life's losers as Saint-Exupéry might have said.

"It's on what you might call a concrete topic at least. Nothing too abstruse or obscure. My thesis is quite pictorial, actually."

"You're in art history?"

"Well no, not exactly. I suppose you could call it more the history of ideas. I'm writing about the glass in York Minster."

"A thesis about stained glass windows."

"That's right. They're really magnificent works of art in their own right, but all with pedagogical intentions at the same time. I've made some rather important discoveries about those intentions, I think."

Arthur wavered for a moment, then set about applying the brush-off.

"I'm sure you could find someone better qualified than I am for that sort of thing. I'm swamped at the moment anyway."

Actually, he was entering a dry spell just then, but thought he knew a dead-end street when he saw one.

"But couldn't you just look at it before you decide? I'm no good at all at promoting myself, you know. The thesis is in much better shape than I'm conveying, and I have slides I can show you too."

The last non sequitur made Arthur wonder if the woman might be unbalanced.

"You could never pay what I'd be asking," he told her.

She gave a short cry of despair. She really had grown quite animated. Arthur had no trouble at all hearing her now.

"Then don't *tell* me what you're asking," she blurted out. "Let me tell you what I can afford."

She named a figure that was so low he almost laughed.

"I can make that in a day," he said.

"Won't you at least come and take a look?"

Come and take a look. He wondered if she was aware her choice of words was fraught with lurid implications. Perhaps when the mind is agitated it resorts to such constructions automatically. But in the end that was exactly why he went. He knew there'd be nothing in it for him financially. He was simply curious to see what the woman looked like.

They agreed to meet after supper the following evening, a Monday near the end of October. She had an office, she said, in an old gingerbread house on Charles Street.

"Standing all by itself at the front of a parking lot," she said. "It was a bequest to the university and even though they'd love to, they're not allowed to tear it down. You can't miss it."

He came out of the Museum subway station and walked east beneath a file of nearly naked linden trees until he found the house, alone, as she had said, and with a very narrow look, forlorn, cramped, and completely dark. Even the light over the front step was off. He wondered if Jenny had forgotten the appointment she herself had been so keen to make.

As soon as he rang the bell light jumped out of the circular gable window at the top of the house, and after a pause the larger window on the second floor grew bright. Then the first-floor hallway filled with light, and he could see her coming down the staircase. She was dressed in an ankle-length skirt and turtle-neck sweater with sleeves rolled back to show forearms almost anorexicly thin.

After springing the lock, Jenny pulled the door open and stepped back with a wary smile, looking him over carefully. Her hair was jet black and short, framing, if hair cut so severely can be said to frame, an angular face dominated by the large, nervous, slightly protruding eyes of a doe.

Before taking him up to her office in the attic, she made a pot of chamomile tea in the galley kitchen at the back of the first floor.

"I'd offer you coffee, but I don't drink it myself and if I used anybody else's my life wouldn't be worth a nickel. Everyone here guards their things so jealously, and they know immediately if you've taken anything, even the tiniest amount. There've been the most horrible rows over nothing worse than a purloined tea bag."

She giggled richly but stopped and looked away when he didn't laugh.

"This house," he said. "It's all offices for grad students?"

"No, I'm the only one actually. I've the third floor to myself. There's a seminar room on the second floor, and the rest of the space is given over to one of the English department's more meagrely funded research projects. The funding grows more meagre every year, as a matter of fact. But they still have a staff of half a dozen people, all of whom are devoted to the project and working like beavers to finish it off before the funding dries up entirely."

"High-powered scholars," Arthur sneered. "I know the type."

The pot of water made a sound that rose higher and higher until finally it sighed and the water rolled and began to boil. Jenny looked idly at the pot, watching the steam pour out of it. She seemed to blank out for a moment, forgetting where she was or that there was a visitor in the room. Arthur waited, curious to see how long the spell would last. After a minute she came to herself and, without leaning, reached across the stove to turn the element off. Her arms were incredibly long, and she had the high bony shoulders of one of Picasso's acrobats. He wondered if she'd been sleeping upstairs in the dark before he arrived. Her skin was paler than candlesticks.

"There's a booth for the parking lot attendant just on the side of the house here," she said, pursuing a train of thought.

"He comes in two or three times a day to call his wife. Makes a point of slamming the door as hard as he can, then tramps through the hall to the phone. It's quiet – he's dialling – then his voice explodes, I can hear it plain as day on the third floor – '*Trudie?*' He's an old man, of German peasant stock, and feels he has to shout on the phone or he won't be heard. He speaks in dialect. Nobody here understands a thing he says, but they're forced to listen to every word and at maximum volume. Even though he drives them all insane, no one has ever told him to shut up or clear out. They've accepted him as part of the furniture, in the same way they've accepted the faulty wiring and the toilet that doesn't flush properly."

She swirled the tea in the pot before pouring it into a cup. Arthur waited a moment for her to continue, then realized she had finished.

"The point being?" he asked.

She poured the tea into the second cup.

"I'm not sure there is a point, really," she said. "I'm just trying to give you an idea of what it's like to work in this house. What the other people are like."

"Well, what are they like? You'll have to spell it out for me."

"I can't put it bluntly, the way you want me to, because I can't decide myself, you see. The kind of forbearance I'm referring to – is it something pathetic, or could it be the attribute of a saint?"

Arthur felt as if he'd been slapped on the face or as if someone standing close by had shattered a pane of glass with one blow of a hammer. He understood she was referring more to herself than to the other people in the house. She knew exactly what he thought of her – amusement mixed with pity mixed with scorn

– and was trying to counter that assessment with an alternative. Although he fought against it, he felt himself blushing beneath her gaze, which had turned suddenly steady, blushing like mad. It was a deeply embarrassing moment for him.

The first thing that struck him about Jenny's office on the third floor was the smell of incense, which he had always loathed with all his heart. If nothing else, it was the perfect olfactory equivalent to the taste of the chamomile tea she had given him. The second impression was of barrenness. A single small picture decorated the walls, a reproduction of one of Cézanne's dimmest still lifes. The furniture consisted of a wooden desk, a couple of folding chairs, a filing cabinet, and a small table. The desk was in the alcove for the gable window, positioned in such a way that when Jenny sat at it, her back was to the window and she faced a blank wall.

The light in the room drizzled out of a halogen lamp in one corner. Lying about on the window sill and the desk and table tops were a number of cheap metal candleholders, in each of them a candle burnt right down to the nub.

"Everything is here."

She tapped lightly with her toe a thick cardboard box sitting on the floor beside the desk. It was a gracefully executed movement and the look on her face, as her eyes slid away from his, was almost coquettish.

"These are my notes and the last draft of my thesis."

Looking closer, Arthur saw it was the type of box used to ship produce. "Chiquita Bananas" was blazoned over the top, and beneath the label was a drawing of a nubile, leggy young woman balancing a pyramid of tropical fruit on her head.

"Twelve years of my life are in that box," said Jenny. "Doesn't that seem ridiculous to you?"

Arthur exploded with laughter. It wrenched right out of his guts and rang through the room like a cannon volley. For a moment he thought he wouldn't be able to stop. There was something in the incongruity between the leering sexpot stencilled on the box and the diffident waif standing in the flesh before him that he found much more than ridiculous, it was hilarious. While the laughter was still pouring out of him, he realized she was taking the full force of it right in the face. He saw something in her eyes then of the same censuring look he must have presented to the stranger at the party two nights before. Suddenly he stood reflected to himself as a coarse, middle-aged buffoon wearing a mask incised by alcohol and self-pity. His laughter went out like a quenched candle flame.

"Yes, of course it's ridiculous," he said and shrugged.

Then he seated himself without waiting to be asked. He was dismayed to find he was sweating. The look on Jenny's face made him want badly to bait her. Arthur wiped his mouth with the palm and fingers of one hand.

"I have something to tell you," he said. "Something I think you should know right from the start. I don't care about the existential background of your thesis, the whole sad story and all the rest. And I don't want to hear about whatever emotional crisis it was that prompted you to call me."

"Then what do you want to know about."

She was still standing by the box, lightly kicking it with one foot. She was not looking at him. Tap went her foot. Tap, tap.

"The only thing that matters to me is whether I can do the work that remains quickly enough to make something resembling a profit. Is that acceptable to you?"

Her head came up at once. He detected a mortified expression in her eyes, which he found quite gratifying.

"Yes, of course."

She went behind the desk and seated herself.

"The profit motive. That makes perfect sense. I sometimes think it's what makes the world go round."

"Do you have an outline for me?"

She glanced uneasily at the cardboard box.

"Outlines I have dozens of. But I'd rather not start with the print materials if it's all the same with you. It's not the absolutely best way of approaching my work."

He wondered how she would prefer to proceed.

"I'd *prefer* to show the slides first. They're really the heart of the thesis anyway. You won't be able to understand a thing of what I've written until you've seen them."

The slides again. He recalled how she had introduced them on the phone the night before, as if she were thrusting a handful of them into his face. It came to him then that all the furniture in the room had been carefully positioned in advance for Jenny's slide show. Both of the folding chairs were pointed at the blank wall on the far side of the room. The table had been requisitioned to serve as a platform for the projector, which was already in place and packed with a slide in every interstice.

As he turned to her, the light in the room began to fail. She was manipulating the dimmer for the halogen lamp with her foot, and he saw that she had the device to control the projector gripped in her hand as tightly as a child holds a lucky rabbit's foot. Her head was inclined towards him slightly; she was biting her lower lip. The only jewellery she wore was a pair of cheap earrings made of bits of coral and silver, the kind Arthur's wife had sold on the street for seven dollars a pair. Jenny's hair was freshly brushed, and Arthur, his pitted red nose ever sensitive to even the slightest hint of perfume, could tell she had recently powdered herself with talcum. Her face flared at him as the light died completely and the projector snapped on.

A rectangle of light appeared against the wall. Another snap, and the light filled with colour – a rich red and blue and a yellow that verged on amber. All Arthur could make out was a robed figure with arms raised.

"This is the first day of creation," said Jenny. "When God created light. From the great east window in York Minster."

There followed a series of scenes in stained glass from Genesis and then from other books of the Old Testament. He saw Eve handing Adam the apple, and wrapped around a tree behind her was a snake with a human head. The eyes in the serpent's face were bleary with guile and lust. There was a picture of Cain clubbing his brother to death and of Noah lying drunk and naked. He saw blind old Samson revenging himself on the Philistines and then Goliath raging, decked out in the armour of a medieval knight. The last window in the series presented David's son Absalom hanging by his hair from the branches of a thorn tree and struck through with a whole sheaf of arrows.

To his great surprise, Arthur was taken with the pictures immediately. Not only were the colours of the glass deep and resonant, but the people's faces formed successful portraits, so remarkably expressive that they were as unlike the kitsch he'd grown accustomed to in the churches of his youth as Titian to a greeting card artist.

Each time she changed a slide, Jenny identified the biblical scene and each of the characters involved but said little else. She took about the same amount of time over each slide, establishing a rhythm that Arthur found relaxing. At some point the scenes portrayed changed from the Old Testament to the Book of Revelation. Jenny showed the first of these, an angel winding a trumpet blast, then stopped.

"These are all panels in the same huge window in the Minster," she said. "Laid out flat on the ground, it would cover about as much space as a tennis court. The top third of the window is devoted to Old Testament scenes, while the bottom two-thirds is all scenes from the Book of Revelation. The two sets of panels are related in a number of ways both obvious and subtle – the old and the new, the prophecy and its fulfilment."

While she worked her way through the scenes from Revelation, Jenny explained different medieval theories of scriptural interpretation and the way she was using them to analyse what she called the window's "iconographical organization." Arthur deliberately ignored most of what she said and concentrated instead on her tone of voice, which was measured and flutelike. It became evident she had her material down cold.

He stole a look at her. The glow from inside the projector was much like candlelight, and it made Arthur acutely aware that they had the dark house entirely to themselves.

He had always considered Revelation the one truly hateful book in the Bible. The scenes depicted in the glass panels grew increasingly more bizarre: the Lamb of God prancing about in a martial attitude, a rider with a sword where his tongue should be, the dreary dead rising from their graves like blue flames from a gas burner. But Jenny's voice was so soothing in the dark room that Arthur found himself lulled, drifting off in a reverie, rather as if he were at a party listening to the music and watching the dancers perform for him. Whenever this happened, whenever he entered this sort of abstracted state, he always reverted to the exact same memory, winging to it like a homing pigeon straining to its cage.

It was winter and he was walking down Yonge Street early in the evening to meet his wife. The day had just turned dark and snow was failing in large, dry flakes that settled on the shoulders of the passers-by. When he reached the corner where Sheila had her jewellery stand, she was already packing up. The earrings and necklaces she made were pinned to boards covered in purple felt, and the boards formed a triptych that folded into a carrying case. Sheila had just bent over, very close to the open boards, to blow the snow off a pair of earrings adorned with pheasant feathers.

His eyes caught her face in a moment of easy concentration, completely absorbed in the task at hand, intent on responding properly to the predicament of snowflake on feather. There was no hint in her expression of contempt or deception, nothing of self-justification or the desire to exult at the expense of others. Arthur had feasted on this image for years, but after Sheila ran off his reverie always ended with the same verbal response.

"What a whore," he said. He said it right out loud and ground his fist into his thigh, just as he always did. "What a goddamn whore."

"What is it you are saying?"

Arthur came to with a start and found himself staring into the face of God the Father, who held an open book across his breast on which were printed the words, *Ego sum alpha et omega*. The painter had drawn the divine eyes large and set them deeply beneath an expansive brow that was majestically stern and commanding. At the same time, a habit of mercy or sympathy was evident in the wrinkled forehead and around the lips, which were unusually long and fine and seemed about to open in speech.

Arthur said nothing, but neither could he take his eyes off the face before him. The telescopic eyes and poised lips gave the image an animated, mesmerizing effect.

Jenny, for her part, stared at Arthur and took a moment to collect herself.

"This," she said, "is the panel at the summit – the apogee – of the window. It's what ties all the other panels together as part of one grand concept. The Latin inscription is taken directly from the Book of Revelation. It indicates that all of history has been laid out beneath in the confines of this one window, the beginning and the end of time."

A jubilant note entered her voice as she realized how fascinated Arthur was by the picture.

"This panel always reminds me of a certain passage from Exodus," she said.

"Yes. What passage is that?" He was bemused but still unable to break the spell.

"When Moses begs God to show himself in all his glory, but God says to him, 'My face shall not be seen.' That may have been how the ancient Jews responded to the mystery of God, but these medieval artists thought differently. They really did believe it was possible to convey an idea of God in several different ways, concrete ways. And one of them was through the human form. It would have seemed to the people on the pavement below that in this window God had condescended to show his face."

On an impulse, Arthur turned and cupped her chin in the palm of his hand. It was the first time he had touched a woman's skin since Sheila had run off. He turned her face to bring her eyes around to his, but she refused to look at him. She didn't close her eyes but kept them turned away and down. He twisted her face harder towards him. She groaned. Appalled, he released her immediately.

The silence that followed was so painful, he would have said anything to break it. The only sound was the humming of the projector. God's face still stared at them from the wall, but the eyes had assumed a startled look.

"How much time do you waste up here," Arthur said. "Gazing at these pictures? The candles, the incense. It's like a church service for you, isn't it? Isn't this why you don't get anything done? Why you can't finish?"

She said nothing.

"Well, isn't it?"

"I can't get past it," she admitted, all in a rush. Her voice was thick with despair.

"I had a sort of experience one night when I was going through the slides and came to this one. I don't know how to express it exactly, but it made everything else seem so futile. Why am I wasting my time, I thought. Banging my head against a brick wall for nothing."

She switched off the projector, and the wall went blank with darkness. Without something to look at, Arthur felt threatened by claustrophobia. He was sick of his own clumsiness and wanted nothing more than to get out of the house and find something stronger to drink than chamomile tea. He mumbled an "excuse me" and stood up to leave.

With the first step he took, his foot slammed into the cardboard box she kept her papers in. The pain and surprise were sharp enough to draw a curse from him. Twelve years of her life, she had said. All of her effort and all of her discoveries he experienced as simple dead weight, something in the way. Jenny asked where he was going, as if surprised he wanted to leave, but he kept on his way without another word.

Each step downward on the ancient wooden staircase cracked out like a rifle shot. The same set of acoustics that so enthusiastically sucked the old German's voice up to her forbearing ears on the third floor now performed the identical service with Arthur's retreating footsteps. He felt a sudden upsurge of bitterness. The trouble with God, he thought, is that he can't hold a candle to his own creations.

When he opened the front door and stepped out into the October night, he realized he was soaked with sweat. As he adjusted his coat and scarf, the heat from his body billowed about his face and Arthur caught the scent of his own fear. By the time he reached the sidewalk across the street and turned to look, the whole house had gone completely dark again. It stood to itself as black as the sky above, where, hidden by banks of impenetrable clouds, hung the splendid moon and an infinitude of stars.

## LIBBY CREELMAN

# *Cruelty*

Lila is sitting on her hands on the edge of the dining room table while her parents dress upstairs. They rarely go out any more, but when they do, her father needs the extra quiet time to shower and shave. Lila's mother doesn't want anyone coming up the stairs with a load of questions.

Lila can see the back yard, which is deep and narrow and suffers from a thick canopy of neighbouring trees so that even in summer it will be cold and overcast. Although snow remains now only in patches, it is not grass that has emerged but green boggy moss.

The phone rings and Lila hears the clip-clop of her mother's shoes as she moves over the hardwood floor in the upstairs hallway.

"Yes, hello, this is Marian."

In the back yard stands a handsome wooden swing set Lila's father put together from a kit. A monument soaked with dampness but free of snow. He hammered his finger that day and Lila's mother ran up and down the stairs looking for Band-Aids. Her mother worries about splinters, but Lila hides them, along with the blisters, by making fists of her hands. Her mother distrusts the outdoors, in particular, back yards.

"Rick, it's for you."

There is the whispered shuffle of Lila's father in stocking feet as he travels to the phone.

"Careful, Rick, you'll slip. That won't be good for your back."

The maple trees are brown, and the tulip beds, the fence, the undersides of clouds. Her mother calls this another disappointing spring day. Her mother is from Ontario and visits there sometimes alone, but comes back with a sad face and new clothes for everyone, saying there is no one left. A place called Kingston has become a foreign land.

Joy appears in the doorway. "Something's going on. Listen."

Joy is eleven and does not sit on her hands while their parents dress. She sits in the kitchen and crayons.

Upstairs their mother says, her voice elevated and slightly frightened, "You're only telling me this now?"

"No, Marian. *She* was only telling me this now. On the phone, just then."

"Is she crazy?"

"Marian." Their father is beginning to sound as though someone has applied glue to his tongue. Perhaps he is experimenting with a new painkiller. "Marian, it was an innocent and kind suggestion. She does have children of her own. But if the baby-sitter is here, let's forget it, shall we?"

"Has she already made their supper?"

"She didn't say. Is the baby-sitter here?"

"Do you hear the baby-sitter nattering away downstairs?"

"Lila's on the table."

"If she's already made their supper?"

"She didn't say. Lila." Her father comes to the head of the stairs. Lila sees his navy socks. "You can hop down now," he calls.

Joy puts her arms out and Lila slides down into them, then stands fanning her hands. In a few years she'll wait in the kitchen with Joy while their parents dress upstairs, but in the meantime she is not unhappy with her stinging hands; they are, to her, like two plants pressed lovingly between book pages: feather-light, fragrant, bruised.

Upstairs, there is the hollow clip-clop of their mother, and more slowly, the slithering hush of their father. The room where Lila and Joy wait is growing dark. The lights are not on and neither girl has the courage to touch their mother's antique lamps. The view onto Monkstown Road is aglow. In the sky above dozens of crows are beating their way back from the dump to Kenmount Hill where they will spend the night. Lila knows this because her father has explained it to her. He has stood at this window and counted hundreds passing overhead.

"Girls?" He is there, almost ready, his hair combed back and still wet from his shower. He'll need help with his shoes. "How would you two like to head out with us tonight?"

"Yeah!" Joy says.

"Lila?"

"I've called the baby-sitter, Rick," their mother shouts from upstairs. "But I'm having second thoughts. Someone find your father's shoes, then everyone go wait for me in the car."

Lila's father puts a hand on Joy who, understanding the gesture, immediately pouts. "Let your sister get them this time," he says. "It means a lot to her."

"Did anyone hear me?" their mother yells.

"Yes, Marian. Loud and clear."

"It's only common courtesy to make that acknowledgment, all of you."

His shoes wait side by side at the back door, smelling of leather, shoe polish, pain. As she lifts them Lila has the desire to crawl inside one, down to the tips of the toes.

What Lila comes to understand on the drive over is that they are visiting a woman who works where their father did before he had to give up working. A woman with three sons, but no husband.

"I believe he went to California," their father explains.

"California? Good Lord."

"I believe he works as a mechanic at Disneyland. But don't quote me on that."

"Could he get us in free?" Joy asks. "Some kind of a deal?"

"Anything's possible."

"Oh, Rick, don't get their hopes up like that," their mother says with soft laughter. "Your father's talking out of the side of his mouth. Is this it?"

They park behind two cars in a single lane driveway. On the left is a dusty turquoise house while on the right a chain-linked fence travels past the cars and up a slight incline, bordering a back yard mostly mud. Lila moves forward in her seat and sees a single tree in the middle of the yard. In the bare arms of the tree hangs a boy.

"What's that?" her mother asks.

"Back of the brewery," Lila's father answers.

"Does it always stink this badly?"

"No idea. Come on now."

A woman steps through the back door and waves.

"She's pretty," Joy says.

"I guess I was thinking a little more formal," their mother says.

Their father looks at the woman, then at his wife. The woman is wearing leggings and several layers of shirts, the outermost a men's red hunting jacket. His wife is wearing a new beige corduroy skirt and her boiled wool jacket.

"Don't sweat it," he says.

"I just wish I had known," Lila's mother says, swiftly removing her earrings and pocketing them – a sure sign that all is lost.

Lila watches her father's jaw clench, from irritation or pain or both. He wets his lips, as though to make a fresh start. "Come on, everybody out now."

As they move towards the house a black dog charges around the side of it, barking and leaping over invisible barrels.

The woman, who has been smiling and shifting her weight from foot to foot, possibly to stay warm, stops and puts her hands on her hips and shouts, "How did Mackie get loose?" She seems to be addressing the boy in the tree. As though the black dog understands this, it immediately heads that way, its tail batting the air unrhythmically. A German shepherd rises from the dirt at the base of the tree and yanks hard against the rope at its neck. The two dogs grapple briefly, and the black dog is off again.

"Brrr," the woman says, hugging herself as Lila and her family approach. "So you brought the kids. Super. Watch out for Mackie. Down boy!" She turns and hollers, "Alfred!"

"I'm stuck. I can't get down," the boy in the tree answers. He does not shout or raise his voice yet speaks with such forceful clarity he could have been standing at Lila's ear.

"What a liar he is," the woman tells Lila and Joy. She seems to find this funny. "Alfred's after living in that tree. Mackie! Down boy."

The dog is avoiding the woman. Lila's father reaches for its tail, misses, and lurches awkwardly. He puts his hand on his lower back and his family stops breathing.

"Now you've done it, Rick," their mother says. "Do you want to go home?"

"Of course not," he snaps. "We only just got here." Then he winks at the woman and jokes, "I'm used to living with phenomenal pain."

"Sure?" the woman asks, alarmed. Turning swiftly, she seizes the dog by its neck and twists one of its ears until it slides onto its haunches at her feet and whimpers, its tail a submissive thud-thud on the wet ground. "Oh, now, will you look at your paws. Down boy. Get down out of that!" She straightens partway, still holding the dog, and smiles. "How's it going, Marian?"

"I can't complain."

"Come on in. It's freezing out."

"Two dogs," Lila's mother says loudly. "That's two more than I could handle."

"Don't be talking! It wasn't my idea." The woman opens the door with one hand and drags the sitting dog over the steps with her other, then puts her foot on its rear and shoves it the last distance. Lila's father and mother follow. Joy moves with her mother as though connected by a rope.

Lila doesn't budge and they disappear inside without her. She turns and stands a long time watching the boy in the tree as he climbs up one side and down the other and then back into the centre. Suspended in the branches around him are items she guesses belong to him: a beef bucket swinging by a yellow rope, a checkered cloth bag, torn ribbons, Sobeys bags and partially deflated balloons. He's wearing a jean jacket over a grey sweatshirt with the hood snug over his head.

"Can't you climb a tree or what?" he finally asks.

Lila's been waiting for this. Although she has never climbed a tree in her life and she's wearing a dress and she's cold, she runs over to the tree. The German shepherd rises like a wave.

"That thing won't hurt you. She's a big baby. Give her a pet. That's what I'd do."

"What grade are you in?" Lila asks, hanging back.

"Grade three. I hates it."

"I'm in grade two."

"Sure, you don't look old enough for preschool."

Lila has heard this before. She won't look at the boy now. She studies the dog digging at the ground with a single paw and panting so frantically its tongue skims the ground. Suddenly it barks and Lila jumps back and falls. She looks at her dress.

"Hey, don't cry," the boy says, scrambling down through the branches. He swings from the bottom branch and lands gracefully on bent knees, his arms extended before him. He lowers his arms, straightens his body, then bows so slightly Lila almost misses it. "Don't go in."

But Lila has no intention of going in. The first thing she notices about him when he squats beside her is the space between his two front teeth, which are new and not as white as the others. She says, "It's just my dress is dirty is all. My mother will kill me."

The boy looks away down the yard, squinting at the back of the brewery – a mustard-coloured building. He turns back and looks again at Lila's dress as though he can't quite make up his mind about it.

"What's your name anyway?"

"Lila."

"Wanna come up in the tree?"

Lila points at the German shepherd. Alfred nods and stands, takes a few steps towards the dog then charges it, leaping onto its back and pinning himself to its neck. It whines and tosses its head.

"Run," Alfred urges, though his voice is calm, almost gentle. "I can't be holding Girlie forever."

She gets to the tree and stops, unable to reach the bottom branch. "See the nails?" Alfred says. "Use 'em as steps."

"Nails?"

"In the bark there."

Lila has never touched a nail. She remembers her father hammering his hand, the search for a Band-Aid. Both her parents had been shouting.

"Look at the bark," he says, still patient. "Jesus, Girlie, you're gross. Give it up."

Lila glances at Alfred flat on his back in the muck with the dog planted over him lapping his face. Hot gratitude rushes through her. She puts a foot on a bent nail lodged into the bark. When both feet have left the earth and she's reached the bottom branch she hears him say, "There you go," and she knows she'll be unhappy now for a long time for not being born into this family.

He swings back up into the tree and joins her. "We're too low," he says. "Them piranhas can still get at us."

She follows him up to an opening where the bark is well-scarred and Alfred can reach his things. He takes a knife out of the beef bucket and scratches something into the branch between his legs, then offers Lila use of it. She shakes her head and he tosses the knife back into the bucket, saying, "Maybe another day then."

He lets go with both his hands and leans back, his legs grasping the branch like hands. She wants to shout. Or touch him. His hood slips off and jacket falls open. She sees his torso tighten and his expression gain years as he grabs at the checkered cloth bag hanging from a branch behind him.

"My music bag," he explains, sitting forward again. Inside the bag is a Sobeys bag and inside that several Oh Henry! bars. "I'm the only kid I knows still has Halloween candy."

She says, "My mother won't let me go trick or treating." He gives her a short satisfied nod and she knows she's said the right thing.

Cars are pulling up and people getting out and coming up to the house. Lila watches her own car become blocked in. The people wave at Alfred and Lila in the tree as they pass, but Alfred ignores them. "Jerks," he mumbles, his mouth full of candy bar. He's fishing around inside his pants, scratching himself and grimacing. He pushes his pants down and handles a small nubby object that seems to be irritating him. He slaps it.

He looks at her and smiles. "Just my old penis breath." He shoves it back into his pants, then slaps his zipper.

"Who were all those people?" Lila asks.

"Jerks. Have you ever been to Disneyland?"

She grins. "I know."

"What do you know?" He sounds cross.

"Your father has a job there."

"You know I visits there whenever I wants?"

She stares at him.

"Nearly."

She's hoping he'll invite her. She's hoping so hard, she doesn't notice him lean over and take hold of a strand of her hair. He yanks it out.

"Did that hurt?" he asks.

"No."

"It was hanging in your face."

"I wonder if it's time for supper?" she whispers.

"Sure, could be finished by now. Were you expecting someone to call you in? Gotta just go. Hold it." He puts his hand out, as though waiting until satisfied that Lila is fully attentive. "Girlie's not asleep yet, I wouldn't make no move. You've got another loose hair. Did that hurt?"

"No."

The next Saturday Lila is playing in her bedroom when her mother comes in and says, "That was Alfred's mother on the phone. Remember the little boy you got so dirty with? He wants you to visit him this afternoon." Her mother scrunches up her face. "That's not really something you want to do, is it?"

Lila has been thinking about Alfred and his tree all week. "Oh, Mommy, yes, please!"

"Let her make up her own mind, Marian," Lila's father says from somewhere.

Her mother frowns. "All right. But I'm going to put out pants and a wool sweater for you. Their house was freezing. And wet."

"Why was it wet?" Lila asks.

"Shame you never uttered more than two sentences, Marian," Lila's father calls.

"Because she had just washed the floor! There were puddles in fact. I took off my shoes to be polite and then my feet got wet and I froze. I don't think they had the heat on, quite frankly."

"Marian."

"Yeah, yeah, yeah. I'm just explaining why she needs to dress warmly. And don't remove your shoes inside their house."

"We'll probably play outside," Lila says carefully.

"No climbing trees," her father says.

"Where are you, Rick?"

"I'm resting my back."

"Of course no climbing trees, Lila, that goes without saying. Children are forever falling out of trees and breaking their arms."

Her mother walks to the doorway and looks down the hall. "Is that comfortable?" she asks him.

"Nothing's comfortable."

That afternoon while Lila is at Alfred's her father checks himself into the Health Sciences. He drives over himself without change for the meter or telling anyone beforehand, then calls just before supper, medicated and humble.

Lila's mother drops the supper plates before the girls, hurls the pots and pans into the sink, the leftovers into the refrigerator. Everything she touches she seems to hate.

"Are you mad at me?" Joy whines.

"No, treasure. Your father. He's set on doing everything his own way. Again. Now I'm going over to that hospital and we'll have two cars collecting tickets. I mean, why didn't he just ask me for a lift?"

"You're going to the hospital?" Joy asks.

"Well, I think I better. They might operate." For a moment her voice lightens, as though she's amused by the idea of not rushing to her husband's side. "Although, frankly, this place. The medical care. It takes forever to get anything done. I mean, a simple X-ray?"

Lila puts a finger into each of her ears. But she can still hear the crying Joy will begin any moment.

"I could have dropped him off this afternoon then picked you up at Alfred's, Lila. It was right on the way." Their mother slams the refrigerator door and on top of it the ceramic bowl of apples bounces nearer the edge. "No, he has to do everything his own way. Now settle down, both of you."

The phone rings. It's sitting right there in the middle of the table and they all jump. Joy and her mother both reach for it but Joy is quicker.

"Just give it to me," their mother hisses.

Joy hands the phone to her mother who immediately tries to interrupt. "If I could just . . ." she begins, then stops, her head thrust forward with the air of someone struggling with the incomprehensible. She looks so annoyed Lila thinks she might bite the receiver. "Sometime maybe. Maybe. I'll get back to you." She hangs up and looks at Lila curiously. "So you know about this? You want to have a sleepover at that boy's house? That woman is really getting on my nerves. From the moment your father tried to collar that mutt of hers he's been paying for it. Of course they'll never operate. Not after three operations already. Nobody'll touch him. Not here."

Alfred has long lashes and black hair that his mother trims with the scissors on her jackknife. She also uses the jackknife to open cans of tuna fish and tomato soup. Lila is fascinated by the speed at which her hand circles the can.

Today Alfred showed her his rocks. He keeps them on a wooden shelf on his bedroom wall. Lila didn't think much of the collection at first, the rocks were so dirty and crumbling. She would have expected a fleck or two of silver or gold, this being Alfred who has been to Disneyland. The game they played with the rocks involved putting a bunch in their socks and underwear and down the backs of their shirts, then going out into the tree. Alfred took a while selecting hers.

As they approached the tree Alfred tackled Girlie, urging Lila to hurry. She scrambled up through the branches despite the rocks under her feet and between her legs, so thrilled when Alfred praised her that it was easy to make peace with her pain.

As it was later, when he plucked out her hair or took her hand and bent it forward at the wrist until the tips of her cold pink fingers brushed her coat sleeve.

"Does this hurt?"

"No."

"Does this?"

"No."

"You got a gift there, girl."

She looked away, afraid he'd see her smile. It came to her naturally, this gift.

Her father returned from the hospital unopened, grey and muted, with a new prescription which made him feel so stupid he tossed it out within a day.

Lila's mother's enthusiasm for housework immediately began to wane; she roamed the house glum and short-tempered until at last she decided to make a visit back to Ontario.

She stood at the door with her bags and said, "I've just got to get out of here, Rick."

"I understand."

"I'm not trying to punish you."

"Have a good time now. Enjoy yourself."

"I don't know why I'm going. I can't relate to any of those people any more."

"Go on. Don't worry about a thing."

"Yeah, yeah, yeah. Oh, look at your poor daughter."

Joy was coming down the hallway, sobbing.

"I'm counting on you and Lila to help your father. Don't hang off me, treasure."

Lila was sitting at the top of the stairs. She wouldn't come down. It was always a little scary when their mother left, shucking her role as though the antique lamps and polished floors, the daughters with pressed dresses and unscarred skin, had never meant anything to her.

Although the last thing in the world they did was help their father. He shuffled around the house in his pyjamas, ordered Chinese food and pizzas, and let the house get turned upside down. It was understood that their mother expected to come home to a frenzy of domestic chores.

With her mother away Lila began to visit Alfred more often. She rarely saw his brothers, but his mother would be there, the cordless tucked under an ear as she patrolled the house busy at some new project, like washing all the windows with vinegar and newspapers. She'd laugh and nod and carry on, and gradually the house bloomed with an acidic odour that clung to Lila's clothes long after she was home again, a reminder of that foreign world that was her secret.

Alfred's mother had relaxed rules about food, and without argument allowed them to carry off whole bags of Mr. Christie's Favorites or Raspberry Temptations. Perched beside Alfred in the tree, Lila could only eat two or three – the smell of the brewery so close it was as though it were routing its way through her own bloodstream and slowly escaping her lungs, but Alfred could finish the bag. Occasionally he dropped one onto Girlie, who would be moving around on her belly in the muck below, her yellow eyes turned up to them with longing.

"You and me," Alfred said one day, removing a rusty wire dog brush from his jean jacket. "We could be married."

"Now?" She held her breath.

"No. What are you saying?" He pinched her. "When we're grown up. Pinky swear?" He offered her his little finger, crooked like the letter C, and she put her own into it.

That night Lila dreamed that she and Alfred had climbed high into his tree. Overhead the crows were going home to roost, calling out in unnatural voices that reminded Lila of her father's electric razor. The sound seemed to attack the tree, convulsing the branches and scaring Lila, so Alfred set to wrapping her in his bedclothes, which smelled of flat Coke and mown grass but were as soft as anything and radiated heat. She had been so cold before. Then he tied his rope around her waist and lowered her, face first, towards the earth.

She dropped over Girlie, who whined, the sound of it echoing off the back of the brewery, which was so near the tree that Lila could see where the last coat of paint did not quite cover the first. Then Girlie opened her mouth and, without warning, her face became the face of Lila's father. He stared up at her with the dog's shining yellow eyes, trying to speak.

It had been sunny all day. In fact, it had been sunny two days running and in the morning Lila's mother had opened a window to admire the daffodils that had emerged, slightly crooked, in the back yard. She stood there, inhaling deeply, bestowing upon this view such a rare generous smile that everyone felt they deserved to be happy. After that she spent several hours going up and down the stairs, humming "I'll Be Home for Christmas," cleaning house, and fetching things for Lila's father, who moved from room to room, floor to floor, looking for comfort.

Lila had been to Alfred's in the morning. When she got home she changed into her nightgown and got into bed and lay facing the ceiling, her hands tucked flat beneath the small of her back. Her body hurt from the rocks and the dog brush. Her scalp seemed to belong to someone else.

"Lila?" Her mother came into her room with an armload of dirty laundry. "Did they give you lunch?"

Lila nodded. "She can make six sandwiches out of one can of tuna fish."

"Like I'm surprised. Why are you in bed?" Her mother moved across the room gathering up Lila's clothes at great speed. After a while she let everything drop back to the floor except for Lila's underwear, which she shook timidly, and together Lila and her mother watched the broken rocks fall to the carpet.

She had to call Lila's father several times and when he appeared he looked sad and his body thoroughly askew. Lila's mother showed him the underwear, and at once the two of them began glancing at each other then back at the underwear like a couple of hens, until he took it in his hands and looked as though he might lift it to his nose, but Lila's mother said sharply, "Rick!" and he stopped.

Lila watched her parents. It was like stepping into another world to see the skill with which they could suddenly communicate.

"Dear," her father began casually, but Lila wasn't fooled. "Who took your clothes off?"

"No one did."

"You did?"

"No."

"Treasure, they have dirt in them."

"I put rocks in them. And my socks. And the back of my blouse. I did it."

"Could you tell us why?"

"It's Alfred's game he taught me."

"Just Alfred?"

"Yes."

"But why did you put rocks in your underwear?"

"To protect me."

"From what?"

"Alfred, see, he's worried about piranhas. But I liked the way it felt. I like the pain."

Her father stepped back to rest against the wall. Her mother folded up the underwear. Both seemed less interested now and Lila was in agony that they would leave the room. They didn't understand.

"Pain," her father said. "Christ almighty. Why would anyone want pain?"

"I do. I want to live with it. It's like . . ." She lowered her voice, wanting only her father to hear. "It's like I want to marry it."

"Huh?"

"That's all you were doing?" her mother said. "Putting rocks in your underwear? This is just a little too peculiar for me, Rick. I don't want her over there."

"Neither do I."

"I hope you realize this is your fault."

"Give me a break, woman."

"But, Daddy, you live with pain."

"Not by choice, I sure as hell don't."

She had expected admiration, reward, a tight hug. "But Daddy."

"I didn't choose this life! Do you understand me?" He was angry. When he was angry, he hurt more. "Does everyone understand me?" he shouted.

Although her father rarely raised his voice, Lila was not surprised, but it exacerbated her cuts and bruises so that her skin seemed to leap from her bones. She closed her eyes. She thought of asking them to leave if they couldn't be quiet.

"You could try another doctor," her mother said, angry in her own way, which was more knife-like and brittle. "You could try another province. Or maybe you like hanging around this house year after year making us all miserable with your belly-aching."

"You just have no idea, do you?" And as he spoke he travelled across the room, gritting his teeth because he was having such a bad day, and shoved Lila's mother down and kicked her in the backside.

Lila's voice was gravelly as though it had been injured in some way, but her shouting served to draw her father off her mother and back to her. As he came towards her, his misery and rage shining, Lila realized that this was the father she had been a long time expecting: the man inside the man who without complaint stooped crookedly at the back door to remove his shoes, rose slowly from a bed, or cleared the corner in the upstairs hall in stocking feet just seconds ahead of disaster.

## JANE EATON HAMILTON

# *Graduation*

The day of my high school graduation prom my mother signed up for a lifetime of exercise at Vic Tanny's. She was almost forty. She had instructed my brother and me to kill her off at forty-eight if she hadn't already done it herself, that she'd keep a gun in the linen closet. Loaded in the linen closet, she said. She'd already had a face lift and was encouraging our little sister, thirteen, to have breast augmentation. Didn't we understand? Turning fifty was impossible. It could happen to other women, she said with her lip curling in distaste, but no one was going to drag her there: she was born to be twenty.

"You boys," she sighed. "It's not the same for you boys." She smoked Virginia Slims and the red of her lipstick ringed her white, flowery filter. "You boys have the whole world in your hands. You'll just get better looking."

Barry was two years my senior and at university studying sciences, hoping eventually to become an oceanographer. He was only home for my graduation accidentally, because his year was already over. The night before, Mom had dragged him out dancing, telling him he should pretend she was his girlfriend. Mom as Barry's girlfriend cracked me up.

Mom showed us the membership for Vic Tanny's. It was costing her big bucks. Then she said, "It's right next to Albert's. Dennis, your girlfriend was in Albert's having her hair put up." She winked salaciously.

"She's not my girlfriend," I said. I was taking Susie Miller to the prom. I had a wrist corsage waiting in the fridge and Barry's MGB idling in the driveway. I was sort of antsy and aroused since I wanted to take Susie down to Sulphur Springs after the dance and get her stoned and do unspeakable things to her body. But she probably wouldn't let me. She had a reputation as a virgin. "She's just some girl."

"She looks very sweet," Mom went on deliberately. "Sweet" was no compliment; coming from our mother it described someone just this side of sub-human. Almost no one in town had the money Mom's father had, which meant anyone Barry and I dated had to be from the wrong side of the tracks. Mom thought our girlfriends were amusing. She expected them to amuse us like toys.

"I went out with Susie Miller's father," Mom went on. "I saw him last winter for a month or two."

This made my stomach dizzy. Susie Miller's father was married to Susie Miller's mother. But I knew Mom wasn't gunning me off: all sorts of fathers of my friends showed up at our house. Sometimes I saw them and sometimes not. I tried not to.

"He hates that woman he's married to. She drags him down." Mom patted my hand. "You tell Susie from me that at least she has a good father. Not much initiative, of course, but decent, overall."

Barry made a disgusted noise and got up to make a salad. He'd come home from McGill a vegetarian and did a lot of weird things with milkshakes.

"Mom," I said, "lay off." There was this constant thing around our house of Mom trying to be a teenager. She kept hash in the sideboard and liked The Who.

"Barry," she went on, ignoring me, "if you're making that food again, you'd better clean up after yourself. If you've got any of that tofu junk, I'm not touching that tofu junk."

"Yeah, yeah," said Barry, lifting sprouts from a jar. He was wearing a blue terrycloth bathrobe Mom sent him for Christmas when he refused to come home. She'd also sent him a quadraphonic sound system in big cartons. I got a lava lamp and an executive toy consisting of a series of suspended silver orbs that banged meaninglessly against each other. I'd also gotten a Pet Rock. Our sister Lisa had received a gift certificate to have a modelling portfolio compiled by one of the best photographers in Toronto.

I took a deep breath and blundered out with what was on my mind besides Susie. "You know the graduation ceremony next Tuesday, Mom? Uh . . . I invited Dad."

"You invited your father to your graduation," Mom replied and fixed her glasses on her nose.

"That's right."

Mom showed no emotion but said, "Your father who saw you last, when, three years ago? Your father who is fourteen months behind on his alimony payments? Your father who couldn't care less if you'd flunked out? That father?"

Barry took his salad into the den.

"That's the one I invited, all right," I admitted.

"The one who trained private detectives on us for seven years. The one who kidnapped Lisa when she was in kindergarten. Would that be the father you invited?"

"Come on, Mom. I'm graduating."

"I'm not good enough for you?"

"That's not it," I protested. "They gave me five tickets. I thought Dad might come." I had very few memories of my father and had actually had to call Mom's lawyer to find out where to send the invitation. My father left when I was three; I just didn't remember him ever living with us. But I thought he had rights.

"If he goes, I'm not, I'll tell you that for sure. What came over you, Dennis? Why on earth would you do something so stupid?"

"I don't have any arguments with Dad," I said sullenly.

"Well, Mr. Superior," Mom said. "You'll just have to decide between us." She lit another cigarette and regarded me shrewdly. "He isn't coming, is he?"

I shrugged. There'd been no word.

"He won't come. He was never interested in you kids."

"Maybe," I said, unwilling to concede the fairly obvious point.

"You'll have to phone him and tell him you've reconsidered."

"I haven't reconsidered," I said. "Why do you always think I'll change my mind? I'm not changing my mind."

"If he goes, I mean it, Dennis, if your father's there, I'll get out my gun and blow him to pieces. Then where will you be?"

Mom loved melodramas.

"Orphaned?" I said.

"I'll go to jail and you'll see where that leaves you. What will poor Lisa do?"

Poor Lisa managed quite well. Poor Lisa had already run away from home three times. She'd probably love it if Mom killed Dad, especially if she inherited money.

"It doesn't matter," I said. "He won't come anyway, you're right."

"No, he hates you kids. You remind him of what a shithead he is." She smiled happily. "You call him and make sure, though, or I'm not going."

This mother of ours was no PTA mother; there was only a slim chance she'd attend anyway. Other things would come up, other things always did. She'd develop a rare melanoma or be needed, absolutely required, at her favourite dress shop, Giselle's, for a fitting. This last I could almost understand since she bought whole shipments of couturier clothes, often the same sweater or dress in three or four different colours. After Barry went to college she took over his room as a walk-in closet. No one minded; she needed the space.

I had to go downtown to pick up my rental tux, and when I got home near dinnertime Mom had Lisa in a stranglehold on the den floor in front of the hi-fi. Barry was nowhere in sight but Tom Jones was on the radio telling us it wasn't unusual to be loved by anyone. Lisa wasn't in any danger, so I sat down and told Mom I'd seen her archenemy Carol Dugan in the city. I thought it would take her mind off killing my sister. Mom was screaming at Lisa about stealing her bangle bracelets and screaming at the Afghan hound, Katie, who was interfering, growling and snapping and getting her big floppy limbs everywhere, but she stopped all right, just let go of Lisa's throat and sat back. She ran her hand along her chin where she'd worked up a sweat. Lisa scrambled free.

"Carol Dugan?" Mom said. "You didn't talk to her, did you?"

"Lisa has marks on her throat," I said as my sister ran out.

"Never mind that. What was Carol Dugan wearing?"

I shrugged. Carol Dugan was Barry's friend Steve's mother. Long ago she'd accused Barry, a toddler, of biting her son – Mom had never forgotten it. Mom was a great grudge keeper. One of her friends married money and hired three housekeepers and Mom never spoke to her again.

Just then Lisa came back in with her face red and her hair all over. She had a pair of scissors in her hand and she went slowly towards Mom, raising them. Mom ignored her.

I told Mom that Carol Dugan had said she had terrible taste in clothes.

"She what!" Mom extended an arm towards Lisa but didn't look at her. "She really said that, Dennis? I don't believe she really said that, she wouldn't have the nerve."

"She said she heard you joined Vic Tanny's," I went on. "'Some of us need it,' she said."

Lisa dropped the scissors on the floor.

"Why that low-down cow," Mom said getting ponderously to her feet. "I suppose *her* son's at a prestigious university like McGill?" She knew very well that Steve Dugan was taking accounting at a community college. "I suppose *her* husband's never fooled around. Well . . . we know better, don't we?"

This last referred to another of Mom's affairs, one she considered a coup.

"On the other hand," I remarked, "her kid's not a vegetarian."

"It's only a phase Barry's going through. You watch, Dennis. This time next year he may have a ponytail down his back, but that Steve Dugan will have a brush cut, mark my words."

Lisa said, "Gross me out."

"What's for dinner?" I asked.

That night at the prom, Susie Miller looked like a little boy's fantasy of a fairy godmother. Her dress was blue like a sky and glittered; as we danced I kissed her neck again and again. The Prom Committee had decorated the gym with crepe paper flowers and had even hung a swing from the ceiling and built a wishing well in the floor's centre. It was hard to imagine it as the scene of so many basketball games and assemblies. I was into it; I was into the whole thing. I was home for one last summer then off to Western and an engineering degree. I was so glad to be getting out of Parnell High and Vocational School it made me feel generous. Tonight was the pinnacle: Susie Miller in my arms smelling like a wrist corsage; music, strobe lights, and the end of my childhood.

Before we went to any of the after-grad parties, I drove Susie down to Sulphur Springs. I cut the car radio and we sat there under the smoky, late night sky. Other cars were parked, too, their windows already steamy. Susie unfurled a scarf from her hair.

"So," I said, my voice ratchety like one of the crickets we could hear sawing, "did you pick where you're going next year?"

Susie looked at me strangely, all whites of eyes, all clouds. I leaned my head back and closed my eyes. Her school, Western or Waterloo or Queen's, was clearly not on a straight path to seduction. She said, "I told you. Queen's."

I moved my hand over the stick shift and placed it on the side of her seat. "You decided on your major?"

"Economics," said Susie Miller. Her dress rustled.

"Right," I said.

"Well," Susie said.

I opened my eyes. "Well."

"Uh, are we going to –"

I interrupted. "What?"

"You know."

I knew. I twisted behind the steering wheel, leaned over and crushed her in my arms.

"Dennis," she said huskily and licked my ear.

This is the truth: on grad night at Sulphur Springs, with the smell of rotten eggs all around us, Susie Miller the virgin licked my ear. "I want," she said breathlessly, "to do it."

Her dress had spaghetti straps and they were down in a second. She wasn't wearing a bra. She fumbled at my zipper while I sucked one of her nipples. The feel of her other breast supported in my left hand made me lightheaded. She found me and held me. Our breath was harsh. I reached down to the floor-boards and the hem of her prom dress. I felt her ankle and calf and knee and thigh. I was moving up from there, along her soft pantyhose with the glittery fabric of her gown harsh on the back of my hand, when I came, crying out.

"Oh, Dennis," Susie said, pulling away.

"I love you," I said. "Oh Susie, Susie. Susie."

"Dennis, really," she said. Her legs clamped together like a vise.

I came in bleary-eyed and hungover at ten in the morning. Lisa had already gone to school, junior high having an extra two weeks, and Barry was eating yogurt with sliced-up avocados in it at the kitchen table.

"Where's Mom?" I asked. I gave Barry his car keys back.

"She went to get out of her contract with Vic Tanny's. She decided to get a nose job instead."

I pulled a box of Cheerios out of the cupboard. "Did you ever stop to think we have a very weird mother?"

Barry shrugged. "How'd it go with Susie?"

"You wouldn't believe me if I told you. Let's say it was good." I preferred to forget the last part. I took the milk to the table. "Let's say it was a superior experience."

For Christmas Barry had sent me a book called *Leo the Late Bloomer*. I knew he was on my side.

I dug into my Cheerios. I'd already eaten at Bill Waterby's house, ham and eggs and bacon at eight, but I was ravenous.

"So did Mom tell you?" Barry asked.

"Tell me what?" I said. I'd just gotten such a clear picture of a particular moment at Sulphur Springs my skin was prickling. My scalp was prickling.

"She's getting married," said Barry smiling.

"Mom's getting married?" I tried to make sense of this. "Right. Anyone we know?"

"Some architect she's been seeing. He proposed last night."

I shook my head. This was unfamiliar territory.

"Lisa says she's running away. This time I think she means it. She's got bruises on her neck."

"She took Mom's bangle bracelets."

"She hates the idea of having a father, though. She thinks she'll have a curfew."

I poured a second bowl of Cheerios. "When's the big day?"

"Dunno," said Barry and he got up.

I told him thanks for him loaning me his car.

"No problem, bro," he said.

Susie avoided me. When I called, her parents said she was out. When I went over, her kid brother Dean told me she had mono and I better get lost. I knew from the grapevine Susie just didn't want to see me. I actually missed school. At school I could have cornered her in the hallway or lunch room. This way I was at totally loose ends, just hanging out at the bowling alley and the drugstore hoping she'd show up. Which she didn't. I called three of her best girlfriends. Two hung up and the third said, "Listen, Dennis, why don't you just get the message?"

I called my father. When I asked did he get my invitation there was a long silence before he said that he had.

"Graduating. Well," he said. "Congratulations. On the honour roll, are you?"

"That was Barry," I said. "Can you come? Mom wants to know."

"Is your mother going?"

"I dunno, I guess. Maybe. You know Mom."

"I didn't go to your brother's graduation," Dad said quietly.

"It would mean a lot," I told him.

"Everyone there all right?" he asked. "Lisa okay?"

"Sure," I said. "Mom's getting married."

There was a longer silence until Dad broke it. "I see."

"Dad, I want you to come. It's important to me."

"I see," he said. He said he'd try.

The night before my graduation ceremony the next week, we met Mom's intended. She invited him to dinner and kept Lisa home from school to polish the good silver. Neither Barry nor I was working, so before company arrived, we peeled potatoes and carrots. I reminded Mom about the graduation thing. Since I had a good idea Dad wasn't coming, I told her he'd said he couldn't make it. I wanted one of them.

"Your father can't hurt me," Mom said. Her hair was newly done and the kitchen smelled of floor wax. The housekeeper had been in two days in a row. Everything shone.

Lisa said, "Screw this noise. I'm leaving." She got up and threw her soiled cloth on the table.

"Sit right back down, young lady. You aren't half done."

Barry sighed.

"What, you're going to stop me?" Lisa asked.

"Go then," Mom said. She looked at us boys. "I'm getting married, and today I find out I probably have leukemia –"

Mom was hopelessly hypochondriac.

"– and your sister the tramp is walking out."

She turned back to Lisa. "Go, I don't care. I'll be dead when you get back anyway. See if I'm not. I'll kill myself."

Mom had swallowed bottles of Secobarbital four times that I knew of. If the leukemia didn't get her, the barbiturates still could. Or the gun.

"Good!" screamed Lisa. "I hope you are dead. I hope you do die!"

Barry passed me carrots. He turned to Mom. "Listen, Mom," he said. "If you're planning to off yourself, could you at least set the timer so we don't overcook the roast?"

Mom laughed and Lisa sat back down.

The architect Mom was marrying showed up right on time. We had a gracious evening. He looked about Mom's age; even so, he seemed to like it when she got giggly with him. He made a big deal about giving her a ring in front of us and asking our permission. Even Lisa said, "Sure, marry the guy." It wasn't exactly high in our priorities, whether he did or not, but Lisa liked his Porsche, I liked that maybe he could handle Mom and Barry liked that he was a liberal, so really, why not? Mom obviously liked him. He said he'd pay for Lisa's breast augmentation.

Before Barry and I went out to play snooker, I reminded Mom again about the graduation. She was holding what's-his-name's hand across the table. "Dennis, please," she said. "I'm not stupid. I remember from when you reminded me before dinner." She smiled at her fiancé.

"Right," I said and nodded. "I'll see you then."

"You'll see me," Mom said.

Mom wasn't home when Barry and I got back. Lisa was asleep in front of the TV, so Barry and I did the dishes and wrapped Mom's silver in its soft green and purple felts and put it back in the pantry cupboards.

"You think she'll really marry him?" I asked. "You think she'll remember the ceremony's today at two?"

Barry said, "Stranger things have happened."

That was entirely correct. Stranger things happened daily and could again.

The graduation ceremonies were to take place in Parnell High and Vocational's auditorium. It was so new the carpets still smelled. It was built like a playhouse, with pull-down padded chairs ascending to the entry doors. We all wore caps and gowns. Susie was there; I kept trying to get near her. Her girlfriends, though, had her cordoned off. They kept tossing their heads my way and looking mad. I looked for Mom and Dad. I couldn't see either of them, though Barry and Lisa waved from near the back. I kept turning around restlessly. I generally took all of my parents' stuff without a pang but this time, I didn't know why, I felt lonely and sad. Later, Mom would say something like, "Oh Dennis, dear, I'm sorry. Your graduation just went right out of my head!"

Up on stage, the principal and the vice principal and the secretary and some old guy, probably the guest speaker, and Herbie Smith, the valedictorian, sat stiffly. The room quietened.

Then I heard a ruckus up back. I think I knew it must be Mom. I heard a harsh man's voice and then a voice all too familiar shout out, "Yoo hoo! Dennis! Dennis Talbot! I'm here, sweetheart, but they won't let me in!"

I felt instant heat under my skin. Everyone was whispering, then pointing and staring. Even Susie and her girlfriends were looking. I got slowly up. Barry and our physics teacher Mr. Edly were already beside Mom. I saw right away what the trouble was. Mom, wearing an unseasonable mink coat, had brought Katie, the dog. Katie the moronic Afghan hound dog. Katie saw me and pulled the lead loose from Mom's hand and bounded down the aisle. She was none too coordinated. She looked like a galloping blond mop. People were shouting and laughing. Katie got to me, leaped and missed, and fell with all four legs splayed out straight, a cartoon dog.

I bent to grab her leash. A hand cupped my elbow under my gown.

"Son?"

It must have been my father. A large man who looked vaguely familiar.

My mother minced towards us. "That man!" she yelled, pointing a long, dangerously sharp fingernail at him.

I held Katie's leash tight and she whined miserably.

"This man," my mother shouted as she drew close. She looked around to her audience. "This man is a *criminal.*"

She extended her hand for Katie. I passed the dog over. I was on the decline below her and had, therefore, to look up. Mom said, "You *promised* your father wasn't coming."

I smiled sheepishly.

"Tell me, Dennis," Mom went on. "If you had to choose, if I made you choose right now, which one of us would you pick? This *man,*" she said, "or me? Him or your mother? You can only have one."

I couldn't say a thing. Barry and Mr. Edly were standing behind Mom.

"Dennis?"

I looked up. Mom dipped her hand in the pocket of her coat and pulled out her gun. I heard gasps.

I stared hard in her eyes and answered her. "Dad," I said.

It was a mistake, I guess, because Mom shot me in the leg.

I woke up in the hospital with Susie Miller leaning to get something behind the bed's headboard, and my first cognition was of her left breast brushing my nose. Whatever I'd done, she'd apparently forgiven. When she noticed I was awake she kissed my nose and told me about my leg. They'd taken the bullet out and there was some muscle damage that would take the summer to heal. She added very solemnly, since after the shooting I'd fainted, that my mother was "somewhere they could help her."

"You're back," I finally said. My voice was thick and my mouth swollen and furry. I raised myself on an elbow.

Susie nodded. She smelled pretty, like apricots. My leg throbbed but at least it was there, it wasn't amputated.

"Your mother's really nuts," she said.

"No," I said slowly. The words were difficult to form. I was slurring. "She just . . . she's only unhappy."

"Well," Susie said.

"Well," I said.

Susie squirmed in her chair. "I could . . . you know . . . nurse you," she suggested. "I mean, if you want me to. This summer, 'til you're on your feet again."

She was wearing a tank top and her shoulders and the top of her chest were freckled from the sun.

"Okay," I said. I knuckled my eyes.

"The doctor says you'll be out of here in a couple of days. You'll have to come back for physical therapy twice a week, but you can go home. If there's someone to come in and help you while Barry's at work."

"I'd like to go home," I said.

"Lisa moved in with your father."

"That's fine," I said groggily. I didn't know if it was or not. I felt a stab of resentment that Lisa got to go to Dad's. My vision was blurring and I could hardly keep my eyes open. I sank back down.

Susie got up and patted my hand. Vaguely, I saw her back away. She said, "I'll go tell the nurse you're awake. And your family's waiting."

"Susie?"

"What?"

"I'm awake," I said. I kept blinking to get her in focus.

"I know," she said.

I fell asleep without realizing I was about to. I dreamed that I was very small, maybe seven or eight years old, and that my mother was in the kitchen. She was a beautiful mother. She handed me a plate with a brownie steaming on it. She ruffled my hair. I could hear robins singing in the sun outside the window. As I chewed, my mouth filled not with soft chocolate but with chunks of glass. I cried out. My mother, laughing, bent and cupped her hands. Blood and glass spilled from between my lips across her smooth, lovely hands.

When I woke again my father, Barry and Lisa were in the room. Barry and Lisa were slouching by the door and Dad was bending over me. "Dennis?" he said. "Dennis, are you awake?"

"Hi, Dad," I said. I wondered how he could be my father and barely recognizable.

"You're all right, son," he told me.

"Dad?" Tears were coming up fast into my eyes. I tried to blink them back, to get control of myself, but I couldn't.

"I'm here," he said. "I'm right here."

He was right beside me and I saw him, large and real. I began to cry. "Dad?" I kept saying. "Dad?"

## DENISE RYAN

# *Marginals, Vivisections, and Dreams*

"How's your mother," my father asks, his voice cracking ever so slightly. I stare at his stethoscope – it hangs where his heart should be – I shrug and say nothing. What is there to say? What is the point of asking now? How could you not understand her then, when she was having a hard time? I remember him running home with roses, the cheap kind grabbed at the last minute from the stand outside the pharmacy. Roses wrapped in plastic. He is a doctor, but he arrived at the scene of his marriage too late to save it, and with too little in his hand. There is nothing to say now. Two years have passed, and we both know that this time she won't be back.

I draw a fresh sheet of white paper over the padded vinyl examination table, folding a sharp edge and ripping it off. Clean and precise. He has always taught me the art of precision. Like when you slide a needle under the skin to take blood. How to hit the vein without digging around in the flesh leaving bruises and blood leaking between the tissues. He offered his own body to me for practice, he taught me to puncture flesh quick and clean as a snakebite. He held his palm open, then tightened it into a fist. He coaxed me under his skin with quiet words and the sterile pinprick of a syringe. I took his blood. Like a good daughter, I learned.

"Letting go is the only way of moving on," he says as he washes his hands in the stainless steel sink. On the counter is the plastic speculum, used on Mrs. Willis, dripping with jelly. He has left it there. Without thinking, I grab it and toss it into the garbage can. "Careful," he says. "She thinks she has herpes." I scrub in the sink under hot water. There are a thousand ways to kill him in this office, I think. I have worked in his office since I was fifteen. He has shown me every drug, every instrument, the path of every nerve in the back of the neck. But not today. I have to study. I am going to be a doctor.

He is proud of me. He is sure that I will be a good doctor, like him. I study where he studied. Although he is a family practitioner, he is delighted that I have chosen neurology. He says that I have a brain for money. I don't tell him that I have doubts. I don't tell him that I give away my heads. I can't stand splitting the cranium with a saw. I can't cut away a face, strip off an eyelid, a lip, scrape smooth the bone of a forehead. Scooping out a brain like pudding is the worst part of the Anatomy Lab. I don't have the stomach for it. John, my husband and lab partner, manages, though. He dissects my heads for free, he charges the other students ten dollars each. It isn't cheating, really. John calls it "subcontracting." He does it so enthusiastically that I am pulling A's in this class (B's and C's in everything else this year). He has bagged, weighed, and measured my brains perfectly. Until now. Last month we separated. Last week some gust of spite blew through him and he told me that even this was over. I am on my own. He won't cover me in Anatomy any more. I offered to pay, like the other students, but he said that obviously I didn't understand. And I don't.

My father cooks dinner while I am shut in his guest room staring at honeycombs in my textbook, memorizing molecular structures. Everything in nature has a pattern. I close my eyes and see starbursts. I open them and see stripes. Curtain, beige, blue, and mustard. Something my father took home from the hospital when they re-decorated the oncology waiting room. This room is not mine. I am staying here in order to give John the space he says he needs. He has asked me to leave, and I don't think he wants me back.

My mother left her marriage many times, sometimes with my brother Terry and me, sometimes without. My father never asked her to stay. He always knew she would be back. I most remember the first time she moved out. Terry and I were in the back seat of the Volkswagen. We were both in the back because we had argued so loudly over who got the front seat. Our father stood on the front porch, stiff and smiling, waving goodbye. Tough, unwilling to bend. I turned away, gulping down the bologna sandwich that was gagging up my throat. I pressed my face against the window, fogging it up with my breath, drawing happy faces with my finger. "Don't worry, Mom, we'll be happy," I said as she pulled out the choke and the car stalled. "No, we won't," said my brother.

Happiness, I am told by my psychiatrist, is the source of all suffering. Happiness is a talent, like walking on water. Christly few have it, fewer still survive it. It is a mirage that shimmers and evaporates, calling only to those who crave it, to those who want. The craving, she says, is a symptom of my problem. Dr. Chase is helping me learn not to want. She tells me that there are things other than happiness. There is satisfaction. There is pleasure. There is pride in accomplishment. There is security in knowing that not everything works out. There is realism.

"Your mother is not a realist," says my father as he scoops a forkful of blue cheese dressing from his salad. He turns back to his *New York Times*. He knows she won't be back, but still he waits for her as if she is a fussy child who will return to the dinner table, hungry and grateful. We eat what he has prepared tonight, his Friday favourites. I am getting fat. There is a salad dressing slimy with sour cream, French bread soaked in butter and garlic. A rare roast beef with a slab of bacon laid over it for flavour. Frozen peas boiled in a bag. A letter came for me today, from her. This bothers him. I read it while he reads his paper and worries about her influence on me, her savage heart, her attachment to dreams. "She ruined your brother. Don't let her ruin your marriage," he says, as if he has read the letter, as if he knows that she has written *daughter, I dreamt you called my name.*

I don't flinch any more when he mentions my brother the ruin, his personal Pompeii. I remember the last time Terry came to dinner here, over a year ago. My father handed me and John a cheque for three thousand dollars to help with tuition and rent. At that time, Terry was living in a basement apartment, not working, having troubles with coke, and with his boyfriend who had never been invited to dinner. That night, Terry asked our father for a loan. He was refused with the usual suggestions of going back to school and doing something useful for society. Something like what John and I were doing. Something like what he had done when he was Terry's age. I know now that I married the man my father wanted for a son. While I walked Terry to the bus stop, John stayed at the dinner table, drinking Armagnac and talking to my father. Terry borrowed some change from me to get on the bus, and as I handed it over he leaned his head into mine and sobbed. As his tears dripped down my neck I stroked his hair and whispered that everything would be okay. He said no, no, that he didn't know how to make things okay, that he could never make things okay. Then he asked if I would split the money with him. I said I would. I lied.

My father looks up from his paper now. "How is Paris, anyway?" he asks. He wants to understand. He imagines my mother as she was thirty years before, when they first met. Leila, drinking red wine with lovers, and laughing, her voice clear as April light singing through glass. He doesn't imagine her as she is, with an untended abscess swelling in her mouth, a cold-water sixth-floor walkup, washing her clothes in the toilet, treating herself to a little brandy once a week because that is what she can afford, because she'd rather be poor in Paris than anywhere else.

"Paris is fine, I guess," I reply. My eyes idle on the carving knife that drips and gleams on the sideboard. I am remembering a dream, dreaming that I held a knife like that one, that I slid it under my father's skin. A vivisection. My hands are shaking. When did I dream that? I push away from the table. I know that the Anatomy class is doing this to me. Making me crazy. I am learning to cut people up, to dissect and conquer. But most of the corpses come from the city morgue, bag ladies and lonely people wrapped in fat, their organs pocked with disease. I encourage my friends to donate their bodies to medical research. I imagine cutting into someone lean and young, like unwrapping a gift. Inside, a perfect liver the colour of a plum, and a young heart that shows me what a heart can be. I am tired of cutting through the bellies of junkies and homeless people. The unclaimed and uncared for. *We do it so we can learn to care for those who deserve care*, says my father. These stray bodies were people once, people my father calls *marginals*, people whose greatest contribution can only come in death. Each death is a relief to society, a boon to medical science. Terry, he said once, was a marginal. It isn't that he doesn't love Terry, it's just that, as a doctor, he tries to see things for what they are; cell structures and molecular webs that function or don't function. He is a professional and we are all humans, some with greater capacities, some with lesser. He is waiting to rescue Terry. He thinks he has rescued me.

I excuse myself from the table. I am going back to study. I take after him, he has always said, I have the edge required for survival, he thinks, an intellect that divides me from the others of our species, the Terrys and Leilas. Terry, he has always said, takes after our mother. Tender, and imprecise. I am thinking about anatomy and the fever that runs through me when I cut open a body. I am afraid I will disappoint him. He smiles beneficently as I leave the table. He is happy to have rescued me. He thinks he is providing me with an opportunity. That I will be reasonable, I will learn what it is that John wants, that I will do the right thing. He thinks this rescue is a triumph, something my mother has not been able to do for me or Terry because she has been too busy thinking about herself.

Of course she couldn't do this. He is right. She walked away with nothing, she walked away because, as she put it, the love was gone. But love, love says Dr. Chase, is a fiction. It doesn't exist except in the imagination and sometimes on paper. There is only the need for companionship, the exchange of warmth and fluids from one body to the other. The desire for partnership is a desire for ease, and if it isn't easy then a person is right to leave, as John has.

I think of our joint counselling sessions, how sympathetic Dr. Chase was to me until she met John. He swung into the office with the same easy smile that had won me over at nineteen. He was a charmer, and she was charmed. She saw his point of view about everything – my inability to keep a house, the laundry piling up, my refusal to put aside my own education until John finished his. In private sessions, Dr. Chase assured me that she didn't think John was right, but that we were both right. John needed space and I needed help. In our joint sessions she agreed with John that we should separate. They laughed together, while I twisted Kleenexes into balls and excused myself for my appearance – it is hard to keep up appearances when there is so much work to do for school, although John doesn't have that problem. He always looks great, even when he is splitting open heads. Me, no matter how much I shower I can't scald the smell of formaldehyde from my skin.

Dr. Chase tells me now that perhaps I should learn to settle for less. She brings up my mother as an example of someone who couldn't settle for less. She says that my mother didn't understand that men were weak, that they strayed, that integrity sometimes means less than security, that she had walked away wanting more and has ended up with nothing.

I am homeless, I realize tonight as I pull back the sheets on the guest bed. I re-read the letter. My mother has written that she has a job, part-time at the consulate, working as a cook. She is a good cook, she writes. She thinks her confidence is coming back. She took no alimony, but she left with no regrets. She is reading a lot. Could I lend her some money to get her tooth fixed? There is a couch, she writes, so Terry and I can visit. There are markets that smell of coffee and orange peels, markets where roses are piled as high as her head, where people buy bull's balls to sauté for dinner, and prostitutes walk cobblestone streets wearing fur coats, naked underneath.

Tomorrow, I know, will come with its carcasses and bones. There will be an appointment with Dr. Chase, a meeting with John to decide who gets the stereo and the kitchen table. Tomorrow I will dissect a lifeless head alone, weigh what must be weighed and measured. But tonight I go to sleep dreaming that I split open my own head, that blood pours out like roses, smelling of Paris, smelling of happiness.

# MADELEINE THIEN

## *Simple Recipes*

There is a simple recipe for making rice. My father taught it to me when I was a child.

When I was young, I sat up on the counter near the kitchen sink, watching the patterns of rice, then water, then hands rising up from the pot, then rice again, then water. My father's hands rose then fell, the rice slipping away like pebbles on the shoreline, a million grains falling between his fingertips. Over and over again; there is a rhythm to it.

The instructions are simple. After you have finished washing the grains, you measure the water by resting the tip of your index finger against the surface of the rice. The water should touch the first line of your first knuckle. That is the perfect amount.

My father did not need instructions or measuring cups. He closed his eyes and felt for the water line.

If I wanted, I could close my eyes, too. I know where the water should touch. Even though I have not seen my father for many years, even though it has been many years since I last watched him, his hands circling up and underneath, rice falling away and scratching the bottom of the pot, I know that I could do it. I know the recipe the way I know the weight of my own hands. I could close my eyes. I know how high the water should rise.

My father stands in the centre of the kitchen. He is holding a plastic bag filled with water. Inside the bag is a live fish.

The fish is the length of my arm from elbow to fingertip. When my father lays it down on the counter, I reach up and touch it through the plastic bag. My index finger traces a line from gill to tail, traces a circle around the open eye.

We fill the kitchen sink with water. My father opens the plastic bag and the fish slips smoothly into the sink. It curls its body around and swims in place. I watch, my fingers pressed against my lips, and the fish moves, then stills, then moves again. I listen to the sound of the water lapping, and the sound of my father in his bare feet padding back and forth across the linoleum floor.

For many hours at a time, it was just the two of us. I was ten years old and my father walked me to school in the mornings, then stood outside my classroom door at three o'clock to walk me home. Often, we spent hours together without speaking. I walked beside him, my legs stretching to match his steps. I was overjoyed when my feet kept time with his, right, then left, then right, and we walked like a single unit.

In our house, the ceilings were yellowed with grease, too many years of oil rising up from the wok to cling to the walls. Even the air was heavy with it. But at that time, I did not know any different and so I loved the weight of it, the air that was dense with the smell of meals cooked over and over in a tiny kitchen.

My father was born in Malaysia and he and my mother immigrated to Canada the year I was born. My father was born in the wash of a monsoon country; I was born into the persistence of the Vancouver rain. When I was young, my parents tried to teach me their language, but they never could. My father ran his thumb gently over my mouth, his face kind, as if trying to see what it was that made me different.

My brother was born in Sabah, in Malaysia, but when he immigrated with my parents to Canada the language left him. Or he forgot it, or he refused, which is also common, and my father was angry. "How can a child forget a language?" he would ask my mother. "It is because the child is lazy. Because the child chooses not to remember."

So my brother only came home at the dinner hour, even when he was only twelve. My mother came home from work then, too. She was a sales clerk at the Woodward's store downtown, at the building with the revolving "W" on top.

The fish in the sink is dying slowly.

My father lifts me up, sets me down on the kitchen countertop. The fish has a glossy sheen to it, as if its skin is made of shining minerals. I want to lean over and touch my index finger to the round eyeball. When the fish slows and comes to rest at the side of the sink, I want to prod it with my hands, feel the muscles of its body curve against the pressure of my fingers.

Beside me, my father chops green onions quickly, using a cleaver that he says is older than me by many years. I watch the edge of the knife roll forward and backward, loops of green onions gathering in a pile beside my father's wrist.

Nearer to dinner time, my father comes and stands in front of the sink. He pulls back his sleeve and his hand cuts through the surface of the water. He loosens the plug, and pulls it loose. The water drains quickly.

The fish in the sink circles and we watch it in silence. The water slips below its eyeballs, beneath its transparent gills, beneath its belly, and then the fish is lying on its side in the sink. Its mouth is open and it is gasping for breath. The fish no longer moves gracefully. A part of its body snaps into motion, and then another, and another. There is a persistent drumming as its body slaps against the aluminum sink.

Eventually, these movements ease themselves out, the drumming becomes more and more broken, until it finally stops. I have not closed my eyes and I am looking at the space at the fish's mouth, where its lips have remained open.

My father reaches into the sink with his bare hands. He lifts the fish out by the tail and he begins to clean it. His hands are gentle as he begins scraping the skin. He moves as though he does not want to bruise it.

In my apartment, I keep the walls scrubbed clean. I open the windows because I do not like the smell of cooking in my home. When I use the wok, I turn the fan on so that the air does not become clogged with oil. My father bought me a rice cooker when I first moved out, but I use it so rarely it stays in the back of the cupboard, the cord wrapped neatly around its belly.

Sometimes, I still dream about my father, his bare feet flat against the floor, standing in the middle of the kitchen. He wears buttoned shirts, and sweatpants drawn at the waist. Surrounded by the gloss of the kitchen counters, the hard angles of the stove, the fridge, the shiny sink, he looks out of place.

My father used to tell me stories about Malaysia, about pulling coconuts down from the trees, about ripping durian from the branches, how the smell as you ripped one open would fill your lungs to choking. He described the durian's spiked skin, the twenty-six varieties of bananas. He described drinking coconut milk straight from the shell.

Now, when I close my eyes, I can see him. My father's hands, dark and beautiful. My father circling the kitchen, retracing his footprints around and around, the smell of a million cooked meals rising up to encircle him.

My brother, Edmund, comes into the kitchen and his body is covered with dirt. He leaves a thin trail of it behind as he walks. He is twelve, and has been playing soccer with his friends from school. He says nothing to my father.

At the stove, my father pours a thin line of oil down onto the wok. It begins to burn, and when my father flicks a stream of water into it, the oil bursts and rises up like ribbon.

He lifts the fish up from the counter and drops it into the wok. Smoke billows up and my father's hands rise out from under it, and the sound follows his hands, the oil hissing. The steam wraps around my father, and the sound of the fish cooking drowns out every other noise. My father steps out from the smoke, alarmingly close, and ruffles my hair with the palm of his hand. "Spoon out the rice," he says, as he lifts me down from the counter.

Edmund sulks around the room, knees the colour of dusty brick, hands soiled, soccer shorts fluttering against the backs of his legs. He makes a face and sits down. My father ignores him.

Inside the cooker, the rice is flat like a pie. I spoon it up and over and the steam shoots up in a hot mist and condenses on my chin. I begin spooning the rice out: first for my father, then my mother, then my brother, then myself. I listen to the sound of the fish steaming. My father moves his arms delicately over the stove. He stirs cauliflower in a pot of crockery.

Edmund slams his fist into the table.

My father looks up from the cauliflower pot. "What's the matter?"

Edmund is silent for a moment, as if considering. And then, "Why do we have to eat fish?"

My father answers slowly. "You don't like it?"

Edmund crosses his arms against his chest. I see the dirt lining his arms, hardened. I imagine chipping it off his body with a small spoon.

"Nobody else eats fish."

"Who's nobody else?"

"Edmund!" My mother appears. Her name tag is still clipped to her blouse. It says, Woodward's, and then, Edna, and then, Sales Clerk. "Wash your hands," she says, hanging her purse on the back of the chair.

My brother glares, just for a moment. Then he begins picking at the dirt on his arms. I bring plates of rice to the table. The dirt flies off his skin, speckling the tablecloth, falling into his plate of rice. "Stop it," I say, crossly.

"Stop it," he imitates me.

"Hey!" My father slams a spoon down hard on the counter. He points at my brother. "Stop it," he says. "Go wash."

My brother looks at the floor, mumbles something, and then shuffles away from the table. As he moves further away, he begins to stamp his feet. Still, my father ignores him.

My mother eases into the kitchen. She takes her jacket off, and it slides from her shoulders. She says something to my father in the language I cannot understand. He merely shrugs his shoulders. And then he replies, and his words are so familiar, as if they are words I should know, as if I knew them a long time ago in a different place. The language that they speak is full of soft vowels, of words tousled together, spoken without breath.

I stick my spoon in my rice and listen.

Edmund comes back to the table. He stares at the three of us, my father, my mother, and me. Then he pounds his fist against the wall and he screams something wordless, something incomprehensible.

My father stops and looks at him. But still, he ignores him.

My mother told me once about guilt.

Her own guilt she held in the palm of her hands, like an offering to my father.

But your guilt is different, she said. Imagine this, she said, her hands running along my forehead, through my hair. Imagine, she said. Picture it, and what do you see?

A bruise on the skin, wide and black.

A bruise, she said. Concentrate on it. Right now, it's a bruise. But if you concentrate, you can shrink it, compress it to the size of a pinpoint, a birthmark. And then, if you want it, if you see it, you can blow it off your body like a speck of dirt.

She moved her hands along my forehead. From somewhere far away I could hear screaming.

My father gently breaks into the fish with the edge of his spoon. The skin breaks and underneath, the flesh is white, and the juice runs down along the side.

My father lifts a piece and places it carefully onto my plate. A gift.

Once more, his spoon breaks skin. Gingerly, my father lifts another piece and moves it towards my brother.

"I don't want it," he says, and he breaks the spell.

My father's hand wavers, and a sprinkling of juice falls down onto the tablecloth. Still, he ignores my brother. And then slowly, always slowly, he places the piece on my mother's plate.

There is silence. Only the sound of spoons against porcelain dishes. The smell of food fills the room.

My father eats slowly, savouring each mouthful, head tuned to the flavours in his mouth. My mother eats with her head bowed down, as if in prayer.

My brother lifts a stem of cauliflower to his lips. He breathes deeply, chews. And then his face changes, eyes wide, mouth open. He coughs. And suddenly, he retches the mouthful back onto his plate. Another cough, and then again.

My father slams his fork down on the table. In a single moment, he reaches across, grabbing my brother by the shoulder. And the other hand sweeps by me, hard and open, and bruises into my brother's soft cheek.

There are no sounds. My mother flinches. Edmund's face is red and his mouth is open. His eyes are wet.

He grabs a fork, points aimed at my father, and then in a wild moment, he heaves it at him. It strikes my father in the chest, and then drops.

"I hate you! You fucking chink, I hate you!" Edmund holds his plate in his hands. He smashes it onto the table. Something rises into the air. "I wish you were dead!"

Again, my father's hand falls. This time pounding downwards. And I am afraid, I am so afraid that my brother will disappear under the weight. I close my eyes.

All I can hear is someone screaming. There is a loud voice. I stand awkwardly, my hands covering my eyes.

"Go to your room," my father says.

And I think he is talking to me so I uncover my eyes.

But he is looking at Edmund. And Edmund is looking at him, his tiny chest heaving. I look into my brother's eyes, and I see his fear.

My mother begins clearing the table.

I remain seated, my heart pounding.

My mother sees nothing, only dishes littered with bones, transparent white fish bones delicate as thread.

I drop down from my chair. Past my mother. Onto the carpet, up the stairs.

Bamboo is smooth. The grains, fine as hair, are pulled together. At intervals, they are jointed like knuckles.

My father holds the bamboo between his hands.

As my brother lies on the floor, my father raises it into the air.

I want to cry out. I want to fall into the room, on the ground.

It is like a tree falling. I see it, beginning to move, beginning to fall. My father's hands, huge and soft, a slow arc through the air.

The bamboo falls silently. It rips the skin on my brother's back. There is still no sound. His skin reddens, breaks. And I see blood ebbing gently across his body.

The pole rises, and again, it comes down. Falling. I am afraid of bones breaking.

Again, he raises the pole.

My brother cries into the ground. His body paws at the carpet, hands pulling his knees into his chest, the crown of his head burrowing down. His back is hunched over and I see his spine, a million tiny pieces, cradled against skin.

The pole smashes into bone. And the scene in my mind bursts into a million white pieces. We begin to fall.

My mother picks me up off the floor. She drags me across the hall, into my bedroom, into bed. Everything is wet, the sheets, my hands, her body, my face. And she soothes me with words I cannot understand because all I can hear is screaming. Only someone screaming.

She rubs her cool hands against my forehead.

She covers my mouth.

In the morning, I wake up to the sound of my father easing gently through the kitchen, to the sound of burning oil, and the smell of French toast. I can hear my mother bustling around, adjusting skirts, blouses, jackets.

And no one says anything when my brother doesn't come down for breakfast. My father piles French toast and syrup onto a plate and my mother pours a glass of milk. She takes everything upstairs to Edmund's bedroom.

I follow my father around the kitchen, like always. I track his footprints, follow behind him and hide in the shadow of his body. Every so often, he reaches down and rustles my hair with his soft hands.

We cast a spell.

The spell breaks when he stops moving, when he stands in place, his feet a beautiful dark tan against the white floor. His hands drop as if he has forgotten the ritual, and then he is lost. And the edges of the counter, the sanded down cupboards, the glossy shine of the oven, glass, aluminum, they wear him down.

If he looks too hard he can see distorted reflections of himself in every space, in every glossy mirror.

He stands in the middle of the kitchen, confused.

And soon, soon my mother comes and puts her arms around him, and she holds him. And she whispers something to him, words that to me are meaningless and incomprehensible. But she offers them to him, sound after sound, in a language that was stolen from some other place, across some uncrossable ocean, until he drops his head and he remembers where he is.

Upstairs, I stand in the doorframe and listen to the sound of a metal fork scraping against a dish. My mother's voice rises and falls.

Light is pouring in through the window and it marks my brother's bed in loops and patterns. My mother is moving the fork across the plate, offering pieces of French toast to Edmund. I move towards the bed, the carpet rising between my toes, the wooden frame smooth against my hands. I go to my mother, reach my fingers out to the buttons on her cuff. I twist them over to catch the light. "Are you eating?" I ask.

Edmund starts to cry. I look up and find him, his face half hidden under the blanket.

"Edmund," my mother says softly, "try and sit up."

He only cries harder, but there is no sound. Only his mouth opening and closing, and his eyes pinched shut. The pattern of sunlight on his blanket moves with his body. His hair is pasted down with sweat.

His tears, they are running down into my hands. I do not know how my hands reached his cheeks, but now they are holding him, and he is crying into me. His head moves forward and backward like an old man's, but his eyes do not open.

I can hear my voice ringing on the walls, the walls that are as hard as open hands, as sticks of bamboo, notched and broken.

I know my father is standing in the doorway, but I cannot turn around and see him. He is broken, but I am holding my brother in my arms. I will hold him until he stops rocking, until his breathing becomes regular, and his crying subsides.

My mother has stepped away from us and she is standing with my father. She has placed her cool hands in his, and she is speaking to him with soft words. But my brother and I are speaking now, and so I am afraid to turn to them. I am afraid that if I listen too closely, I will be able to understand.

I can cut all the threads from my family to myself. But in the end, what does it do? I have my father's eyes, I have his mouth.

When I close my eyes, I can see him standing in front of me, and he is sad. He wants me to love him, the way I used to when I was a child.

A face changes over time. It becomes clearer.

In my father's face, I have seen everything pass. Anger that has stripped it of anything recognizable, so that it is only a face of bones and skin. And then, at other times, so much pain that it is unbearable, his face so full of grief it might dissolve. How to reconcile all these things and still love him? For a long time, I thought that it was not possible. You do not love your father because he is complicated, because he is human, because he needs you to. A child does not know yet how to love a person that way.

How simple it should be. Warm water running over, the feel of the grains between your hands, the sound of it like stones running along the pavement. My father rinsed the rice over and over, sifting it between his fingertips, searching for the impurities, pulling them out. A speck, barely visible, resting on the tip of his finger.

Somehow I think it should come down to knowing how to make the perfect bowl of rice.

If only I could do it, a cupful of rice in my open hand, a smoothing out, finding the impurities, then removing them piece by piece. And then, to be satisfied with what remains.

Somewhere in my memory, a fish in the sink is dying slowly. My father and I watch as the water runs down.

# TIM ROGERS

## *Scars and Other Presents*

Mason thinks we should find the highest point along the first meridian. The first meridian, he says, is the line where the future happens and becomes the past. We should find the highest point along that knife-edge, where the sunlight first touches the trees and rocks and eyes, if there are any, every morning. That would be the oldest place, says Mason – the place where morning happens first.

"We could be the first ones to see the new year. Maybe bring our guitars and hold a concert or something." Mason's eyes are neither closed nor open when he says this. They are looking elsewhere, not into the future really, because he knows this won't happen. He's looking sideways into another present where it could happen.

I have asked Georgie and Mason what we should do to celebrate New Year's Eve. It is December 1999 – a science-fiction year, a year of Martian Invasions and starships and prophecies of bad things. Georgie will disagree. She is already arguing with Mason about meridians, her mathematician's mind filled with the arbitrary nature of lines and dates of all kinds.

She is slumped in my father's reading chair. Mason lies on the den floor on his back, looking at a little spot somewhere between his nose and the ceiling. I'm perched on a barstool looking down on both of them. Whenever we are together, this is how we arrange ourselves: Mason on the bottom, me on the top, and Georgie, the level head, somewhere in between. I will ask a question and watch it percolate down, via Georgie, to Mason. Three points define a plane, unless they lie in a line. I suspect that Georgie, Mason, and I lie in a line, defining no level surface.

And I think: *What is the atom of time? Does it pass in fixed quantity? Is there, shall we say, an indivisible moment that can collect like flour in a cup, adding up to this, a second, or this, a lifetime? And if so, then what fundamental instant separates me from that child I used to be?*

When I am sixteen, Mason and I go to Georgie's cottage on Lake Nowhere. This lake is so shallow you can walk from shore to shore without going over your head. It's warm as bath water, and filled with parasites. Seagulls poop the tiny eggs into the water, and unless you are careful, they will grow under your skin like measles.

Mason is outside, floating on the lake. Not *on* it, he will tell us later, but pressed between media. A bubble in the seam between air and water. The sky and lake conspire to hold him in a plane. The wind howls, trying to pick him off. To get closer to the lake? Are they lovers? Is Mason holding them apart?

Georgie and I are inside, listening to her father's old jazz records. The sounds from the scratchy record skip out the verandah and off the lake like flat stones, to echo from the trees on the far side. Georgie is lounging on the beanbag furniture with a magazine. Sometimes a gust will riffle her pages, run its fingers through her hair. Fickle wind, hungry for anything. I am looking over the dusty bookcase. There are unloved books here, that smell like buried treasure. Old ones with things pressed between the pages. There is a dictionary the size of my chest. I ask Georgie for a word beginning with X and she says, "Xenophobe," without looking up.

The dictionary is filled with blood. No. With leaves. Mostly bright red maple leaves, some orange and yellow. Pressed hearts. Some lemon-shaped leaves and some oak leaves. Waxy and permanent, embalmed in the middle of change by the dictionary weight of words and definitions and gravity. The wind barges in again and shakes the book, perusing furiously, maybe looking for words to express its outrage. Leaves jump into the air like red bats, then dance with me. I'm laughing, laughing. It's snowing red, yellow and orange. Georgie is watching from the couch, smiling. Outside, Mason keeps between the sky and lake, chaperoning.

And in October, Georgie and I go back for a weekend alone, to close up for her parents. The first snowfall, red and yellow leaves everywhere. I ask Georgie whether it is winter or fall, and she says it's spring in Australia.

That night for the first time we press our bodies together like pages in a book. I have never done this before, Georgie has. Outside, the lake and wind are alone together too, but are growing cold to each other. I fumble and clutch. We are opening quotation marks, curled together to begin a statement. I wonder if we have pressed something beautiful between our souls, some blood-leaf, and can we preserve it. Is there pressure enough pulling us together? Later I wonder was Mason already there, in the seam between my belly and her back growing like a parasite in the heat between our skins?

There are scars to remind me of these things. We trace them with greedy fingers, learning to have fun being naked together, learning the script of our bodies. Each blemish is a word in a story. Here is the sissy-test scar I got when I was nine. Mason taught me the sissy-test: you scratch and scratch until you bleed. If you can do it until you bleed, you're not a sissy. I remember Mason and me pressing our wounds together, blood brothers, how it stung when we pulled them apart because they stuck at first like lips, kissing. The scar looks like a little pink birthmark. Is Georgie impressed or dismayed? She calls it the idiot-test scar. But this is only one of many hurts binding me to Mason, sticking to his own pains and to an assortment of shared memories. The summer we did the sissy-test was the summer Mason's parents got divorced, the summer we peeked in Betty Freid's bedroom window, the summer I threw up in the swimming pool at the Y. Over here is the appendectomy scar, knotty and brown, more like a scar is supposed to look. I make Frankenstein jokes. My appendectomy happened in grade nine, I failed history.

Georgie has knee scars from running and falling. A round scar on the ball of her thumb from whittling. A chicken-pox scar right between her eyebrows. She had chicken-pox when she was ten, the same Christmas she got Disco Barbie.

Just down my right bicep is where Mason's scar will go, when he cuts me the second time. Georgie's fingers are there now, tracing lightly up and down and making the little hairs stand on end. Then she lifts her left breast and shows me a tiny, paper-white line.

Where did you get that?

That's where you opened me up to take my heart, she says smiling, and I buy it. I don't think of it as an injury, something I could regret in the future.

At Mason's flat I knock. Mason often takes a long time to answer the door. He has no sense of time, he says. He can talk to past and future selves. From the future, he receives advice; the past, in turn, he advises. Do I tease him for this eccentricity? How can I? Everything works out for Mason. I'm ready to sit cross-legged, to hum strange mantras, to smoke a hookah pipe. But I am untrustworthy of the advice I may receive from future selves, and can think of nothing to say to my past.

The door opens on a smirking Mason, a yellowish towel mostly wrapped around his lower half. Georgie is in the act of pulling up her pants. "Mason!" she shouts before ducking into the bathroom. A long slow punch in the belly.

"Nothing he hasn't seen before," Mason jokes. "Don't throw up," he tells me.

Mason's apartment only has one room and a bathroom. He has lived by himself since he was sixteen in the same little space, so now it smells like him: old Kraft dinner. There is a drafting table, a small fridge, a bookshelf, a futon, a hot plate. A barred window above the futon only lets in light of the worst sort. Covering the walls are glossy naked fold-outs of Mason's women. He corrects the flesh of the wayward models of *Foxtrot* magazine, erasing all scars and pimples with his airbrush. I can't imagine how Georgie feels walking into this room of breasts and legs. She should be shocked or disgusted. But stuck in Mason's bathroom mirror are several snapshots of Georgie naked and in various erotic poses which I can't quite believe. Shy, mousy

Georgie who told me she couldn't have orgasms. Mason is offended by propriety, he wants us all to be proud of our nudity. I wonder if his parents ever come to visit, and whether they use the washroom when they do.

She emerges from the bathroom fully dressed and also blushing, thank goodness. Mason slaps her on the behind as she walks past and guffaws rudely, making her smile. Instead of fleeing, I ask if they've decided what we should do for New Year's Eve.

"Actually," Mason says casually, "I think Georgie and I will spend the night alone together."

I see him with his cupped hands out towards me. In them he holds a wound. Take this, he says. Put it with your others.

The first time Mason cuts me, it is an experiment to see what I will do. We are fourteen and in art class. Outside is the first day of spring-like weather. I remember the mailman walking by in his shorts, so old-fashioned those shorts with the three blue stripes down the side and showing that long expanse of winter-white thigh. The trend this year is baggy shorts down to the knee, but mailmen aren't expected to know this. In class, Miss Bell has told us to cut out different geometric shapes from coloured bristol board. Later we will glue them together to form a sculpture. I have chosen my colours and shapes carefully. They are more complicated than Mason's, which look as bored as he does. See how well I remember these details. In the middle of my octagon, Mason leans over as though to confide something, and very deliberately presses the blade of his X-acto knife into the fleshy mound below the thumb on the palm of my left hand, the mound of Venus. The blood wells up ominously quickly. It is a much deeper red than my bristol board. Dark coins appear on the table. I look up at Mason, to find him watching me curiously. He has slid his X-acto under the table. We observe one another for a small moment, before Alma James across the table sees the blood and puts up her hand. "Miss Bell, Jordan has his period," she snickers and everybody laughs. I throw up on my artwork. Miss Bell bustles over to the table and says, "Oh dear." She helps me up and ushers me out of the room. As the door shuts I hear Mason's laugh with the others, a girlish titter.

"How did it happen?" Miss Bell clucks on the way to the infirmary. I say, "I cut myself with the X-acto."

This cut has healed to a thin white line about an inch long. I showed it to a palm-reader who told me I had been deeply wounded by a loss in love. I told her that the scar wasn't accidental, that it had been inflicted intentionally by a friend.

"My boy," she said, "that's how it works."

"I need a ride to the hospital," Mason says over the phone. "Something's wrong with Georgie." I hang up the phone gently, roll over and switch on the light. My mother has appeared in the doorway looking frightened. She is holding the neck of her robe closed and looks old. How long will it be before the sound of the phone at night worries me?

"What's wrong?" she asks.

"Mason needs a ride to the hospital." Only a year ago my mother would not have let me go alone. Now she looks at me for a long minute, and then says, "Call if you need help." She abandons me in my little room, which has been left behind. The time passed keeps me from touching these things: the old stuffed monkey, the comic books, the marionette. I have travelled backward in time from a bleak future. I must warn my earlier self. Watch out, I'd like to say. Good advice under any circumstance. I pulled on a pair of boots and put on a jacket. I was still wearing my pyjamas.

Mason has not bothered to dress, his yellowed towel is draped about his skinny hips again. I am gratified to see he is frightened.

Georgie is lying on the futon in the middle of the small room, naked and bright blue from the neck down, except for a round flesh-coloured circle around her crotch. Because none of this is real, I show no surprise. Nothing will surprise me. For once I am collected, and show no signs of throwing up.

She is on her back, gasping hard and shivering. Her short hair is dripping with sweat, but her teeth are chattering. Her lips are a beautiful blue-purple, not the bright blue of her body, but blueberry blue. Her eyes are wide open and scared.

Mason and I stand observing for a moment as though looking under the hood of a stalled car. Neither of us knows anything about cars or medicine. Then Mason looks at me, and this look divests him of responsibility. He hands me the power and the blame with his eyes. I lap it up and adore it.

"Georgie?" I ask as I bend over her shaking blue body. "What's wrong?"

"I'm fuh-fuh-fuh . . ." Her chattering teeth. ". . . freezing. Can't *breathe*!" Her wide eyes are starting to cry, scaring me. I try to pick her up, but her skin is cool and rubbery, like a snake's. Against my will I recoil, and stumble backward over an open paint can. Bright blue scum leaks over the dusty hardwood floor, and Mason almost drops his towel.

"Watch it," he says. "That stuff won't come off!"

"What is it?"

"Latex," Mason mumbles. He looks away for a rag, or just away.

*"You painted her with Latex?"*

"We have to get her to a hospital," he says. I shove him hard, right in the middle of his bony chest, because I'm allowed in this situation. I watch him fly backward. He trips over his futon and collapses against the wall. Amazingly, he bursts into tears. I turn back to Georgie and scoop her up, lizard-skin and all. I'm a super hero. She's also crying now. I head for the door, making shushing baby noises, cherishing this moment which allows me intimacy, permits my little kisses and clucks.

By the time I reach the car, Mason has caught up with me again and I am secretly relieved. My crazy anger has worn off, and also I can't figure out how to get the car keys out of my pocket without dropping Georgie. I'm afraid I might drop her anyway; my arms have turned to sticks of wood. Mason digs the keys out of my pocket and we shuffle Georgie into the front seat wordlessly. He climbs in back, still wearing his towel but with a jacket and a pair of sneakers now. Georgie is shivering more than ever. Maybe the Latex will keep her warm.

The ride to the hospital is a cartoon. I've started to giggle. I can't help it. What if I get stopped for speeding? What will the cop make of our pyjamas, towel, rubber? What kind of crazed sex maniac have I become? "Will you shut up?" Mason says from the back seat. Those are the only words anyone speaks in the car.

In the waiting room Mason passes out and splits his head open on the marble floor. They whisk him away and leave me with old magazines. This will be a night to remember. A man walks in with what appears to be a vacuum cleaner attachment stuck to his groin. Even this doesn't make the woman at the registration desk smile. The man sits next to me and strikes up a conversation.

"What's your problem?" he asks.

"My ex-girlfriend was painted with rubber and had a panic attack." I can say this without affect now. Perhaps I could work at the registration desk.

"Can I get her number?" he asks.

At 3 a.m. a doctor comes to tell me that Georgie is sleeping. They got all the rubber off with a special solution. "But she's still a little blue," says the doctor, and I can't tell if she's joking. I ask about Mason. They are doing some tests. She suggests I go home and sleep, but I tell her I'll wait. At 6 a.m. a new doctor wakes me up, Dr. Salinas, who took out my appendix.

"Mason will be fine," he tells me. When I ask him what was wrong, he says, "Parasite."

There is no one else in the waiting room any more, so I lie down on the bench and try to sleep again. I dream about my appendix. Dr. Salinas saved it for me to see when he took it out. I did not believe it had been a part of me. I thought about the little space inside me it must have left, and what other alien things were growing next to it. In my dream there is a monster in there. It's getting bigger and bigger, and I must find the seam inside where the monster stops and I begin, or I will disappear.

Georgie breaks up with me on the same day that Mason cuts me the second time. She has been sending me mental signals for some weeks but I have cleverly refused to acknowledge them. She says, "You're the coldest person I've ever met," and, "*Must* you smack your lips like that every time you eat?" When I kiss her, she turns her cheek at the last moment or scrunches her lips into a dry peck. But I am sly, I say, "Thanks, Granny," and "I'll only smack for you, sweetheart." She calculates: how close to the border must I push him before he topples? I have the idle thought that our relationship has become a competition. Against my will, I am participating. Internally I can sense the beginnings of an enormous, undefined fear, expanding like a bubble. Waiting to be popped.

"I went out with Mason last night," she says in homeroom, thrusting her jaw forward like a shield. She looks physically braced, as though I am a strong wind in her face. The confrontation. I have been anticipating it like a dentist appointment. How did I happen to arrive at this moment? Then I realize, this is what it will be like to die.

"I don't think we should see each other any more," she says in a softer tone of voice. But I am stricken! I can imagine this moment branding itself into my memory so that as I lie dying, it will replay itself again and again. Various dramatic deaths occur to me. I am falling from a cliff in darkest Africa, and thinking of this moment.

"There ought to be a word for the instant when the anticipation ends and the experience begins," I tell her. "Don't you think?" The bell goes off. Georgie looks blankly at me, but I can't say anything. I am captivated by the image of myself on my deathbed, unable to stop this moment from occurring, a victim of the present.

Georgie kicks me in the shins. She is crying, gathering up her books.

"*Feel* something, goddamn it!" she shouts before storming out of the room.

By lunch time my epiphany has vanished and I have developed the strange feeling that I should be starting a fight. Surely this is the proper course of action. Is that what people are expecting? Why are they all watching me so intently? Can the news have spread so fast? I have been catapulted into a soap opera. Somebody has scripted my reactions. My own emotions are indistinguishable from those I feel I ought to have.

Mason is outside smoking with his new friends. Cataloguing my grievances with Georgie, I note that she has driven him away. I hardly recognize him now with his cigarettes and jean-jacketed cronies. Does she seriously want to date him? Only now it sinks in. But how can she? Look how shallow he is.

When he sees me he smirks and looks sidelong at the others. In his hands is a hunting knife. He turns it over and over and it winks at me.

"Cool, eh?" he says, daring me with his eyes to deny it. If he's caught with this shining tooth, he will be suspended. That's where the danger lies, not in the knife but in the possession of the forbidden. How juvenile, how unworthy. Mason's sly posturing offends me. I want to reach out and strip it away, hurt him and embarrass him, cut him with words.

"You stole my fucking girlfriend," I tell him. Mason's lupine friends come into sharp focus, suddenly appealing. Lackadaisical and threatening. Their toughness is contagious. It seeps into my speech, hunches my shoulders, curves my spine. I am becoming casually dangerous. The circle shuffles and expands like a dance, leaving Mason and me in the centre. I don't know this choreography, but I want this to happen. I want to attribute blame, infuse Mason with my inadequacies and tear him apart.

I give him a little push, an experiment, and he shoves me back hard. "Fuck off, Baum," he says, and, "What's your problem?" Unfriendly arms propel me back into the circle. The knife is still in his hand, injecting seriousness into every motion. But he's not brandishing it yet. He's still half joking. I rush at him flailing my arms and screaming. I think this surprises him. He holds me back with his knife hand, and says, "Hey!" The flat of the blade is flush with my left bicep, just above the elbow joint.

And then with utter clarity it strikes me that there is another kind of moment. A single action may fix a path among infinite futures. I am in this moment, I realize it in the way you realize sometimes that you are dreaming, and that understanding gives you power. It is luminous. I have hold of Mason by the shirt collar, and I foresee all consequences. I may choose among them. He is pushing me with his knife hand, trying to get away. I act. Quantum uncertainty resolves. The present happens. My arm closes on the knife blade. He flinches back and draws the blade across my bicep. The blood is thick and furious. "Oh, hey," he says again. I take advantage of the hesitation, and punch him in the eye. He falls on his butt and says, "Ooof!" and I begin to laugh. My knuckles hurt like hell, more than my arm which is now dripping with blood. Little black spots appear before my eyes. Someone pulls the ground out from under my feet. But I don't throw up.

Mason is expelled. I get three weeks of detention because I am seen as the victim. At the end of this period I graduate from high school. Next September I will leave for university. During the summer, Mason and I will take turns trying to be friends again, never quite making it.

Georgie wakes me up at 8 a.m. on December 31st and tells me she has been discharged. Can she please get a drive back to her apartment. It strikes me that this is the last day of the twentieth century.

In the car I ask her if she has heard about Mason, who is still in the hospital. She says, "He has a tapeworm. It's disgusting, I'm breaking up with him." Is this my Christmas present, this small bomb that I can pass off to Mason if I want? I wonder what I will do with it. Here, take this hurt. Cradle it, hold it close to you. Keep it happy, so it will breed.

But when I visit Mason in the hospital, and he says, "Can you get me my clothes?" vulnerable in his hospital johnny and ridiculous towel, I can only think of the long white snake in his belly. Who knows how long it has been there? Maybe it knows me intimately, maybe it has eaten the baloney sandwiches I used to trade with Mason at lunch, watched me from within, hidden but not far away, only four inches into Mason's skinny body, eating and growing fat like an evil secret.

"The doctor says it's about twelve feet long," he brags with a wide grin. "Twelve feet all curled up in there, imagine that." He pulls down the covers of his hospital bed and exposes his white gut. When he puffs it out it looks like a giant blind eyeball, or a huge breast. "Maybe I can get the doctor to save it for me, that would be cool."

Yes, Mason likes to have his secrets put in jars and set out in the sun. He's proud of them. I don't have his kind of bravado, and I decide to keep my own little worm to myself.

In Mason's apartment, I do a strange thing. His can of latex has dried to a rubber pulp, but in the closet I find six more. Without any real intention I begin to paint one of the naked women on his wall. I paint over the flawless airbrushed skin, over the eyes and face and breasts and legs and hair. I leave only a circle of crotch unpainted, surrounded by a sea of bright blue. It's a shaved crotch, looking for all the world like a swollen eye. Then I start on the next picture, and before I know it I have used up an entire can of latex. I only hesitate a moment before opening the second can. After six hours, I have finished the entire apartment. The walls have become planes of sky, dotted with strange fisheyes and bearded mouths. The obscene has become the absurd. I stand in the centre of the room, breathing hard, watched by a thousand pussies. I don't know why I've done this. Is it a gift or a condemnation? A compliment? An insult? I have made a statement without hearing it. I have created this mark that will stand in memory. The eyes look on sightless, the lips are silent.

And I think: *These are the things we use to mark our time: anniversaries, birthday parties, holidays. Rituals that stand at regular intervals through our pasts like meridians. Mountains exist in this temporal geography, which we call passages. At least, certain events occur which we feel ought to be mountainous, and so we elevate them with pomp and circumstance, as though the marching bands and party hats can balance the mess of scars and accidents that normally mark our memory.*

Above the town is a ski hill and a lookout, and that's where we finally decide to bring in the new millennium. We buy several bottles of cheap wine. Mason brings his deceased tapeworm, Biff, in a mayonnaise jar of formaldehyde. It looks like an old scar sealed away, or a scab of dead skin. It is a remarkably mild December afternoon, and we build a bonfire. The sun sinks fast against the horizon and leaks its orange-pink into the clouds. The trees grow high enough to catch these magic rays in their highest branches, become huge flowers. Bad things go away. Tonight, despite all casual cynicism, we allow ourselves to look forward to the future.

Georgie tells us that night only comes because we are standing still. If we could keep up, we could match the sun and it would never be dark. Time would not pass. Mason says we could all get a tan, even Biff. I ask Mason, what do I have to do to grow a tapeworm, anyway.

And this is how we spend the night, joking and talking and getting drunk. We celebrate with our pasts. That's what we are to each other finally, the past, the friendly past and tonight we will love ourselves together for it.

We don't notice when it gets dark. Sometime during the night, midnight passes and the new year begins, but none of us is quite sure when.

IAN COLFORD

# *The Reason for the Dream*

My mother used to spend hours working on her face. Sometimes I'd watch from the doorway of her bedroom while she carefully lined up the bottles, jars, and tubes across the top of the dresser – as if there were some secret order she had to follow – and opened them one by one. She used her fingers and some little brushes to spread the powders and creams over her eyelids, cheeks, neck, and lips. When she was finished, she sometimes tried different expressions and considered her face from different angles, tilting her head up and down, turning it from side to side. When she smiled, I felt a shiver go up my legs, she was so pretty. But this was back in the days when we didn't have any money to do anything, and since my mother stayed away from most people for a long time after my father's accident, she usually spent her evenings alone. With the makeup on she looked like she was all ready for a party. But tonight there was no party. I watched her put the jars and tubes away and take off her clothes. Then she wrapped herself in a terrycloth bathrobe and headed out to the kitchen to boil water for coffee and to read the newspaper.

All that winter she did nothing. She stayed home and roamed from one room to another, pausing occasionally to stare out the window. There was always something puzzled in her expression, as if she couldn't understand how she'd ended up here. I thought she was too pale to be healthy. She seemed so brittle; she looked as if she'd be shattered at a touch or blown away by a breeze. Sometimes she yelled at us for no reason, my sister Julie and me. According to her we were worse than useless, nothing but dead weight around her neck. She complained about the cold too, hugging herself and pouting, sinking into a chair and appearing frail and vulnerable, like a sick child. Then she was silent and didn't speak for hours. Her frustration with the way our life had changed seemed to drain her strength, and Julie and I were left to worry at her frequent trips to the doctor, wondering with solemn glances and much discussion what would happen to us if she should die. She did not die, but we watched her wilt and grow lean. After so many years in a big house with lots of spare rooms, the cramped spaces and cluttered corners of our tiny two-bedroom apartment seemed to cause something inside her to wither, something she needed in order to live. Idle and confined, she struggled to contain her temper – by squeezing shut her eyes, by holding her breath, by counting backward from one hundred. But sometimes nothing could appease her; those were the times that Julie and I fled to our room to wait until the storm had passed. Strange as it seems, we got used to these outbursts and learned to go about our business while she struggled with her demons. I can remember completing a difficult mathematics assignment, performing intricate calculations, all the while listening to my mother sobbing in the next room. At the height of one of these episodes – when she'd been drinking all weekend and eaten almost nothing for days – she told me that she didn't want to continue like this. She said something had to give. I became alarmed at this sort of talk, as I'm sure any child would. But then she took me aside, away from Julie whose extreme youth would prevent her from fully understanding what was about to pass between mother and daughter, and informed me that my father was to blame for all of our troubles.

My father had been in an accident and for almost a year had been lying comatose in a hospital bed. His absolute tranquillity only seemed to make my mother's agitation worse. We hardly ever made the trip across town to visit him any more because my mother said there was no point. He couldn't see us or hear us. So why waste our time and our money on bus fare? I didn't argue. To tell the truth, I was just as pleased not to have to go there. I really don't like hospitals and it was creepy watching someone you know just lying there breathing, with his eyes wide open but not seeing. One day when she was on the phone and didn't know I was close enough to hear her, my mother said that if he had a shred of decency he'd die and let her get on with her life. "It's not fair that he can do this to me!" I heard her complain. "It's just not fair!" She made it sound as if he'd done this to himself deliberately, simply to hurt her, and for a long time I believed everything she said. She had me thinking that *she* was the victim, that *she* had suffered more than anyone.

But somewhere along the way I stopped believing her. I don't even know why really. I just stopped. I'm sure she noticed a change in my attitude; noticed a new adolescent scepticism in the crease of my brow. Sometimes I wondered what she thought when I buried my nose in a book and ignored her or else just got up and walked out of the room so I wouldn't have to listen to what she was telling me. But I never asked. All I know is that after a while she stopped talking about my father. I was grateful, but I never said thank you.

The January when I was twelve she rented a car so we could all go and visit her boyfriend. I hadn't been inside a car for months and so I wasn't prepared for the riveting thrill of being strapped in, the swoon of anticipation at sitting in the front seat for the first time that I could remember. Julie was wedged between us, and it bothered me when my mother let her fiddle with the controls on the dashboard. I wanted to fondle the shining buttons and sculpted knobs and make the digital displays flash too. But I also understood that I was too old to be amused by that sort of thing.

I could remember from before the accident that my mother wasn't a very careful driver, that she talked all the time and kept looking at the people who were in the car with her when she should have been watching the road. Years ago she'd been stopped by the police and ticketed, and I remember my father raising his voice and barking questions at her that she could never answer. Why? Why? Why? Eventually, after more tickets than anyone could count and more than her share of warnings, he took the keys away from her and refused to let her use the car.

I always thought it unfair that she had to get rid of the car so soon after my father's accident because it seemed the perfect chance for her to teach herself how to drive properly.

Because she hardly ever told me anything, there are lots of things about my mother that I only learned by chance or figured out on my own along the way. I don't know much about my father either, and since most of what I *do* know came from her, I haven't decided if I should believe it or not. There was always something incredible about her stories, something that would raise an eyebrow or cause an uneasy sensation in the stomach. She had a habit of making herself look good by putting other people down, and I went away feeling like I'd been given a puzzle and it was up to me to dig the facts out from under all her fiction.

As I understand it, my father was very successful at what he did. He occupied some sort of executive position with one of those department stores you see everywhere these days. Even though he was still young he had a big office and got to be really important. But my mother insisted he would have made nothing of himself without her. Her patience, she said; her commitment. That's what made the difference. He worked hard, granted. He put in long hours and never complained. But she was the one who held it all together with her strength of character and her belief in a higher purpose.

His ambitions were all out of focus before he met her. Before she came along he was mired in a menial routine and didn't even have the sense to realize he wasn't happy. She changed his life and made it possible for him to become something. It was because of her that he achieved the things he did. On his own he was nothing.

That's what my mother said.

She loved telling people what I was like when I was younger, but I can't believe I was really such a snivelling brat. I remember being on my own a good deal and not being unhappy about it. The first time I had to cook supper for my sister and myself was when I was six, and even though it didn't happen very often I already knew how to change her diapers by then.

This wasn't because my mother was too busy or because she had a separate career that took her out of the house. As I see it, she wasn't ready for the trauma of raising children. Her heart wasn't in it. Children fuss and make noise and call attention to themselves, and it never ends. Never. Even *I* know that. But my mother was either unwilling or unable to accept this simple reality. Anything we did, she took it personally. For her, child-rearing was mortal combat. Someone was going to win and someone was going to lose. And she wasn't about to weaken her position by giving in to any of our demands.

Once, on a particularly trying day when the three of us had been scrapping like alley cats, she pulled on her coat and announced, "I've had enough. I'm leaving. You've got no one to thank but yourselves. Cry if you like." For a child, there's nothing quite as terrifying as watching your mother disappear up the street and around the corner, not looking back. When you're that age you can't help wondering if you'll ever see her again. All you can do is stand there and wait for the house to come crashing down and for the whole universe to be swept out from underneath you. I'm sure we felt it slipping as we watched her walk away, slightly stooped in her struggle against the wind, and we were astounded at the ease with which she'd given up on us, stunned by the magnitude of our loss. We both cried as she'd suggested, a copious eruption of tears, my sister Julie and I. It seemed like we would never stop.

It wasn't until a few months after we'd moved from the house to the apartment that my mother made any attempt to sort out her life and put things in order. It was September, wet and dreary, and Julie and I were about to start school in the city.

I'd heard a few rumours about this school from other kids, but nothing could have prepared us for the dirt and squalor we were about to encounter. Children my age and younger carried knives. There was stiff wire mesh protecting all the windows, and a troop of morose security guards patrolled the corridors like it was a prison. The desk where I was told to sit was blackened by age and burn marks, and also by obscene messages and drawings carved into its surface. The classroom was filled with a putrid stench like cigarettes and urine mixed together. The plaster was falling from the walls. The linoleum tiles were peeling up from the floor. And all the teachers had this hopeless crazy look about them, like they were trapped in some nightmare and couldn't get out.

Julie and I had never really appreciated where we'd come from, I guess because for all those years we never knew anything else. Our old school wasn't perfect, but at least it had clean bathrooms and lights that worked. Mostly we'd enjoyed going to school, though I doubt we'd have admitted this even under the threat of torture. It was true that some kids misbehaved, but they were amateurs who didn't get much support from the rest of us.

Here, however, in the city, it was nothing for gangs of kids to push each other around in the classroom and to beat up anyone who tried to stop them. Teachers kept blunt instruments in their desks. This world was alien to me, as were the other children. I had not the slightest interest in any of them. I could not endure their wan faces turned to me: the impudent scrutiny of their distrustful eyes made me shudder. I recoiled from any contact with them. At lunchtime on the first day Julie and I fled home and declared that we would rather die than go back. My mother was furious, but when we described what we'd seen she realized we could never have made it up. I think the sheer volume of tears convinced her that she had to do something drastic. She made some promises and sent us back for a few weeks while she scraped together enough money to get us both into private schools. We were poorer for it, much poorer than before. But, as she said, if we let our standards slip we'd be lost.

My mother was still young and, as far as I was concerned, attractive. She wasn't any older than thirty-two or -three. The last few months had taken a toll, but to me the streaks of grey seemed an enhancement. Something about her reminded me of those china dolls you see advertised in magazines: pretty, but too pretty to play with. All you can do is put it on a shelf and look at it. My mother had trouble getting people to take her seriously. All sorts of problems came her way when she applied for jobs, or when she had to do grown-up things like deal with my teachers at school. Once one of them, not all that old herself but frumpy and crabby, refused to believe that the woman in the tan suit wearing all that rouge and lipstick was my mother. That was the closest my mother ever came to getting into a fist fight with me there to see her. She wasn't the type of person to back down when it came to telling people what she thought of them.

Now, however, after all we'd been through, she didn't like being mistaken for my older sister. At one time, as she freely admitted, provoking shock and disbelief had appealed to her vanity. But not any more. Her vanity no longer served a useful purpose. It was finally time to grow up, she said, without much enthusiasm and with only the barest trace of a smile. Her flirtatious mannerisms vanished overnight, and I watched one day as she carried bags and bags of old clothes out to the garbage and took what was left down to the second-hand store. In an effort to age herself quickly she bought sensible shoes and mature outfits and tried to apply her makeup with greater subtlety, with only hints of colour where before there had been broad streaks.

It took her a long time to get used to this, but she kept repeating that it would work to our advantage. Before setting out in search of a job she modelled for us, asking, "How do I look?" smiling, gaining confidence in herself and her unadorned charms. She looked great. But even so, she came up against a stubborn prejudice in some people, especially men. Because she was small and pretty and tended to giggle under pressure, I guess they assumed she was either stupid or out to seduce them. She told me they said she didn't get the job because her practical experience was ancient history. But, as she argued, she had to have something going for her to even get into the office for an interview. Right? It was these married men, she concluded, these spineless wimps who were afraid to hire someone who looked good in tight skirts. They were cowards, she declared. And probably assholes. Every last one of them.

Insulted, livid, she arrived home fighting tears and cursing them all: all men, all employers, all those sweaty dolts sitting in their shabby offices. She'd assumed that, if anything, her slim and stylish appearance would be an asset. It hadn't occurred to her that it would stand in her way. But I suppose attitudes had changed, and she hadn't kept pace. In desperation she went out and had most of her hair chopped off. She bought a pair of prim, thick-rimmed glasses at Zellers. Using this strategy she got a position as a clerk-typist at the main branch library downtown. The old woman who gave her the job was so pleased. She had such a nice smile, she was told. She could type. And she had university. Such a blessing these days. They put her at the front desk to greet patrons. On Saturdays she took us with her, and I was impressed because she looked so important sitting there. People consulted her with their problems. It was nice – sometimes it was even fun – but it wasn't what she was looking for.

She wanted something more rewarding, something she wouldn't mind doing for years, maybe even for the rest of her life. Eventually she did find other, better jobs. One thing led to another. But nothing was permanent or as lucrative as she would have liked. The search continued. She made certain we knew it cost her a monumental effort each morning just to get out of bed.

Most of all she had her eye open for a man. She dated, casually at first, then when things hit bottom, doggedly, obsessively. She went out with anyone who asked, men she hated, men she found repulsive. She told us once that she was prepared to go to any length, to do almost anything. If she couldn't provide a decent home for her children, then by god it was her duty to find someone who could. She gathered us together sometimes before going on a date and told us not to be too upset if she wasn't home by the time we went to bed. Not to worry if she wasn't in by morning. Not to cry if she wasn't there when we got home after school. We both told her, okay, and tried our best to sound strong and supportive, but we always cried when she left us like that, not knowing when she was coming back. It brought home to me exactly how far we'd fallen and how helpless we'd become. Whoever she was meeting could make her stay away from us for as long as he wanted, and she couldn't say no. It didn't seem fair, all the creepy people she had to go with, all the menial things she had to do just to keep food on the table. But she was desperate almost beyond caring what happened to her. Things had been bad for so long. She said she was finished applying for crummy jobs that paid nothing only to have someone take one look at her and tell her she wasn't good enough. She didn't want to spend the rest of her life in a dump. She had to make the most of whatever she had left to find a new husband for herself and father for her children.

"Believe me," she said one day as she headed out the door, "It's the only way we're going to get out of here."

She placed an advertisement in one of those newspapers for lonely people: "Petite, chic, intelligent, thirtyish, blonde," and sat back to see what would happen. When the phone started ringing she was right there to answer it. She told them everything about herself, omitting no details. "Yes. I have two children. Two girls." She said if they couldn't handle that she wanted nothing to do with them. Some callers only wanted to talk. But others wanted to meet her. She'd ask a few questions that seemed important: "So what do you do?" "Where do you live?" "What kind of car do you drive?" And depending on the answers she would respond, "No. I'm sorry. I don't think so. But thank you." Or, "Yes. Okay. When?"

Once – it was really early – the phone rang and woke me up. My mother answered it in her bedroom. I got out of bed to get a drink of water and then went and stood just outside her room. When I saw her lying there in bed talking on the phone I decided not to go any further. I'd only gotten up because I wasn't tired. Sometimes in the morning she let me get into bed with her to talk. But it didn't take me long to realize that it was way too early for talking. So I just stood in the doorway, scratching at the painted doorframe, conscious of my feet sticking to the cold wooden floor. I could see her face because she'd switched on her bedside lamp. I was feeling funny because she didn't seem to know I was there, and I sort of felt that maybe I should just go back to bed. I heard her utter a questioning "Yes" in her timid voice, and then a more firm "Yes." Then she just listened. I could see that her hand was moving around under the blankets, over her belly. She murmured, "Uh-huh," as she closed her eyes and her hand moved down further. After a moment her body was moving in slow wriggles and she was making noises into the phone, strange moans and softly muffled grunts. I crept away and crawled back into bed. When she yelled it frightened me out of the warm sleep I'd just started falling into. I turned over just as she hollered again. It almost sounded like she'd stubbed her toe getting out of bed. But I must have fallen asleep soon afterward because I don't remember hearing anything else.

When I came out for breakfast she was excited. Humming along with the radio, her eyes teasing, she nudged a scrap of paper across the table.

"What's that?" I mumbled, barely awake.

"That's him," she said, speaking as if some matter had finally been settled.

"Oh," I said. "Who?"

"That's the one," she said pointedly, ignoring my stupidity. "I've got a date and I've made up my mind. He's going to be your father. So memorize the name. You're going to be hearing it a lot from now on."

She was pushing the hair back from her face and watching me, as if my decision was going to mean something.

I looked at the paper. In her tiny scrawl she'd scribbled a name that I couldn't read, followed by the letters MD and a phone number.

"What's that mean?" I asked. "What's MD?"

Immediately I realized my mistake. Her composure evaporated before I could say I was sorry for being so stupid. Her eyes narrowed with disgust and her hand flew out to sweep the piece of paper away. I gasped at how fast it happened.

"I should have known you wouldn't appreciate anything I do for you!"

She stomped over to the counter and swiped some crumbs into the sink with a cloth. Then she threw the cloth into the sink and stood stiffly still, her hands flat on the counter, her head bent and averted, her body quietly shuddering.

It wasn't the first time I was left sitting there wondering what she expected of me. I tried and tried to think if there was anything I could do to make her feel better. I suppose I *could* have gone over and stood next to her. I *could* have put my arms around her and mumbled an apology. But I'm still not very good at that sort of thing. I kept quiet and ate my cereal. When Julie came into the room I motioned to her to not make a sound and together we crept back to the bedroom to get ready for school.

"You *will* like him, Sara. You know you will. So stop being such a brat. And get ready! Please!"

I didn't turn to look at her.

"How can you be sure?" I asked, trying not to sound like a brat, but probably sounding like one nonetheless.

"I'm your mother. I know all about these things. You'll like him. Believe me. Okay? Trust me. And stop making such a fuss. You're not a child any more."

I knew it was a waste of time to say anything when her mind was made up. But I was only trying to make a point. We were going to stay with my mother's boyfriend for the weekend. He had a big house in the country and we were getting ready to drive out to where it was.

But it was all happening so suddenly. I couldn't believe it, the complete lack of planning. A phone call had come late last night, and here we were this morning, scrambling to get our things together and get on the road. I had homework to do and so did Julie. And to top it off, Julie was complaining that she didn't feel well. But my mother didn't care. I think she was convinced Julie was faking, and she kept telling me we could do our homework when we got there. As if that would be possible. As if the upset of being dropped down into strange surroundings and having to meet someone for the first time – someone who for all I knew was going to be my father – and worrying about making a good impression wouldn't interfere with getting my homework done. The prospect frightened me because I knew I wouldn't be able to sit still. Not for a minute. And that would make her angry.

It was snowing. Julie was lying down and I sat curled up on a chair in front of the window, my feet up off the floor, resting my body against the firm straight back, watching the thick wet snow plaster itself to the street, the signs, the buildings, and seeing the wind whip it into drifts and sculpt it against doorframes and crevices. The window wheezed and whistled and frozen air swept over me with each gust. I had on only a T-shirt and the skin of my arms shivered into goose-bumps.

"Why can't he come and get us and take us there?" I'd boldly ventured earlier. "Wouldn't that be easier?"

"He's out there already, Sara. That's where he phoned from."

"But why can't he come back and get us?"

"Damn it, Sara! Don't provoke me! Okay? Not today. He doesn't want to have to drive all the way back into the city just to get us. And I don't want him to either. It's not safe, with this weather. Understand?"

I nodded. That seemed logical enough. But one question remained.

"But . . ."

"Sara!"

I held my tongue. Why, I wanted to know, wouldn't he come to get us really? It was on my lips, ready to be asked. But the cords of her neck were standing out, her mouth was zipped shut, and her face glowed a deep shade of scarlet. I'd already pushed her too far with my stupid questions. Her movements had become abrupt and choppy and she was making a noise halfway between a grunt and a sigh, as if packing a few things involved tremendous physical effort. As she crammed a bundle of stuff into her big suitcase a paperback book fell to the floor. She bent over, but instead of picking it up she kicked it across the room. "Shit," she muttered. She went and got it and biffed it into the case. A couple of loose pages fluttered to the floor.

She pointed at the mess and said to me, "That's your fault."

She'd been seeing him now for two or three months, but so far there hadn't been enough time to bring him home to meet us. He was so busy, she said, her eyes flashing with pride, you wouldn't believe it. Always working. Always. Always. She spent a lot of time waiting for him to call, but even so she seemed genuinely happy with the way things were going. The old cares and worries were suddenly not worth the effort. She made jokes and laughed at the slightest provocation, and when I hugged her she felt warm. She told us again and again how considerate he was, how thoughtful, and how intelligent. He took her to an opera. They went to some fancy restaurant that she'd always wanted to go to. He even took her along to gatherings of his colleagues who, she said with a soft smile, were all very nice.

But there had been no mention yet of bringing him home. It seemed he couldn't fit it in. He was always so busy. Sometimes he was out of town. This went on for such a long time that I began to suspect he didn't know we existed, Julie and I. I thought that somehow she hadn't made it clear to him that she had these two kids at home, and then somewhere along the way he'd said he didn't like children. And so she was keeping quiet about us and hiding us from him. I knew she sometimes didn't tell people about us. I could remember a few times when people called or showed up at the door and they seemed so surprised to see us. My mother would say, "Oh, yes. I forgot to mention . . ." And then send us away to our room.

Still, I *had* caught myself dreaming about having a new father. The big hands and a warm lap to cuddle up in. That's what I remembered. Only I was too old for all that. Maybe Julie would get to fall asleep in his arms. I'd have to content myself with relating on a more mature level. I'd have to discuss grown-up things and help around the house and quit complaining so much. I could see it was going to be a nuisance trying to fit this person into my life, especially when I hadn't become used to the idea of setting my old father aside. There wasn't any hole there yet for this new person to fill. I knew the situation was delicate. I knew I'd have to struggle with my peevish tendencies and try to not say the wrong thing as I so often did. And then there were times when I wished that she'd never met him. It wasn't going to be an easy adjustment. But as I watched her packing our cases I could admit there was a chance it would be worth it, if he could keep my mother happy and if he welcomed us all into his life. As long as my mother was happy and didn't yell so much I was sure I could put up with anything.

But now we were all going to visit him at his big house in the country, so he had to know about us, didn't he? My mother had gone out the previous night and rented a car. It was parked across the street, covered with new snow. We were all set.

The phone rang. My mother hurried to answer it.

"Yes?" she said breathlessly.

With my back still to her I could hear her voice soften, hear the smile spreading across her face.

"We're almost ready. Oh, Philip! I know. I can't wait!"

I could envision her talking on the phone. I'd seen her so often recently, smiling dreamily, perched on one leg, her other foot rubbing on the back of her knee. Sometimes she plucked at the fuzz of her sock and sometimes she twisted the telephone cord around her fingers.

"Me too," she was saying.

She listened for a moment.

"I know. Yes."

She giggled.

Then her tone flattened and became solemn.

"What do you mean?"

"Of course we're coming. Don't be silly. It's not that bad."

She laughed.

"I will. You know I will."

"Okay."

"Okay. I'll see you in an hour or so."

Then she said quickly, "Just a second. Philip?"

She motioned me over to the phone and handed it to me.

"Just say hello," she instructed.

I took the phone from her. It felt so heavy suddenly.

"Hello?"

"Hello. Is this Sara?"

The line crackled. He sounded far far away and his voice was thin and hollow like an old recording.

"Yes."

"I've heard all about you, Sara. I know how smart you are. I hope you're being a good girl and helping your mother this morning."

"Yes," I tried to say, except my voice cracked. I could feel my knees getting wobbly. I was way too hot and something gummy was stuck in my throat.

"I've been looking forward to meeting you and Julie, Sara. I hope you know that. I can hardly wait."

"Me too."

Then I said, "Are you really a doctor?"

He paused for a brief chuckle, then answered, "Yes, Sara. I'm really a doctor. But I hope that's not the only thing your mother's said about me. I do lots besides just being a doctor."

"Yes. Uh . . ."

"I'll see you in a little while, Sara. Okay? Tell your mother to drive carefully. It might be dangerous out there."

"I will." I coughed.

"Okay. Goodbye."

"Bye . . ."

He hung up.

My mother took the phone and plopped it back into its cradle. Then she looked at me crossly, her hands on her hips.

"I don't know what I'm going to do with you Sara. Sometimes you embarrass me so much. What was all that about? Did you think I was fibbing when I said he was a doctor?" She shook her head, baffled. "I sure hope you can do better than that when we get out there."

I felt myself turn deep red beneath her puzzled gaze. I hated when she put me on the spot like that.

But then all she said was, "Come on. Give me a hand here."

We finished packing together.

My mother whistled as she drove. This was going to be her day. The snow, the driving conditions; none of it bothered her in the least. She ignored the slickness of the road, guided the car smartly around tight corners, glided to a stop at red lights. She took us out of town along Burnside Drive where all the stores and warehouses kept their lights on day and night, and past the hamburger places that were busy all the time. But today everything was deserted and ours seemed to be the only car on the road. I saw a bus go by and the only person in it was the driver. The snow was plunging from the sky in clumps, tumbling over the car and accumulating around the wipers. Already, though, the ploughs were busy clearing the parking lots in front of the shopping malls. It seemed a shame. All those stores and nobody around but us. And my mother had said we weren't stopping. Not for anything.

Still, I was pleased. She'd chosen a bright red Corona – a classy move, I thought. It had a stick-shift and it smelled brand new, like polish or cleaning wax right out of the can. The interior was a rich shade of burgundy and the upholstery collapsed under my weight like one of those pillow chairs filled with foam. I wondered how easy it would be to snuggle down and fall asleep. But then right there in front of me was the leather dashboard, set with dozens of tiny lights and dials, shining as if someone had poured oil over the whole works and rubbed and rubbed. When my mother wasn't looking I reached out and touched it and rubbed my fingers together. They felt slippery but I couldn't smell anything on them.

She glanced over in our direction and smiled, a wonderful, uninhibited, lavish smile. "Everything okay?" she asked, just like that, for no reason. She was proud of herself. I could tell. She'd finally done it. Just like she always said she would.

We were using the directions he'd given her to follow. They were supposed to make the place easy to find, but the map he'd drawn just looked like a jumble of lines to me. After some sharp turns and a long slow curve up a ramp we joined the highway. I checked the map to see if I could figure out where we were in relation to where we were going. I turned the paper every way I could think of, but none of the lines seemed to make any sense. It made me feel stupid because I was sure I was doing something wrong. I knew it was supposed to be simple. Any dummy can read a map. So I kept looking for a clue. At the end, where all the lines joined together to make a funnel, he'd stroked in a great big black X with a caption that read, YOU GOT THERE! But I was still worried because I couldn't find anything that said where "THERE" was. It was like he'd told her to go one place and then given her a map that would take her somewhere else. As far as I could tell, his "THERE" could be anywhere. It could be out in the middle of nowhere. Still, I reasoned it had to be somewhere. I just couldn't find it on the map. I felt so stupid.

I didn't want to say anything. It would look like I was trying to spoil the trip. But when I couldn't stand it any longer and finally spoke up my mother didn't care at all. She seemed to know exactly where she was going, even though she insisted she'd never been to this place before. When I told her I couldn't find the highway on the map she just said, "Keep looking. It's there." As if someone could lose a whole highway.

I kept looking, for a while anyway. But I soon lost interest in trying to decipher a map that was like a puzzle with no solution. I finally let it drop into my lap and turned to watch my mother. I knew it was a dangerous thing to let my mind wander too far, but I had to start thinking sometime and it occurred to me that I knew very little of what was actually taking place. For one thing, it didn't seem reasonable for us to be out here in a snowstorm risking our lives. I wondered why, if he really loved her, if he really cared so much, why was he making her drive all this way in such rotten weather? He was already out there. Okay, but if it was so important for us to get there too why didn't he just get in his car, drive back to town, and pick us up? And if the weather had made this impossible, then what were we doing out driving in it? Surely this weekend visit could be safely postponed until another time. Julie and I had survived this long without meeting him. We'd last another week or two. Why was it so urgent?

I had so many questions. But instead of asking them I shifted myself in the seat. I couldn't take the risk of annoying her. I didn't want to throw off her concentration. We were going slowly now, inching our way along through snow falling so thickly it looked like fog. Her hands were wrapped around the wheel, the knuckles knotted white. She was leaning forward, the lines around her mouth rigid, its expression severe. I had to say something, just to get it started, but I realized that making her angry would not work to our advantage. I certainly didn't want her to imagine I was badgering her or trying to provoke an argument. So I asked a question I thought was harmless, one that had been on my mind for days.

"Mom, are you really going to marry him?"

She didn't hesitate.

"Why do you say it like that, Sara? Like you can't believe I'd actually go through with it. You don't want me to, do you?"

"I don't know."

"You're selfish. That's your problem, you know. You don't want me to get married because then I wouldn't have as much time for you. And don't you look at me like that, Sara. I know the way you think. You're worried about not having me to yourself any more, aren't you?"

"I don't know," I said quickly, shifting my weight around, wishing I'd had the sense to keep my mouth shut. "I'm just not sure about this. I guess I don't know if I want a new father yet. That's all."

"Well, get used to the idea real quick because you're going to get one."

I had to look at her this time.

"So when *are* you getting married?"

She glanced at me and then at Julie who had fallen asleep between us.

"It's just a matter of time now," she replied, her voice losing its edge. "We haven't really made any plans yet."

I nodded. That seemed to be the end of it. I didn't want to aggravate her further so I turned to watch the trees and snow through the side window. The rhythm of the moving car began to lull me to sleep. I felt my head nod, and my eyelids became heavy. But then I heard her start talking again, taking up where she'd left off in the voice that I always found so soothing.

"You have to be so patient with these things, Sara," she said. "You don't want to push too hard or muscle in on someone's life. It only scares him away. You have to hold back and work on it slowly. Let him know you're there but don't let him see what you're doing. Tell him you're there for him always. Anytime at all. Philip can call me in the middle of the night and I'll go to him. He knows that. I've offered him my love and my support and whatever else it takes. I'm ready to live with him for the rest of my life."

She laughed.

"I know it sounds kind of nutty to say something like that after only a few months, but it's the truth. It's how I feel. I've let him know I'm prepared to make a commitment, and I am. I'm ready. You know, at first I thought it was just meeting someone new. The novelty of seeing a different face across the table. I felt myself falling for him right away and I thought, you know, there's no way I'm letting anyone get under my skin this easily.

So I resisted what I felt. I even tried to tell myself it was my imagination. I tried to make myself believe I didn't feel anything at all. But that doesn't work for very long. Fooling yourself. Falling in love is a lot like falling asleep. There comes a time when you can't do anything to stop it. It just happens. I was in love long before I was ready to admit it to myself. I just couldn't believe it could be true. Not after all this time. I thought maybe I was sick or something. Now I can see I didn't want it to be true because of how it changed everything. Before, I wouldn't have cared if he never called me again. It would have made no difference. But God! When I realized how I felt, it was like the whole world could go straight to hell and it wouldn't have mattered so long as he phoned. I know, Sara, you don't really understand much of this yet, but take my word for it, you will. You'll learn. We all have to learn. But you can never describe what it's like. Not really. It's different for each of us. For me . . . God! . . . it's like his voice is water and I want to let myself drown in it. Or like when you're dreaming and you sort of know what's going on, and it doesn't make any sense but that doesn't matter because you're there in the middle of it. You understand how you got there and you know why you're there and what's behind it all, the reason for the whole thing, for this dream, and you're about to do something you wouldn't normally do but you can't stop yourself. Well, that's sort of what it's like. That's what love is. The reason for everything you do, the reason for the dream. After a while it keeps you going." She put out her hand. "I know this probably just sounds silly, but it's impossible to explain, especially when you're going through it. Love doesn't follow any rules or anything. It just makes you feel alive. And when I'm with him I feel more alive than I ever have. You'd be surprised. We can have so much fun together just holding hands and walking down the street. Or sitting in a restaurant. Or just lying there looking at each other. I know, I know. It's silly. But I want you to at least try to understand how important this is for me. He asked us to come out to his place for one reason. And when he asks me to marry him I want you to know that I'm going to say yes."

I was sure she didn't really mean for me to say anything, so I didn't. I kept my eyes on her though. She was happy, she'd just said so. But now here she was not smiling, her eyes fixed grimly on this chosen object, this one desire. She wasn't letting anything stand in her way or alter her mind. She couldn't wait for it to happen and far from holding herself back she was doing everything she could to speed it up. I wondered, with a distant tremor in my stomach, if the snow looked any different to her than it did to me.

After a minute or two she said, "This is going to mean a few changes, you know. I hope you don't mind having some brothers and another sister."

She said this casually, as if it were nothing.

"I guess I forgot to tell you he's already married, didn't I?"

I sat dumbly trying to fit this new information in with what she'd already told me. "Brothers?" I asked. My mind grew heated.

"Yes. Philip has two sons. William is fourteen and I think Donald is eleven. I haven't met them yet but I'm sure they're nice boys. His daughter Elizabeth is ten."

I put out my hand and, as if the car had been struck from behind, felt the dashboard pound me. I choked while trying to swallow but I still managed to ask, "Are they all going to be there?" knowing that my horror was apparent and that it would irritate her. I'm not sure why I asked that particular question or if I even really wanted an answer. What if she told me yes, they would all be there? What could I possibly hope to do about it?

I couldn't help wondering too why she'd chosen to wait until now to mention this. Had she been concerned I would have refused to come had I known?

"I'm not sure, Sara. He didn't say. I sort of expect the children might want to stay in the city with their mother today."

"Their mother?"

"Yes! Their mother!"

All at once her voice cut me. Julie moaned in her sleep and pushed up against my arm.

"Don't you dare say another word! People get separations and divorces all the time. There's not one thing wrong with it. And there's nothing wrong with being in the right place at the right time. Philip told me he's been wanting a divorce for years and now I've given him a reason to go ahead with it. I can help him.

I really can. He said so. She yells all the time and won't let him be. She doesn't do anything but make them all miserable. He only wants to get away from her. He told me she's so crazy and hateful that she'll never get to keep the children. That's why when we move in with him there's going to be seven of us. So you better think twice about making a scene. You're going to do just what I say. You're going to smile and be polite no matter how many of them are there. And I don't care *what* you think. I don't want to listen to any whining. I'm not letting you ruin this weekend for me, Sara. If you try I'll stop the car and put you out in the snow. How would you like that?"

I said nothing. I already had enough to think about.

She started fiddling with the radio dial but all the signals were muddled. One station drifted in and out until there was nothing left but hiss and screaming pulses of static. She kept the volume cranked way up as she twisted the knob and when it wouldn't go any further she slapped at the dial and switched the thing off.

"Shit," she muttered.

Julie rubbed her eyes and murmured. My mother glanced coldly in her direction, unconcerned.

We drove in silence.

The snowfall had slackened almost to flurries and for the first time since we started I could sort of make out where we were. On every side clusters of trees rose up and here and there rectangles of cleared farmland slid by. Spirals of smoke drifted from farmhouse chimneys. Normally, this kind of scenery was charming, but today because of the snow it all looked flat and desolate. I couldn't understand why anyone would want to build a big summer house way out here.

Abruptly, without warning, my mother reached across Julie and snatched the paper with the directions from my lap.

"Give me that," she said.

She held it close to her face and then squinted into the distance. Up ahead was a green road sign, but I couldn't read the letters until we got closer and she slowed the car. Then I saw it was two signs on the same post. One said "Exit 62" and the one underneath said "Justine" which I guess was the name of a town. Beside each was an arrow pointing right.

"This is it," she announced as we approached a road branching off the highway. She eased the car on to the ramp.

I held on.

We curled downward and at the bottom she braked to a stop and once more consulted the map before turning left. The unploughed snow lay thick and at first the tires spun uselessly before catching on something and pitching us forward. We drove for a while before I noticed a sign that said, "Justine 20," and after rounding a bend I saw the white landscape laid out flat before us, miles and miles of it. Off to one side a crooked farmhouse tottered behind a busted-up wooden fence. A big tractor lay on its side, rusted to a husk, as if long ago flung there by giants. I looked around but there was nothing else to see. Just flat land and the odd tree, exposed and misshapen by the wind. A few broken boards lay in a heap, the remains of a shack. I didn't panic exactly, but I *was* having trouble breathing. I had to wonder if there wasn't an easier way to get there.

I watched my mother closely for a minute or two. She was pushing her hand through her hair like she did sometimes and for some reason she kept wetting her lips. It occurred to me that we'd brought no food along and I was starting to feel hungry.

"How much further do we have to go?" I asked.

"Not much," she said.

She tried to smile at me, but the smile quickly faded and to hide her face she turned to glance out her side window. I saw her lips move as she spoke to herself.

Between us Julie was still sleeping, her body slumped over with her head resting on my shoulder. She felt hot. My mother stroked her hair briefly, brushing it back from her forehead.

"She's okay," I heard her murmur.

We drove on. It was all farmland and it was flat. I didn't see any other cars, any other movements. A few times the wind tugged at the car and tossed more snow onto our path. I saw another farmhouse. This one was dark and rickety and had no glass in the windows. Snow was heaped up inside.

"How would you like a little brother or sister?"

My mother was watching me and smiling. I shifted Julie's weight from my shoulder and wrapped my arm around her.

"Huh?"

"You heard me. Don't be rude. How would you like to have a little brother or sister?"

Had I missed something?

"I thought you said he had two boys and a girl."

"I'm not talking about that. Use your head. A little brother or sister? A baby?"

"A baby . . . ?"

"That's right. I only found out the other day. God! When I told Philip he was so happy. I couldn't believe it. I thought for sure he'd be mad at me. Anybody else would have. I was trying to reach him all day at his office. I must've left a hundred messages for him to call me. But I guess he was too busy. So I just came out with it when I finally got him. I had to just say it because I thought any second he's going to have to rush off again. So I said it without even letting him catch his breath. 'I'm going to have a baby,' I said. You know what it's like when someone tells you something like that. Something you never expected in a million years. It knocks you off your feet. Poor Philip. He was pretty shocked. But then he was so happy. He didn't seem to mind that I'd called him at his office, even though he told me never to do that."

She shook her head. The smile on her face stretched so wide it hardly seemed real.

"He was so happy," she repeated.

I couldn't think of what to say.

The snow had stopped. Somewhere overhead the cloud cover split open and sunlight sprayed over us. For a moment it warmed my face. I even lifted my hand to shield my eyes. But then, with jolting swiftness – as if a door had been swung shut – the light was cut off. Shadows closed in and it was suddenly so dark it could have been night. There was nothing here. The land was flat and dismal and looked like the ragged end of something. A few buildings were scattered here and there, but they were all beaten down like feeble old men, and some had actually burst open, spilling their contents like rotten fruit. My stomach gurgled. I got the feeling that we'd wandered off the right track and it almost made me think we'd stumbled into one of those nightmare movies where the world looks the same as it always does but somehow you know it's different. It was like falling into a dream and finding yourself to be nowhere, nowhere at all.

I noticed then that the paper had slipped from her lap to the floor of the car. It seemed to me that she'd want to consult it quite soon, when we finally got close to where we were going. But when I bent down to pick it up she said, "Don't bother, Sara. Please."

"Huh?"

"Leave it be."

I paused just long enough to be sure she really meant it. When she didn't say anything else I said, "Okay," and sat back.

At this point I didn't really care what she did. If she felt she could get there without looking at his directions it was fine with me. She'd taken us this far without anything happening; I had no trouble convincing myself she'd take us the rest of the way. But I *was* wishing she wouldn't worry so much. It was like she imagined someone standing right there at the other end waiting to take it all away from her. I knew she'd worked hard for this; I knew it was only because of her that we'd made it this far. But I wanted her to relax for once. She couldn't do anything else now anyway except keep driving.

I wasn't as selfish as she thought. I knew that my happiness wasn't the most important thing in the world. I wasn't about to ruin anything. I was sure I could adapt myself to this new life she was concocting. Wherever we finally ended up, I knew it wouldn't be as bad as where we'd come from. One way or another we'd all be better off even if our gains were modest.

I looked at her again. This was one of those times when she should have been happy and smiling. But her mouth was all flattened down and her lips were pushed together into a sour pout. I saw her eyes darting back and forth. She squinted into the distance and then started muttering to herself. It seemed strange that even after finding someone she liked and getting him to like her, she still behaved as if everything were on the line, as if she had no idea what sort of trouble she was getting herself into. And I thought what a great pity, because who could tell when another moment like this would come along?

## ELISE LEVINE

# *You Are You Because Your Little Dog Loves You*

I'm going to come clean here. This is how it works.

First you're ordering drinks, nuts, thinking Merri or Melinda will be green as fish guts. Before the jet's off the ground you're in the rear bathroom with Jimmy or Steve, doing what you do best. Later, higher still, you find crushed velveteen – purple, blue, or black – in every seat. Also, cut-out stars, the moon. Sequins. Satisfaction. Girl, give your head a shake!

Then more drinks, hits to be dropped. The plane's a tin pot banging against a hot-sink sun. Dick or Mick or Steve – the glory-boy with the curling mane – says, The bitch. He announces this carefully, very British. You think you're so out of it you're not sure what he means. But what you really are is lying across the aisle, and someone lays a boot against your throat in a curious slow-time pulse as he forgets to apply pressure, then with a start remembers again.

From inside the plane the sky looks like nothing, upending blue blank as a baby's first dream. Tin-skin, that blue leaking in. Nothing to get through. Nothing to lose. Mystery. Sheen on your arm from the drooly boys. Somewhere someone's puking. And thirsty. Someone says, The stinking bitch.

Fifteen's already old, older than you are now at 36. When you're 15, and your dim mother's ditched you in Vancouver, and it's a

West Coast winter raining everywhere all over you, what's the story going to be?

You were hatched from a bombshell of a woman who'd torn through her early life like it was a house on fire, until the doors to all the rooms in her head clapped shut against mayhem rising like a wail. By 30, she was easily exhausted. She had the fatty eyelids and slow lips, the rounded Barbra Streisand rear of the eternal émigré, Montreal to Toronto to the land of milk and honey where she waited tables in the dining room of the Sylvia Hotel on Vancouver's English Bay, a place of only money and no-money, grey wandering rain.

You were seven when you washed up with her on that shore. She had named you Mimi, after *her* mother – an extravagant gesture from a woman for whom the past was a vanishing point, a scrap of an old language murmured in the ear to quiet a child, something odd, *Shpeelt, zit ah-zoy goot, ah fawks-trawt*, please play a fox-trot, a leftover from an erased world. What did she see when she looked your way? You were half her, half not – in a world where half was nothing, not one thing and not another.

You lived in an efficiency in the back of the Sylvia, facing a parking lot. During the day you'd drift along the seawall walk in front of the hotel, too-big red rubber boots like boats on your feet, an umbrella with pink and blue poodles floating above your head. Other children in brightly coloured raincoats and pants bobbed between sandy ribs of beach like balloons tethered to diligent mothers. The rain-scored horizon like steel wool.

At night, windows shut tight against raccoons prowling the ledges, red eyes blinking from between the vines that smother the Sylvia's façade. Lights out, the TV on, its blue buzzing your mother's wood-red hair until you think she might disappear in a cathode rush. Take that, Toronto! the weatherman says in winter. Fifty-seven here in Vancouver today. The rustling notes, each pinprick of sound, pushing pictures whole into your head. Take that! Your own giddy brain your mother's bright TV dream. Slow dissolve. Fade to black.

You see this mostly in black and white, the occasional swab of colour: a man on stilts. He unfolds like a flower from the side door of an old van parked next to the seawall in front of the hotel. With great bows and flourishes, his oversize Stetson slipping back and forth across his small head, he mounts a six-foot-tall candy-striped bicycle.

Wind whips sand to tumbleweeds along the walk. The sky is barely spitting now, though still low and dark. It's three on a winter afternoon. In good weather, portrait painters mass like primulas along the walk near Denman Street. But on this day any stragglers have packed it in by 3:15. At 3:17, the wind drops like a stone.

The man wheels past you then stops, carefully placing each stilt on the ground, leaving faint hoof prints behind him. He turns around and nods once, smiling, as if at some fabulous secret.

Beyond him you can see bluish-backed gulls rising and falling in the sky like breath. Beyond them, the blue-chested mountains. For once the rain has fully stopped. The night will be clear, the sunset yielding to a sky plush with stars, the lights of the ships at anchor even now beginning to pulse above the tarry water.

He cocks his head, as if listening to the tankers waiting in the bay. A murmuring wind. Impossible high notes, low notes. Laughter and applause. The clink of loose change tuning up like an orchestra. At this moment everything seems possible.

He turns his head towards you again. That same slow smile, his mouth such a miracle of makeup you think each syllable he utters stitches the newly arisen half-moon to the night, as if it had been a prop waiting backstage. His teeth like polished seashells. Through a tear in the left leg of his pink pin-striped pants you can see wood, metal, something long and cold, hard.

In the months that followed, your mother managed to unglue herself from her TV, unwrapping herself like some fresh thing from skeins of fatigue long enough for Mr. Long Legs to woo her. As if some dimly remembered past echoed in her ear. *Please play a fox-trot.*

Stiltless, without his costumes (which he made himself), your mother's beau was tiny, delicate. Also, breathtakingly penniless, buying roses with money he stole from your mother's purse while she showered. He had the heartbreak allure of the cheerfully insolvent, the seductiveness of their fugitive ease.

Mimi, my lovely girl, he'd say, slipping a slender finger and thumb into your mother's wallet, Is the coast clear?

Let the show begin! He moved out of his van and into the Sylvia with you and your mother. He brought with him a scrappy white terrier with caramel patches on its face and behind. He quelled your mother's resistance with a radiant upsweep of canary yellow, crepe-clad arms. What's a family without a dog? he asked, standing in the doorway. The dog – called Alfie, after the Michael Caine movie – incautiously sniffed every piece of furniture in the cramped apartment as your mother peered after it, saying nothing. She looked both hopeful and afraid. The alchemy of her lover's dreams could work wonders.

The dog ran loose on the beach every day while Mr. Long Legs worked the seawall walk bestride his bicycle, floridly addressing the mothers of small children he'd take for rides at a dollar a pop. When a bus burst the dog at the seams one milky white morning, delicate entrails festooned Davie Street like streamers.

That afternoon, Mr. Long Legs pulled you onto his lap, drummed his thumbs on your knees. He smelled of the Old Spice your mother had given him. He touched a finger to the tip of your nose.

Hey! he said, as if he'd just had an idea. Alfie still loves you.

You sat very still as a breeze nudged the edges of the heavy beige curtains. Water streamed through the ivy around the window. He seemed to know something you didn't. After a moment you said, Alfie's dead.

Mr. Long Legs pulled his head away, raised his eyebrows, and opened his pinprick brown eyes as wide as they would go. He held his hands palm up and lifted his narrow shoulders.

Dead? he said, deeply shocked. You think so? I think Alfie's in heaven, barking and peeing, trying to sniff the ladies.

He closed his eyes. His lips relaxed, drooping at the edges. He looked tired and sad.

Just think, he said. Heaven.

For your mother, each time Mr. Long Legs left it was forever. He'd be gone for weeks at a time. He always came back broke.

Your mother would unfasten herself from her TV long enough for tears, wall pounding. Once he stood by helplessly as she ripped up his pink pin-striped pants. When she finished he held the shreds to his face and wept, stopping every now and then to glance sorrowfully at the craters in the wall plaster. Suddenly he brightened. He lay the rags on the kitchen table. He took out a polka-dot hankie and wiped his eyes, blew his nose. He put his hankie away. He puffed out his slender chest and the creases fell away one by one from his just-past-its-prime brow.

You could almost hear the fresh cha-ching as he gazed tenderly at the pink strips on the table. Money, money, money. He'd milk this one for sure.

His eyes were shining. So what do you think it's worth? he said.

When forever came for good you were 12. Three years later your mother had scraped up enough to return alone to Ontario, tail tucked between her skinny varicosed legs.

She didn't have enough for the taxi to the airport, an extravagance you paid for with your earnings from your after-school and weekend job at Record City. You made less than minimum wage, but you saw the position as entry-level. You hoped to get an office job at a record company when you turned 16.

As you stood on the sidewalk outside the Sylvia, your mother rolled down the window of the taxi. Her face looked puffy, her drawn-on eyebrows faintly askew. Rain grizzled the beach across the street. Much of the bay itself had vanished from sight.

Did you hate her then?

She was your mother. She rolled up the taxi window, which immediately covered with steam.

You, age 15: ready for the bright hereafter. Left to your own devices you made yourself over as if you were the high alembic of every sulky *Creem* queen, each Bebe and Miss Pamela and Patti. Kohl-eyed, lips frosted high-glam white. If you weren't one thing, then you could be another.

Magic. All the way down the coast you learned the hit and bang came first and last. In between you learned about girlish boys, their rainbow perfection. Working your way up. Competing with Fawns, Dawns, and Merri Madrigals for the well-bred L.A. record exec who before the age of 13 thought there was no such thing as a poor Jew. The lowly drummer with his high hats and jelly rolls. A long-tongued slender-hipped lead guitarist. A Jimmy, Mick, or Keith. *Both* Keiths. Wheeling above you, huge as constellations.

Colour this red for passion.

The biggest prize? To be queen for a night on the private jet, the high priestess of higher love, for which you'd leave Lady Jane and Prudence below, weeping in the wings.

This was what you craved, in order to have something over other people: the *up there*, honey and smoke. The ample horizon a streak of blue beyond money and reason, glimpsed from between a guy's skinny legs, his velvet-clad butt and stick-figure bulge. Dry ice machines lisping eternity. Everything you can't quite remember – magic, mystery, an electric-blue boot bruising your throat while all the boys love you – a feckless drug of choice.

You never knew nice.

Hello? Earth to? You were 25, overripe. You couldn't decide whether Toronto's spill of light from above Pearson International was the circuit board for some third-rate sound and lighting show hard-wired to your limbic system or merely a sorry child's spill of beads. You were broke, electric with it because the truth is, poverty can elevate: that snap and crackle of fear can take you right out of your mind.

You called your mother from the airport. She hung up on you. When you walked into her apartment in Whitby she slapped your face, then she cried hard.

Eye concealer shone beneath her eyes like half moons. Her once-beautiful hair stuck out uncertainly from her head, a dry sprig of curl here, a greasy tendril there. Her nose was dripping ferociously. She held her arms out to you then quickly dropped them.

It's me, Mimi, you said, not sure she recognized you. You'd always had this shyness with each other. That same shyness you'd come to recognize between people who've slept together long enough to find themselves in that remote place where the touching stops – each of you bedding down with the other's fantasy, someone else's breasts sliding in ones or twos across your body as clouds might drift across the sky – and where all you are is part and parcel of these loveless moments, grasping the metal bed frame to keep from falling, swaying to beat hell, bleating *mumma* like a lamb, wounded bear.

Baby, you'd say to whoever you were with. Or some other girlfriend would. These guys always had someone.

What you have is this: the sins of the mothers, for you are of a generation that never forgives. Whose pain exceeds? Outlives? In a world where half is nothing, love only endures.

Place is a thing to be moved through, like so much backdrop. At 25, your choice was classic Canadian: Toronto or the boonies in a southern Ontario of subdivisions, a culture of commuters and megamusicals, the province itself one vast bedroom community endlessly unfolding like a house of cards gone amok. To the near north and east of Toronto, a scattering of century-old farms and red-brick houses among the townhouse developments and outlandish executive homes, the new and the old mixing it up. In Whitby, your mother continued her disappearing act syllable by syllable until she couldn't care for herself any more. You moved her out of the tiny apartment and into the local psychiatric hospital. By then you had a job in a Stouffville beauty shop. You bought an ancient white Monte Carlo. One night in an Oshawa bar you clambered on stage to screech along with the house band in front of a mostly auto-worker audience too toasted to notice you couldn't actually sing. With them you could play the loud exotic, queen of the cross-eyed Jacks and horned shills, having slept with the stars, the magicians and kings you once collected like cards. Your veiled past hinting at marvellous futures.

What a joke. Standing up there on that puny Oshawa stage fear would snake around your throat, shredding your voice to rat-shit. It was perfect: you were giving up nothing, all your nothing years, because nothing could be everything in this nowhere place. You imagined the dull grey sounds like ghostly lullabies your mother never sang.

You met your best friend Joy in that bar, on a rainy Tuesday night. The place was half deserted, and between sets she bought you drink after drink.

Mimi, she said, around the seventh Jack and coke. That's a name.

She punched your arm and snorted through her stubby nose, as if she'd said something hilarious. She was short and thick, roughly made up, foundation caking in her laugh lines. At 30 she wasn't hard to impress since she'd never been anywhere in her life.

Just before the bartender cut you both off, Joy gave you her phone number – her brother's, really, since at the time she lived in an apartment in back of his farmhouse where he ran a small boarding stable. He was previously married, had a daughter. He had a couple of thoroughbreds. His name was Walker.

Now you were laughing. Walker – a ridiculous name, as if he were a southern gentleman. You had to hand it to this old-Markham world clinging stubbornly – despite no money and no reason, despite wholesale land expropriations for the never-to-be-built Pickering airport – to its dream of itself, a dream fuelled by a hatred and fear of the immigrant city, the greedy city.

Within a week you drove your Monte Carlo out to visit. You quickly understood how Walker's unstinting bulk and that of his horses could be beneath you. And how Walker could both hate and love you for your boys, for how you'd loved them all, for he was heedless of awe, a stickler for details, each one a stitch of blood on white rayon panties, the red in his head that made him so angry. It was how you got to him – that you knew some of the things people do. Heigh-ho, Silver! Wild girls and horses! A masked avenger, riding to your own rescue, having found a way to still be tall in the saddle. And all that.

Eleven years later you still pretend to do it well, needing at least this much to believe in: that you can still be above it all. That you can still know yourself in this way.

Yesterday, Walker pulled the sliding door to the arena open and stepped inside to watch you ride. The horse shied from him, danced beneath you every couple of strides to the top of the ring. Your legs jerked like a puppet's.

Keep your hands down, he shouted. As if you'd never heard that before. Keep your legs still.

He stooped as you neared the bottom of the arena. As you passed him he uncoiled, tossing oiled dirt that flummoxed your head. That horse's neck like a giraffe's hit your nose. A second later the ground pummelled your chest.

Wasn't the first time you were winded, sucking nothing but queer sounds so unlike singing you feared someone else had entered you. Something else outside going, Shoosh, aroo, shoosh.

Then there was Walker standing over you, looking. He leaned closer. Laughed.

Fucked up again, he said. It was how he loved you.

Later he stood in his kitchen and said, The years haven't been good to you.

What's good? was all you could reply. Your mouth felt reamed with mud.

You, 36 years old, walking slowly across the floor, the tick of the kitchen clock like a warning shout. Dishes drying in the blue rack, bills in a careful stack on the table. You shut the screen door quietly behind you, stepping into sunlight thick as ice-glare.

Good for Walker. Good – that you tried hard for him? A trick for which you've lately lost the knack.

Walker's daughter, Jena, was in the barn when you walked in. She was lounging on the steps to the tack room, twisting a slick strand of dirty blond hair around a finger, using her breath to puff up her bangs from her creamy, slightly moist face. Sweet 16. She tugged at a 10-carat gold chain around her neck and rocked absently back and forth. Her stomach formed rolls beneath her tight T-shirt. You could understand how her mother felt about her.

You nudged one step past the girl and sat down. She tugged harder at the gold chain and stiffened. She half turned her body and twisted her head to look at you. Nothing showed in her small eyes, as usual when she looked your way. You thought how unknown this girl was to you, how opposite you she was. After all, she had Walker's love. You knew one day she would leave, taking it with her.

Get lost! you wanted to say. That's the trick most worth mastering, to become a place the heart can safely grow fonder – an after-image, a faint blush of a thing, some vaguely remembered history of secret feints and thrusts. Even your drably desirous mother roamed each night down Whitby's bleary psychiatric home hallway, an orderly in hot pursuit. Your mother's fuzzy green bathrobe gaping, her skinny breasts wriggling like worms.

In the box stall across from you a horse gently weaved. Barn kittens mock-hunted field mice in and out of the standing stalls at the other end of the barn. By the door, black ants reeled like drunks over the husk of a June bug. The mother cat sat in the dust and groomed her paws. The lardy girl beside you was barely breathing. Maybe she was already gone. You realized with a start that underneath that pale-pink T she was as familiar to you as some pallid straw-stuffed animal you'd misplaced long enough to have forgotten. Love's puling malcontent, soaked in neglect, encrusted with discontent, like an old mattress put out by the side of the road. She could almost be your daughter. For a moment you were as confused as the stammerings and velvety whoofs of the neighbouring horses.

You shifted slightly and placed a finger on her wrist, tapped lightly. She shivered a little, afraid or embarrassed. Maybe hopeful. You thought if you touched her harder she might cry, laugh, confide, opening up to you like a fat piñata whose hidden treasures you'd only squander.

You shoved to your feet, stepping past her into the aisle. You clapped your hands to startle the horse out of his tranced weaving. When he stopped you stroked his nose. Without turning you said, Still here?

She was standing close behind you. You could feel her breath coming hard on your neck. Her face, when you veered your head sharp right to look at her, was splotchy, red and white like a checkered flag. The split ends of her hair seemed to rise and twine, vaporize almost, in the mote-veiled light. When she spoke her voice was thick, a sneer or a choke.

Still here? she mimicked. Like fucking duh. Are *you*?

This morning Walker woke you early. A bird called outside the window. The bed sheets cooled against your feet. He ran his cracked hands over your stomach, up and down your arms. You turned over, rump up. When you woke again the bird was gobbling on the window ledge. Walker was sitting on the edge of the bed, half-dressed. He'd been up already. His head hung low, almost touching his knees. The bed rattled as he coughed. Christ, he was saying. He pressed the heel of his hand to his forehead.

You'd heard the Trans Am pull up in the drive around two in the morning. You'd heard Jena close the door to her room, and something heavy bumping down the stairs with her. You hoped she was gone for good.

Walker's cough worsened. His shoulders heaved. You unwrapped yourself from the bedsheet and sat up. At least you could have this satisfaction: now Walker himself knew what it was like to have someone slip him like sunlight in November.

The bird outside the window had stopped singing or had flown away. You put a hand to Walker's grey wavy hair. Well?

Well what? he said. Happy now?

You had to stop yourself from grabbing a chunk of hair and yanking.

Fuck me to tears, Walker said, dropping his head into his hands, rubbing his face. Get the fuck out.

When you got up you smoked and peed. Smoked. Otherwise your hands were empty.

You got dressed. Went outside, got in your car. Drove around for hours. Past the Stouffville flea market, out to Musselman's Lake. Up and down the concession roads, past red-brick farmhouses with crumpled barns. The radio on though not loud.

Barely listening. Trying to figure what you could still get away with. Trying to tell yourself you could still enjoy the show.

Only hours ago you parked your ancient Monte Carlo in Walker's drive. You knocked softly on his kitchen door. When he came you turned your head away. His small bay mare stood quietly under the big maple in the front paddock, half asleep, though her tail swished unceasingly.

When you glanced again through the screen, Walker was looking at you through half-shut eyes, his naked belly massively overhanging his jeans. You could hear him suck his cigarette and move it from one side of his mouth to the other.

Give it up already! You slammed the door to the Monte Carlo. Through the open window you yelled, Still a treat, aren't you, Walker. He moved a little behind the screen, like the shadow of a boulder. He'd always been like that for you, a rocky overhang beneath which you slipped along the stony scree of your failures and his: that he was the wrong one for you, the right one. The right one.

You turned the engine on and drove past, heading towards the first barn. You heard him behind you now on the drive, shouting, Don't tell me your troubles. Your tongue rasped in your mouth. You opened your hands, flexed them like a cat might its paws. You turned the car off and leaned your head against the steering wheel, Walker's ducks and geese barking like dogs, a dog barking. Crow. Wind in the trees. You'd never heard such stillness, falling in lush sweeps like a first heavy snowfall, the air softly smacking your skin. The afternoon shadows a cold locket of memory in which a man on stilts groans backward like an old machine, into the terrible distance before floating upward to fade above the stars and waiting ships of English Bay.

You are still poor as the day. The crisp 10s and 20s, the crackling Gs of Ontario fall from you like dead leaves. No one in this dying province has the heart to sweep them away. This was the dominion you thought you'd never bargained for, where the future closes over you like a curtain of snow.

Then Walker, his shadow another blindness brindling the drive shimmery with heat.

Get real, he shouted. Don't you know when to quit? You take that fucker on the road I guarantee he'll come back without you. Leave you in the dirt.

He turned back towards the house. He jerked both arms out at his sides, waved them above his fat head. The big bastard was still yammering.

So go on, he brayed. But I told you. End of story.

Walker's wrong. Out on the road there's sky spanked by cloud. The stillness of the late afternoon. The playful buck the horse gave when the two-ton passed hauling a flat-bed trailer. After, the horse hanging loose, empty as a balloon beneath you. Your hands – which you remember to keep down – are light on his mouth. Between your legs he's jittery with flies and nothing else, not even the hot afternoon shivery with breeze. No end in sight to this bright blister of day.

Maybe the dead don't want you to rescue them. Maybe the dead just want to sleep, in their rattling dresses and shard suits, chattering with cold under the noonday sun. Scant-witted in their bugbear stupor, they're wedged deep in the earth you have always loathed. Maybe they think you've got it all wrong.

Your mother is there and late this afternoon you'll grab her arm and yank hard. You idiot, you'll yell, How could you be so stupid? – because for your mother love was a fat ruinous thing, pancake makeup, dimpled cooing in late afternoon, nothing you think that should matter to her any more.

Mom, you'll screech, How could you? So much for nothing!

Drop the lathered reins. The horse cascades his neck to drink from the nearly dried-up creek. On the low bank above, wands of dry grass candle the ground. The horse chuffs, smoke-eater, big beast between your legs to shake a bouldered shoulder at so small a fly.

Don't move. Never let go. Keep your hands low, as Walker always says you should.

City traffic from nearby Steeles Avenue chimes coolly but here it's August hot. The tall trees creak. In the neighbouring fields a great demon baling machine parts the blond grasses and dust vapours the road. You've stopped to linger in the cemetery and at this moment you're sitting pretty while your mother leaks secrets into the earth. From the ninth concession line traffic makes a slow cortège into a city of dust where at night sirens unravel sound from the faded stars as bats scratch the dark air. If this were late fall your breath would hang in front of you, heavy white sheets wet from so much drinking. You'd think the boys you love have left you.

Your mother was a rough woman, given to fits and starts. Yanking you along an icy Toronto sidewalk when you were five, gripping your arm so tight it hurt. Riding a two-wheeler for the first time when you were six, you reached out to steady yourself, dizzy from the sudden spectacle of hard ground. First thing you grabbed was her arm. She bruised easily. It was always like this: neither of you knew what to do once you'd grabbed hold.

A dry breeze twitches the uncut grass. A sudden alertness in the world. Thrash chords, you think. A whisper-bright tremolo. Anything. You can almost hear the dead sigh damply beneath you and sink lower into the earth.

For now you're saying nothing. Your mother's saying nothing back.

Maybe the dead don't want to be saved, the memory of them stashed away like so much coin, booty for the half-living. Maybe the dead hold on to their hats whichever way the wind blows, to keep their hands from waving goodbye. Or hello.

# About the Authors

**John Brooke** is a writer/translator living in Montreal. He has had three essays published in the "Facts & Arguments" column of the *Globe and Mail*, and recently completed a three-part "moral mythology" entitled *The Book of Aliette*. "The Finer Points of Apples" is his first published short story. He is at work on a collection about life in Montreal around the time of the 1995 referendum.

**Ian Colford** has had stories published in Canadian literary journals such as *Grain*, *Event*, and the *Antigonish Review*, and online in the *Blue Moon Review* and the *Gutter Voice*. He has completed a novel and collection of stories and is currently working on a second novel. From 1995 to 1998 he edited *Pottersfield Portfolio*, a literary journal based in Halifax, Nova Scotia, where he works as a reference librarian at Dalhousie University and lives in a 130-year-old house with his wife, Collette, and their cats, Gatsby and Seamus.

**Libby Creelman** is a St. John's writer. Her fiction has appeared in *TickleAce*, the *Fiddlehead*, and *Pottersfield Portfolio*. She is currently at work on a collection of stories, entitled *A Walk in Paradise*.

**Michael Crummey** was born and raised in Newfoundland, and now lives in Kingston, Ontario. He has published two books of poetry, *Arguments with Gravity* and *Hard Light*. His first book of stories, *Flesh and Blood*, was published in August 1998.

**Stephen Guppy** has published a book of short stories and a collection of poems. His book-length poem *Blind Date with the Angel: The Diane Arbus Poems* will be published in the fall of 1998. He has recently completed a second book of stories, *The Origin of Country Music*, and a lengthy novel, *Skyhooks*, set in

Richland, Washington, and the Funeral Mountains of western Nevada. He teaches Fiction and Poetry in the Creative Writing program at Malaspina University-College in Nanaimo.

**Jane Eaton Hamilton** is the author of a children's book, *Jessica's Elevator*, two poetry books, *Body Rain* and *Steam-Cleaning Love*, and a volume of short fiction, *July Nights*. Her writing has appeared in such places as the *New York Times* and *Seventeen*, and has won numerous awards, including the Federation of B.C. Writers Fiction Award and the *Event* Non-Fiction Award. She is currently working on a novel.

**Elise Levine**'s short story collection, *Driving Men Mad*, was published in 1995. Her work has appeared in *Coming Attractions 1994*, *The Journey Prize Anthology 7*, and *Concrete Forest*. She lives in Chicago, where she is currently working on a novel.

**Jean McNeil** of Cape Breton, Nova Scotia, was born in 1968. Since 1991 she has lived in London, England. Her novel, *Hunting Down Home*, was published in the U.K. and Canada in 1996, and is forthcoming in the U.S. She is also the author of the *Rough Guide to Costa Rica*, and a co-author of the *Rough Guide to Central America*. A novel and a collection of short stories, *Nights in a Foreign Country*, are forthcoming. "Bethlehem" was the co-winner of the 1997 *Prism international* fiction competition.

**Liz Moore** lives in Kingsville, Ontario, where, thanks to a grant from the Canada Council, she is working on a collection of short stories. She has been published in *Pottersfield Portfolio* and the *Antigonish Review* and twice won the Atlantic Writing Competition.

**Edward O'Connor** works as a textbook editor with a publishing company in Toronto. His stories have appeared in a number of magazines, including the *Antigonish Review*, the *Dalhousie Review*, the *Seattle Review*, *Prairie Fire*, *Quarry*, and the *New*

*Quarterly*. He is assembling a collection of short stories that are divided between settings in Ontario and Florida.

**Tim Rogers** grew up in North Bay, Ontario, and is now attending graduate school at Carnegie Mellon University in Pittsburgh. He published his first story in *Aberrations* (San Francisco) and received an honourable mention in *Books In Canada*'s undergraduate writing contest in 1993. He was the winner of the 1994 Tom York Award at the University of Waterloo. His first Canadian publication was with the *New Quarterly*. Currently he is working on a short story cycle, of which "Scars and Other Presents" is the first.

**Denise Ryan** is a recent graduate of the Creative Writing program at UBC. Her fiction has won numerous awards and appeared in *Prairie Fire*, *B&A*, and *Event*. Born in San Francisco and raised in Toronto, she has lived in Paris, Mexico, Manhattan, and Flin Flon. She makes her home in Vancouver, with a sweetie named Chris, and a cat named Gordito. Denise is a regular contributor to *Vancouver Magazine* and the *Georgia Straight*.

**Madeleine Thien** lives in Vancouver where she works as promotions assistant for Press Gang Publishers. Her fiction has appeared in *Event*, and she was a finalist for the 1997 CBC Canadian Literary Award for fiction.

**Cheryl Tibbetts** was born in Halifax and has been living in Toronto for several years. She twice won first prize in *Storyteller*'s Great Canadian Story Contest (1997 and 1996); and also won first prize in the 1996 Short Story Contest of the *Toronto Star*. Her work has also appeared in the *Globe and Mail*, the 1996 *Winners' Circle* anthology of the Canadian Authors Association, *Contemporary Verse*, and other publications. She has received a Toronto Arts Council Grant for her first novel, which, along with a collection of short stories, is currently in progress.

# About the Contributing Journals

**Event** is published three times a year by Douglas College in New Westminster, B.C. It focuses on fiction, poetry, and reviews by new and established writers, and every spring it runs a creative non-fiction contest. *Event* has won national awards for its writers. Editor: Calvin Wharton. Fiction editor: Christine Dewar. Submissions and correspondence: P.O. Box 2503, New Westminster, B.C., V3L 5B2.

**Grain,** "Food For Your Brain," magazine provides readers with fine, fresh writing by new and established writers of poetry and prose, four times a year. Published by the Saskatchewan Writers Guild, *Grain* has earned national and international recognition for its distinctive literary content. Editor: J. Jill Robinson. Prose Editor: Connie Gault. Poetry Editor: Tim Lilburn. Submissions and correspondence: Box 1154, Regina, Saskatchewan, S4P 3B4. E-mail: grain.mag@sasknet.sk.ca Web site: http://www.skwriter.com

**Kairos** is a literary/arts anthology that was started in 1989 by the faculty of the Language Studies Department of Mohawk College in Hamilton. It is now published independently and released annually in the fall. *Kairos* looks for previously unpublished short fiction, excerpts from novels, non-fiction, short (or excerpted) plays, and poetry. Submissions: P.O. Box 33533, Hamilton, Ontario, L8P 4X4.

**The Malahat Review** publishes mostly fiction and poetry and includes a substantial review article in each issue. It is open to dramatic works, so long as they lend themselves to the page; it welcomes literary works that defy easy generic categorization. Acting Editor: Marlene Cookshaw. Assistant Editor: Lucy Bashford. Submissions and correspondence: University of Victoria, P.O. Box 1700 Stn. CSC, Victoria, B.C., V8W 2Y2.

**The New Quarterly** publishes a lively and eclectic mix of fiction and poetry plus views from the inside of the writer's craft. Winner of the gold medal for fiction at the National Magazine Awards for the last two years, as well as making regular appearances in *The Journey Prize Anthology*, *The New Quarterly* shows off the work of established writers alongside that of newcomers. Good talk, a good read, and all at a good price ($21.40 for four issues)! Submissions and correspondence: ELPP, PAS 2082, University of Waterloo, Waterloo, Ontario, N2L 3G1. E-mail: mmerikle@watarts.uwaterloo.ca Web site: http://watarts.uwaterloo.ca/^^mmerikle/newquart.html

**Pottersfield Portfolio** is a tri-annual journal publishing fiction, poetry, essays, and book reviews. Founded in 1979, it accepts submissions from any geographical region and has published the work of Governor General Award winners along with writers publishing for the first time. The type of work published in *Pottersfield Portfolio* ranges across a broad spectrum from the traditional to the unusual and innovative. Editor: Ian Colford; Fiction Editor: Karen Smythe. Submissions and correspondence: P.O. Box 27094, Halifax, N.S., B3H 4M8. E-mail (for queries only): aw486@chebucto.ns.ca Web Site: http://chebucto.ns.ca/Culture/WRNS/pottersfield/

**Prairie Fire** is a quarterly magazine of contemporary Canadian writing which regularly publishes stories, poems, book reviews, and visual art by emerging as well as established writers and artists. *Prairie Fire*'s editorial mix also occasionally features critical and personal essays, interviews with authors, and readers' letters. *Prairie Fire* publishes a fiction issue every summer. Some of *Prairie Fire*'s most popular issues have been double-sized editions on multicultural themes, individual authors, and different genres. *Prairie Fire* publishes writing from, and has readers in, virtually all parts of Canada. Editor: Andris Taskans; Fiction Editors: Heidi Harms, Susan Rempel Letkemann, and Joan Thomas. Submissions and correspondence: Rm. 423-100 Arthur St., Winnipeg, Manitoba, R3B 1H3.

**Prism international** has published, since 1959, work by writers both new and established, Canadian and international. Its editors look for first-class, innovative fiction, poetry, drama, and creative non-fiction, in English or English translation. *Prism* instituted the annual Earle Birney Prize for Poetry in 1997, and runs one of the most popular and long-standing annual fiction contests in Canada. In addition, *Prism* publishes one-third of each issue on its website at http://www.arts.ubc.ca/prism/; it was one of the first periodicals in Canada to pay contributors for electronic rights. Currently the editors are Jeremiah Aherne, Natalie Meisner, and Miranda Pearson. Request for guidelines or submissions: *Prism international*, Department of Creative Writing, Buchanan E462-1866 Main Mall, Vancouver, British Columbia, V6T 1Z1. E-mail: prism@unixg.ubc.ca (e-mail submissions are welcome; query for guidelines).

**Storyteller**, "Canada's Short Story Magazine," aims to help bring the popular short story back into the mainstream of Canadian fiction. It publishes a wide variety of styles and genres, with the focus on entertainment. Comedy, mystery, Canadiana, adventure, science fiction, and more combine to produce a different package every issue. This diversity, along with the large number of stories published, makes *Storyteller* unique among Canadian magazines. "The Flowers of Africville" won *Storyteller*'s 1997 Great Canadian Story Contest, an annual event which invites writers to produce a story that could only happen in Canada. Subscription and submission information: *Storyteller*, 43 Lightfoot Place, Kanata, Ontario, K2L 3M3. Web site: http:// www.direct-internet.net/~stories

**This Magazine** is Canada's best-known alternative magazine of politics and culture. Thirty-two years old, *This* publishes a unique mix of literature, poetry, investigative journalism, and analysis, plus literary journalism and arts reporting. Devoted to publishing the best new work of emerging and established writers and poets, *This* continues to win both National Magazine Awards (nine in 1997 alone) and other kudos for its intelligence, wit, and innovation. Editor: Andrea Curtis. Submissions and correspondence: *This Magazine*, 401 Richmond St. W. #396, Toronto, Ontario, M5V 3A8. E-mail: thismag@web.net

**TickleAce** is a semi-annual literary magazine that publishes fiction, poetry, book reviews, interviews, and visual art. Now in its third decade, the award-winning magazine focuses on the words and images of contributors in its own province but includes as well a fine selection of good work from across Canada and beyond. Decidedly eclectic in subject, form, and flavour, *TickleAce* offerings include pieces by the internationally renowned, the emerging artist, and the talented first-timer. Editor: Bruce Porter. Submissions and subscription information: P.O. Box 5353, St. John's, Newfoundland, A1C 5W2.

Submissions were also received from the following journals:

*The Antigonish Review*
(Antigonish, N.S.)

*Backwater Review*
(Ottawa, Ont.)

*B&A*
(Toronto, Ont.)

*The Capilano Review*
(North Vancouver, B.C.)

*Descant*
(Toronto, Ont.)

*Exile*
(Toronto, Ont.)

*The Fiddlehead*
(Frederiction, N.B.)

*Green's Magazine*
(Regina, Sask.)

*NeWest Review*
(Saskatoon, Sask.)

*Other Voices*
(Edmonton, Alta.)

*Parchment*
(Toronto, Ont.)

*The Prairie Journal of Canadian Literature*
(Calgary, Alta.)

*Queen's Quarterly*
(Kingston, Ont.)

*The Toronto Review of Contemporary Writing Abroad*
(Toronto, Ont.)

## The Journey Prize Anthology
## List of Previous Contributing Authors

* Winners of the $10,000 Journey Prize
** Co-winners of the $10,000 Journey Prize

1
1989

Ven Begamudré, "Word Games"
David Bergen, "Where You're From"
Lois Braun, "The Pumpkin-Eaters"
Constance Buchanan, "Man with Flying Genitals"
Ann Copeland, "Obedience"
Marion Douglas, "Flags"
Frances Itani, "An Evening in the Café"
Diane Keating, "The Crying Out"
Thomas King, "One Good Story, That One"
Holley Rubinsky, "Rapid Transits"*
Jean Rysstad, "Winter Baby"
Kevin Van Tighem, "Whoopers"
M.G. Vassanji, "In the Quiet of a Sunday Afternoon"
Bronwen Wallace, "Chicken 'N' Ribs"
Armin Wiebe, "Mouse Lake"
Budge Wilson, "Waiting"

2
1990

André Alexis, "Despair: Five Stories of Ottawa"
Glen Allen, "The Hua Guofeng Memorial Warehouse"
Marusia Bociurkiw, "Mama, Donya"
Virgil Burnett, "Billfrith the Dreamer"
Margaret Dyment, "Sacred Trust"
Cynthia Flood, "My Father Took a Cake to France"*
Douglas Glover, "Story Carved in Stone"
Terry Griggs, "Man with the Axe"
Rick Hillis, "Limbo River"

Thomas King, "The Dog I Wish I Had, I Would Call It Helen"
K.D. Miller, "Sunrise Till Dark"
Jennifer Mitton, "Let Them Say"
Lawrence O'Toole, "Goin' to Town with Katie Ann"
Kenneth Radu, "A Change of Heart"
Jenifer Sutherland, "Table Talk"
Wayne Tefs, "Red Rock and After"

3
1991

Donald Aker, "The Invitation"
Anton Baer, "Yukon"
Allan Barr, "A Visit from Lloyd"
David Bergen, "The Fall"
Rai Berzins, "Common Sense"
Diana Hartog, "Theories of Grief"
Diane Keating, "The Salem Letters"
Yann Martel, "The Facts Behind the Helsinki Roccamatios"*
Jennifer Mitton, "Polaroid"
Sheldon Oberman, "This Business with Elijah"
Lynn Podgurny, "Till Tomorrow, Maple Leaf Mills"
James Riseborough, "She Is Not His Mother"
Patricia Stone, "Living on the Lake"

4
1992

David Bergen, "The Bottom of the Glass"
Maria A. Billion, "No Miracles Sweet Jesus"
Judith Cowan, "By thc Big River"
Steven Heighton, "A Man Away from Home Has No Neighbours"
Steven Heighton, "How Beautiful upon the Mountains"
L. Rex Kay, "Travelling"
Rozena Maart, "No Rosa, No District Six"*
Guy Malet De Carteret, "Rainy Day"
Carmelita McGrath, "Silence"
Michael Mirolla, "A Theory of Discontinuous Existence"
Diane Juttner Perreault, "Bella's Story"
Eden Robinson, "Traplines"

5
1993

Caroline Adderson, "Oil and Dread"
David Bergen, "La Rue Prevette"
Marina Endicott, "With the Band"
Dayv James-French, "Cervine"
Michael Kenyon, "Durable Tumblers"
K.D. Miller, "A Litany in Time of Plague"
Robert Mullen, "Flotsam"
Gayla Reid, "Sister Doyle's Men"*
Oakland Ross, "Bang-bang"
Robert Sherrin, "Technical Battle for Trial Machine"
Carol Windley, "The Etruscans"

6
1994

Anne Carson, "Water Margins: An Essay on Swimming by My Brother"
Richard Cumyn, "The Sound He Made"
Genni Gunn, "Versions"
Melissa Hardy, "Long Man the River"*
Robert Mullen, "Anomie"
Vivian Payne, "Free Falls"
Jim Reil, "Dry"
Robyn Sarah, "Accept My Story"
Joan Skogan, "Landfall"
Dorothy Speak, "Relatives in Florida"
Alison Wearing, "Notes from Under Water"

7
1995

Michelle Alfano, "Opera"
Mary Borsky, "Maps of the Known World"
Gabriella Goliger, "Song of Ascent"
Elizabeth Hay, "Hand Games"
Shaena Lambert, "The Falling Woman"
Elise Levine, "Boy"
Roger Burford Mason, "The Rat-Catcher's Kiss"

Antanas Sileika, "Going Native"
Kathryn Woodward, "Of Marranos and Gilded Angels"*

8
1996

Rick Bowers, "Dental Bytes"
David Elias, "How I Crossed Over"
Elyse Gasco, "Can You Wave Bye Bye, Baby?"*
Danuta Gleed, "Bones"
Elizabeth Hay, "The Friend"
Linda Holeman, "Turning the Worm"
Elaine Littman, "The Winner's Circle"
Murray Logan, "Steam"
Rick Maddocks, "Lessons from the Sputnik Diner"
K.D. Miller, "Egypt Land"
Gregor Robinson, "Monster Gaps"
Alma Subasic, "Dust"

9
1997

Brian Bartlett, "Thomas, Naked"
Dennis Bock, "Olympia"
Kristen den Hartog, "Wave"
Gabriella Goliger,"Maladies of the Inner Ear"**
Terry Griggs, "Momma Had a Baby"
Mark Anthony Jarman, "Righteous Speedboat"
Judith Kalman, "Not for Me a Crown of Thorns"
Andrew Mullins, "The World of Science"
Sasenarine Persaud, "Canada Geese and Apple Chatney"
Anne Simpson, "Dreaming Snow"**
Sarah Withrow, "Ollie"
Terence Young, "The Berlin Wall"